The Marchand Woman

"Yes?"

She watched the knob turn. She could have spoken; she didn't. Crobey stood outlined in the doorway.

"I sort of was wondering what you'd look like without your clothes," he said.

"Crobey," she murmured, "you've got just twenty-four hours to get out of my bedroom."

THE MARCHAND WOMAN

JOHN IVES

BERKLEY BOOKS, NEW YORK

THE MARCHAND WOMAN

A Berkley Book / published by arrangement with
E. P. Dutton

PRINTING HISTORY
E. P. Dutton edition / November 1979
Berkley edition / July 1981

ISBN: 0–425–04731–8

A BERKLEY BOOK ® TM 757,375
Berkley Books are published by Berkley Publishing Corporation,
200 Madison Avenue, New York, New York 10016.

For Shan:
You must be!

Where there is neither love nor hatred in the
game, woman's play is mediocre. . . .
In revenge and in love woman is more
barbarous than man.
—Nietzsche, *Beyond Good and Evil*

Revenge is a kind of wild justice.
—Bacon, *Of Revenge*

Woman was God's second mistake.
—Nietzsche, *The Antichrist*

A woman always has her revenge ready.
—Molière, *The Misanthrope*

Sweet is revenge—especially to women.
—Byron, *Don Juan*

Part One

Chapter 1

When the telephone rang she made a face. She wound a towel around her wet hair and tucked the edges in and picked it up on the fifth ring.

It was Howard, his voice very low—like a phonograph running at the wrong speed. "I'm glad I caught you at home. I'll be there in twenty minutes. Wait for me. Has anybody called you?"

"At this hour of the morning?"

"Leave it off the hook till I get there. I don't want it coming from someone else."

"Must you be melodramatic?"

"Yes. Wait for me."

By the time the doorbell rang she had fitted into skirt and blouse and sandals; she was putting her face on. She had a look through the Judas glass and saw him lighting a cigarette on the doorstep.

He seemed to have faded a bit with age, like a photostatic copy of himself. She was surprised to realize how long it had been since she had seen him face-to-face; it had all been letters and the occasional telephone vitriol. The things they had said to each other—

She opened the door to him; he neither spoke nor entered but simply looked at her, his eyes swollen. It unnerved her. She cried with completely false affection, "Howard, darling, why is it I *never* see you any more?" But she kept her face blank to put the lie to it.

Howard held up a forestalling finger. She let him in; he turned half around, waiting for her to close the door, holding the cigarette in the manner of an actor preparing to turn toward the audience and deliver a curtain line. But still he didn't speak.

"Darling, you look simply marvelous." An awkward lie. "I love the distinguished way your hair's graying at the sides. It would do credit to an investment banker."

He seemed caught in dumfounded paralysis. She tried again, needling him with her saucy screw-you grin. "How's your ass anyway?"

"Carole, please."

"Well then. " She pointed him with vague weariness toward a chair.

He went to it like an old man, wincing as he sat down. She watched him search the coffee table with childlike baffled concentration. Exasperated—"Good grief!"— she plunged into the kitchen, found him an ashtray in a drawer, dropped it on the table before him so that it rattled. Howard twisted the half-consumed cigarette into it, grinding it out savagely. He looked around the room like a fitful airline passenger anxious to memorize the locations of the fastest exits.

"It's Robert," he said.

"Of course it's Robert. I can't imagine anything else that would bring you here."

"Sit down."

Perversely she drew herself up. "He's dead."

"No. He's not dead as far as I know. Sit down, Carole."

She was furious. "What's happened? You've done your level best to provoke cardiac arrest and there's nothing wrong with him? You've no right—"

"I didn't say there was nothing wrong with him. Well actually as far as I know there's nothing physically wrong with him." He plucked feebly at his pocket. "I happened to be here." Found another cigarette. "In Los Angeles I mean. Meetings with the Japanese." He had to use both hands to light it. "The office reached me at my hotel an hour ago." He inhaled, choked, coughed, recovered. "It's an unhappy coincidence, my being here just now. I'd rather have been in Washington—I think this would have been easier long-distance."

She realized he was groping not for a way to tell her but for a way to avoid telling her. He kept glancing at the telephone as if he expected it to reprieve him. It was so masochistically like him: Never face quick pain if it was possible to choose the long agony of not facing it.

She controlled herself. "What's happened to him?"

He gave her a reproachful look. It slid away; he brooded at the cigarette and his mouth worked ruefully.

She said, "There is, I have to assume, a crisis involving our son—yet you insist on keeping it back so that I can watch you squirm in your own crisis. You're as demanding of attention as a child banging its spoon on the table. You're a bastard, Howard, you really are."

His mouth lifted, one side of it, in a sour smile. "There's such an irony in it," he said. "Hijacked. Terrorists. He's been kidnapped."

He sucked at the cigarette and smoke poured from his mouth with each word: "It's not as if he isn't used to it, is it. I mean at least he knows the ropes, it's not the first time he's been kidnapped."

"Kidnapped." She repeated the word stupidly.

His hands fluttered and he dropped the cigarette and went scrounging for it in the carpet. When he found it he said, "Apparently it was some sort of grisly accident. He wasn't meant to be one of the victims—he just happened to be there, he got swept up in it. No rhyme or reason."

"He's been kidnapped by *terrorists*?"

She watched him stand up; he seemed to loom when he approached her—she wasn't wearing heels. She saw what he was up to in time; she moved away, she didn't want his clumsy embrace. She said, "I don't want comforting, Howard. I want facts. Tell me the punch line."

"There's no punch line. They took him yesterday afternoon. Nobody knows anything. Nobody knows where he is or whether he'd dead or alive. One assumes he's still alive—dead hostages aren't worth much."

"Hostage for what?"

"It's still not clear."

She wandered around the room. "Shall I make coffee?"

"A drink," he said, "a drink would be better."

In the kitchen she drew herself together, helped by the mechanical minutiae: Open the cabinet, take down two glasses, find the Dewar's, pour, return.

Half aware of her movements she sank into the recliner and its footboard flipped up unbidden under her calves. Howard said, "This must be, what, the third time he's been kidnapped?" There was waspish accusation in his tone.

"Let's not get started on that." She tasted the drink but it wasn't what she wanted; she put it aside. "Mexico?"

"Mexico? Yes, in Mexico. Well at least they were kidnapped in Mexico. God knows where they are now. They could be anywhere. State has no idea. It's near the coast and there's flat country all around where they might have landed a plane. The vehicles were found abandoned ten kilometers from where it happened—that doesn't mean anything, of course they'd switch vehicles. The authorities are looking for witnesses, of course, but—"

She watched him inhale deeply. He threw his head back and closed his eyes. "I'll try it from the top. I'm sorry. It was Harrison Gordon they were after. He's the Ambassador. The kidnapers must have been fairly well organized—at least they seem to have had advance information about his itinerary. He was on a fact-finding tour of the provinces. His party was ambushed at a village junction near the coast of Mexico above the peninsula. The kidnappers took Gordon and everybody in his party, hauled them off in buses. Nobody was killed. Apparently one security guard took a rap on the head. A reporter named Ortega happened to be an eyewitness—he's a stringer for the L.A. *Times*."

"What was Robert doing there?"

"According to Ortega he'd hitched a ride down there to plead for medical assistance for the Yaquis. Robert was talking to Ambassador Gordon when it happened. So he was swept up along with the rest of the party."

"Why hasn't it been in the papers?"

"It'll be in the afternoon editions. Washington and Mexico City wanted to keep it quiet but of course they couldn't keep Ortega muzzled for very long. They were waiting for the demands.''

"Demands?''

"Ransom. There are always demands, aren't there? I mean you don't kidnap a United States Ambassador for a lark.''

She said, "It's a mistake, isn't it. A ghastly mistake.''

"We'll know more in time. I asked Paine to call me here this morning if he learns anything. I hope you don't mind—''

"Who are they? Don't they even know who they are?''

"The terrorists? Nobody knows yet.''

She said, "What do we do? Just wait? I don't know if I can bear that.''

"I don't know what else to do.'' His hands wrenched at each other. "It's not much good saying I'm sorry. But I hope you know how much I'm hating myself right now. If we hadn't treated him like a volleyball between us he might not have run away to Mexico with his Peace Corps nonsense and this might—''

"Don't be ridiculous. A thing like this is as arbitrary as a tornado. I don't want to indulge you in a *mea culpa* right now—I haven't the strength. Do you want breakfast?''

"No. But go ahead if you're hungry.''

"I'm not.''

She watched him light his third cigarette. She said, "Shall we just sit here and wait for the phone to ring, then?''

"I don't know.'' She saw the tremor in the hand with which he lifted his glass. He said, "I don't know what to do or what to say. I'm supposed to be in a meeting at eleven. The Japanese trade delegation.''

"Then go to it.''

"And leave you here alone?''

"I'm going to the studio,'' she said, deciding it even as she spoke. "We're still editing the picture.''

"I wonder if it's possible to work. To keep one's mind on anything.''

"I'm not strong enough not to,'' she said. "I couldn't

possibly sit here and stare at the walls.''

"I suppose you're right.''

She looked at her watch. "You've still got time to make your meeting.''

"Can I drop you at the studio?''

"No thanks. I may want my car with me.''

"I'm at the Hilton,'' he said.

"All right. You can reach me at the studio.''

He made as if to stand, but didn't. "Carole, this is awkward but let me ask you: Have you got a boy friend?''

"A boy friend? No. I have a few men friends.''

"Someone you can turn to, I mean.''

"Let me worry about it, Howard. Rest assured if I want a shoulder to cry on I won't choose yours.''

"I didn't mean it like that,'' he said with almost laughable petulance. "But it's just that if you need anything—''

"I know. I'm sorry, I didn't mean to be intolerable. It's kind of you to offer but I'll be all right.''

He said vaguely, "I think I'll ask Paine to fly out today and take my place in these meetings. I'll go back to Washington tonight. I'd rather be there—maybe I can keep my finger on the pulse of things from there. Mexico's not my desk, of course, but I know Mark Blaisedell fairly well. Maybe I can build a few fires. I'd hate to think we weren't doing everything possible to save them.''

"Will you keep me informed?''

"Instantly I know anything.''

She didn't believe him but there was no point arguing with him.

On the turns down Beverly Glen into the Valley she paid rigid attention to her driving; she was running on her nerve-ends and couldn't take it for granted. She was in Burbank within twenty minutes, parking in the slot that had her name on it. When she emerged from the air-conditioned car the heat slapped her face and she hurried across the compound. A red light glowed above the door of one of the soundstage hangars.

She was thinking she'd treated Howard shabbily. But when she went inside the studio office block she thought defiantly that he deserved it. By the time she reached the elevator she had pushed him aside in her mind; she was thinking now of Robert, trying to picture his plight, imagining him talking with nervous energy to his fellow hostages. Robert would be analyzing it. Talking in that staccato fashion that was not quite a stammer, his shoulder jerking at random intervals, his mouth grimacing in rictus tics. Spouting facts he'd absorbed from news magazines about terrorist attitudes and hostage behavior—telling the others how to react, what face to present to the captors. She had no doubt the Ambassador was listening to Robert rather than the other way round. Robert was a font of facts if not wisdom, and incapable of passivity.

In the cutting room Mort Kyle stood about, furiously smoking a cigarette-sized cigar, wearing a trim denim outfit and a suntanned scowl; Edith was lapping .35-millimeter frames on the Movieola and talking cheerfully: "The most incredible hat. Anyhow I think it was a hat, because she had it on her head."

Carole closed the door. In the half darkness Mort searched her face. "What's wrong, darling?"

She told them. Mort and Edith were shocked. Mort stroked his neat beard and made sounds of sympathy; Edith mouthed some of the right things. Carole cut her off: "Look, dear, I need to work. Busy hands, you know, all that. Now where are we?" She had moved adroitly to evade Mort's hands; now he put them in his pockets and scowled again. The scowl was his favored expression.

He picked up the extension. "Darling, this is Mort Kyle. We're in Cutting-room Three. If there are any calls for Carole Marchand, patch them in here, will you?"

Carole said, "It could be for Lundquist."

Mort relayed it into the phone: "The call may come in under her married name, Lundquist."

Edith made room above the Movieola's miniature screen. "We're trying to shave some frames off the skilift sequence. Right here—we could shorten the long-shot, cut faster to the close-up and tighten up around the dialogue.''

''I hate to lose that shot. Cap broke his ass setting up on the ice to get that angle. It's a gorgeous composition.''

Mort was on the phone ordering coffee; he turned away from it, cupping the mouthpiece in his hand. ''It'd do credit to Archie Stout and John Ford, darling, but we're not selling a travelogue. We've still got to snip a lot of footage.''

Edith cocked a knowing eyebrow and Carole tried to smile to reassure the girl but she was having trouble dimpling up just now; she turned away before it became a snarl. When Mort hung up the phone she said, ''Am I going to have to fight you over every foot of this picture?''

''You're going to have to fight me over about sixty-five hundred frames, darling. That's what it's still got to lose.''

The Movieola rattled. Frames jinked across the screen; underlit by that flickering source, Mort's narrow-bearded face had the Mephistophelean look of a silent movie villain's.

''It's my picture,'' she said. ''This time it's mine. I wrote it and directed it—I won't have it butchered by a clock.''

Mort's eyes glimmered from the gloom. ''You don't have final cut, darling. Neither do I. I only produced it—the distributors make the decisions. They want a picture they can screen at seven o'clock and nine o'clock. Go over a hundred and five minutes and you're screwing up their timetables. Look—the studio will cut it if we don't. Isn't it better that you and I do the dirty deed ourselves?''

The little cigar glowed briefly and arced to the floor; Mort's heel crushed the life from it. For a long time they stood in conflicting silences.

Mort gave her a soft smile. He wasn't using his charm deliberately; the charm was there, that was all. ''It's a low-budget picture, darling. I can't see the exhibs bending over to let us have the extra five minutes, can you?"

"If I were a man would you browbeat me this way?"

"Darling, I'd be far more ruthless with a man. Sam Gilfillan refuses to speak to me to this day because he insists I ruined *Pride Goeth* in the cutting room. Face it, Carole, if you were a man you wouldn't have had a shot at directing this picture at all. They're going out of their way to accommodate women and minorities right now. So let's not have any sexist crap, shall we?"

"I'm sorry. It was a cheap shot. I've never done that before. It's nerves."

"I understand, darling. Sure. I also understand you came to work on purpose. You can go home if you want to, but if you stay here we're going to cut this picture. That's what we're all here for. Now find me four and a half minutes to drop. You pick 'em, I'll stand aside. But I want four and a half. Minimum. Fair enough?"

Mort left the cutting room; Carole settled down with Edith to feed stock through the sprockets. She had no real quarrel with her producer; these were the games that had to be played. She knew her craft. *Felix's Kingdom* would have to sell two million tickets before break-even. She didn't have to remind herself she was a movie director, not an *auteur-artiste* defined by the sophomoric *Cahiers-du-Cinema* fools.

It was her fourth picture. Two of the first three had made money; all three had won awards of one kind or another. What Mort had said was not true—she hadn't got this job because of her sex; he'd only said it to goad her. Mort would say almost anything to provoke debate, it was his manner. What mattered in the end was that she knew he liked the picture. She liked it herself: Her object had been to make a movie that she would have bought a ticket to see if someone else had made it.

Felix's Kingdom was an unabashed tearjerker. A man, two women. She'd wanted sentiment, romance: a six-handkerchief movie that would make her cry with heartbreak and cry again with relief and triumph, sappy and trite and wonderful. The critics would lambaste it but screw them. It made her cry.

She hadn't cried for Robert. The realization shook her. Was she so far gone she could be stimulated to tears only by the synthetic?

She couldn't keep her mind on the job. Finally she gave vague instructions to Edith and went out, not quite sure where she was bound.

Mort wasn't in his office. She tracked him to the commissary. He gave her his public smile—a creeping revelation of capped teeth: His party manners and she couldn't tell how he might behave if they'd been alone, unobserved. She hadn't slept with him but at times she'd been curious what it might have been like: He had all his strengths on the surface and from this she inferred he might be a good lover, but good-in-bed was a phrase that had lost its meaning to her because she was going through a phase—at least she thought of it as a phase—in which she had convinced herself that you had to love with your mind and heart as well as your body. Meaningless sex was a stage she had endured in the early days after the divorce. For a while she had believed she had a stunted capacity for loving. She was no longer sure whether that was the case; she liked to think she was mature enough not to believe romantic nonsense (waiting-for-the-right-man-to-come-along) and lately she had begun to suspect perhaps she simply didn't like men very much. She had experimented in her mind with lesbian fantasies but had found them unexciting, uninviting. *Maybe I am just drying up*, she had thought. *Galloping menopause*. Yet she still made herself beautiful before she went out to face the world each day; and she hadn't let her looks go. But was it pretense? She didn't know.

"Sympathy," Mort said, "is easy to give and embarrassing to receive, but I want you to know that—"

"I know. You don't need to say it."

"All the same, darling, if you want a hand to hold."

She listened abstractedly to the commissary's rattle of cutlery, the heavy drone of voices. It was such a mundane scene; it made her feel guilty—Robert somewhere in a jungle, perhaps tied hand and foot: perhaps injured, in pain, perhaps in an agony of hunger or thirst. Keeping his upper lip stiff and bucking up the others, not out of any sense of heroics but simply because that was Robert.

She said, "The one thing about you that's driven me up the wall ever since we first met is that inane Hollywood habit of yours of calling everybody darling."

"I know. I can't even remember where I picked it up." Mort took her elbow and squired her to the cafeteria queue, talking about the picture. Her mind was on Robert and she hardly attended.

When they'd eaten he said abruptly, "Have you ever wanted to get married again?"

"I thought I did once. Briefly thought it. It didn't work out. Fortunately I'd grown wise enough to look before I jumped in—so I didn't jump."

"Cold feet?"

"Yes. Let's talk about something else, shall we?"

"Tell me about your son. I never met him, you know."

"Robert," she said. "Robert the survivor. How he endured the buffeting we gave him I'll never know. That is the overriding guilt of my life—it's part of the reason, I suppose, why I'm having such a hard time dealing with this."

"Nobody could have an easy time with something like this."

"I used to kidnap him from Howard. Did you know that?"

"No. Must have been a while ago."

"Fifteen years ago." She pushed her plate away. "It was one of those asinine custody things. After the divorce I moved out here with Robert and petitioned the court for permanent custody. California court. At the same time Howard was filing petitions in the Virginia courts—we'd been living in Alexandria. Howard still lives there. The upshot was the Virginia courts awarded custody to him and the California courts awarded custody to me. Howard thought I wasn't a fit mother for him. He was convinced I'd ruin Robert's life. I hired

private detectives—they took him right out of an
Alexandria schoolyard and dragged him all the way out
here. It happened twice. What a dismal performance it
all was—the two of us behaving like animals quarreling
over a marrow-bone. I don't think any of us ever
recovered from it. Certainly Robert didn't."

"That kind of kidnapping's not illegal, is it? I mean
you can kidnap your own child and it's not a violation
of the law."

"I'm not talking about that kind of guilt, Mort."

"Your ex is something to do with the State Department, isn't he?"

"It's his career. At the moment he's deputy Under-
secretary on the Australia-New Zealand desk. He'll be
an ambassador one day."

"How'd you come to marry him?"

"You can't imagine how often I've asked myself that
very question."

"Well?"

"It always comes up lame no matter how I parse it.
My brother brought him home one fateful day in
nineteen fifty-one. Howard's very bright, you know,
and he came from one of those nearly Main Line
families, the Lundquists of whatchamacallit. Oh it's all
so tedious. Those cufflinks you're wearing look like
golden manhole covers. Do they signify anything?"

"They're five-dollar gold pieces, vintage eighteen
eighty. A gift from somebody I used to know. Go
on—tell me about you and Howard."

She slumped with memory. "I had a fantastic
pathetic terrible crush on him. I was in school—you
know. In my freshman pleated skirt and saddle shoes.
But I was never one of those apple-pie country girls.
There was a little group of us. We were determined to be
as sophisticated as Noel Coward and as witty as
Dorothy Parker. My dorm came to be known as Villa
Cirrhosis and our little crowd was known all over campus as The Vicious Circle. You know how it is. Kids."

She made a face. "I was very forward and I suppose
quite good-looking in an unformed way. After I got rid

of the braces on my teeth. Anyhow I had all kinds of gentlemen admirers and most of them had acne and fruity drawls, I couldn't stand it. I met Howard and formed a towering crush instantly. My God, I was eighteen, Howard was nearly thirty. Do you know how girls mistake quietness in men for maturity?''

"I guess.''

"He was good-looking. Although actually he's much better looking now than he was then. It took him years to get the baby fat out of his cheeks.''

"I don't think I've ever seen him.''

"You'd like him, Mort. He'd like you. He's easy to get along with—he's got all the social graces, he's up on current events with that engagingly impressive manner of somebody who knows all the inside dirt about anything you'd care to mention. He doesn't drop names; he drops facts. He can tell you the real inside story behind the Rhodesian troubles or the making of *King Kong*, anything. I was thoroughly impressed, and madly flattered by his noticing me. I remember how surprised I was by how hot his face looked the first time he asked me out for a date.'' The memory provoked her wry chuckle.

"So you were married and lived unhappily ever after.''

"We had a good year or two,'' she said in a muted way.

"What went wrong?''

"Everything dried up at once. Robert was born just before Christmas in nineteen fifty-five and I think that was supposed to occupy my complete attention while Howard was off solving affairs of earth-shaking importance in his office. I hated every minute of it. The little snotling wasn't my cup of tea. I was still too damn young—I missed the freedoms I'd had.'' She felt the tears coming. "You can't believe how quickly our marriage degenerated into one of those 'You already owe me three back-rubs' things.'' She plucked at a ragged fingernail. "I find it fascinating to realize that the first time I met Howard I believed him to be a man so smooth you could skate on him. How the polish wore off. It's inconceivable I could have misled myself so completely."

"We're none of us immune to that," Mort said. "I've been married three times."

"A typical Hollywood success story."

He prompted her. "And then you got divorced."

"That was the most humilating part of it. He left me, you know. Not the other way round. Does that surprise you?"

"Some, yes."

"I guess I'd decided to make the best of the bad bargain for Robert's sake. Trying to force myself to grow up and behave like a responsible adult. I was working in documentary films then, in Washington for one of the TV stations. It gave me outside contacts with the world and I was willing to settle for that. At least I had part of a life. Then Howard found a little blonde somewhere. For a little while he persuaded himself he couldn't live without her. It was only an excuse to screw up the courage to leave me. He left one day while I was at work. I didn't know where the hell he was for three days. I had the cops searching, I called everybody at the State Department, I was distraught—not because I missed him but just because I was so completely in the dark. I feel the same way right now about Robert but I'm older and I suppose it doesn't show so much, except for this silly talking jag. Then I got his letter in the mail. I suppose it was easier for him to say that kind of thing in a letter. It was a twelve-page single-spaced diatribe, typed. Meticulously listing all my faults."

"He sounds like a real bastard."

"Not really. Together we were bad—we were terrible for each other, we brought out the absolute worst. We made each other into wretched creatures. I used to think I hated him, of course. Now I'm not sure. Maybe I made him into the thing that I hated. . . . Am I coming to pieces, Mort? Christ, I feel as if somebody somewhere is sticking pins in a wax effigy."

"You're jittery. It'll pass—you'll settle down. You're strong."

"Strong. In the sense that a skunk is a strong animal."

"Oh, come off it, darling."

"There you go again. Didn't I warn you about that?"

"I most humbly beg your forgiveness." He showed her his grin. "You started out to tell me about your son."

"Do you know what I think of when you ask me about Robert? A picture he pinned up in his bathroom. A photograph of General Patton pissing in the Rhine. It was so Robert, so quintessentially Robert. He's so greedy for life and at the same time so alienated by it. He went through a wild period in college, much wilder than mine was. One time I went down to the University of Arizona to visit him, a surprise visit, and got to Tucson fairly late at night. I stopped in front of a fraternity house that looked like the right one and asked a kid if Robert Lundquist lived there. The kid was sitting on the porch reading under a light. He looked out into the darkness at my car and said in a bored voice, 'Yeah, he lives here. Bring him in.' I think he stayed drunk two whole semesters and spent another year or two high on grass. But you know he turned out all right in spite of everything his parents could do to screw him up."

Her voice broke. "So greedy for life."

"How'd he get into the Peace Corps?"

"Howard wanted him to go to law school. Robert didn't want that. He still hasn't got any idea what he wants to do with himself. He told me a few years ago he thought it was ridiculous to have to make those decisions at nineteen. When you're fifty years old, why should you have to spend your life in libraries and courtrooms because some kid decided thirty years earlier that you ought to be a lawyer? And you know he was absolutely right. So he volunteered for the Peace Corps. It was something worthwhile to do while he was making up his mind about the future. That's all—nothing peculiar. But he's got a great deal of dedication. One of the facts he keeps harping on—he's a computer-bank of random facts—is that the governments of the world spend the same amount of money on children every year that they spend on deadly weapons every two hours. Once I asked him why he hadn't joined radical protest groups, and do you know what he said? He said he didn't believe in protests because in order to be a protester you had to take an inferior position to the people with whom you were pleading. When he went off to Mexico he said he was doing his bit to try and help the children win out over the cannons. So if you're asking me if I love my son, the answer's yes. How could anybody not love a kid like that?''

But just then she was thinking about the hope she'd had, and never articulated aloud to a living soul, that perhaps one day Robert would come and live near her. She'd tried to stand back and convince herself that she was making a mistake to count on Robert, even just in those fantasies, to fill the role of strong man in her life. But she didn't really care. All she knew was that she wanted him near.

Mort covered her hand with his own; he scowled earnestly. ''He'll get out of it, darling. I know he will.''

''I hope he does it before I fly to pieces,'' she replied.

Chapter 2

At eight that night she couldn't stand it any more. She backed the car out viciously against the mailbox post and drove away leaving bits of red glass in the street.

She walked into the lobby in high dudgeon, browbeat the clerk into revealing the room number and went up in the elevator with a tourist couple and a bellboy. The Iowans were talking about Knott's Berry Farm. She had to curb her tongue to keep from screaming at them to shut up.

Howard answered the door in T-shirt and shaving cream; evidently he'd been expecting room service. He went all colors at the sight of her.

She thrust past him into the room and kicked the door shut.

Howard said, "I'm sorry. You don't know what a day it's been. This problem came up at the conference and then I had to drive one of the Japanese to the airport and of all the damn stupid things the car had a flat and the idiots hadn't included a spare, and the poor bastard missed his plane and we had a hell of a flap—"

"Soon to be made into a major motion picture," she said with icy disbelief. "You left instructions with the desk that you weren't taking calls from me, didn't you? I've been phoning you for six hours."

"Carole, damn it, I've got nothing to tell you. They've had nothing to tell me."

"It was on the car radio just now. It's been on the news for hours. They're Cubans."

"All right. What of it? Nobody knows where Robert is. Isn't that the bottom line?"

"You might have had the courtesy to call me. At least

19

to let me know they're getting somewhere."

"They're going in circles," he said. "Accumulating useless facts. Don't you think I've been keeping in touch with Washington? There's nothing. Nothing hard."

She sat down, handbag in lap. "If it's not too much strain I'd appreciate your telling me everything you know."

"I could give you twenty minutes of utterly useless information. Would that help?"

"What I want from you," she said with quaking control, "is the stuff that hasn't been in the news. And don't give me any of that need-to-know horseshit. I'm his mother. I need to know."

He went to the bureau where he'd scattered the contents of his pockets; he picked up the wristwatch and looked at it. He actually looked at his watch. She wanted to scream at him.

"I've got a plane to catch," he explained.

"You don't go out this door until you've talked to me."

He wiped the foam off his jaw with a towel. "Over the years it's belatedly occurred to me that you have an abrasive wit and the acidulous instincts of a barracuda but just possibly, behind those defenses, you're as vulnerable as any of us. So I'm going to ignore this fishwife assault. Now if you'll just take it easy for a moment—"

"I don't want your goddamned forgiveness, Howard. I want information."

He found a cigarette in the litter. "All right. If it'll ease your mind. There's nothing in it that helps us. First you must understand that it isn't my department. I've been on the horn with Mark Blaisedell but it's been hard to get a clear picture so early. To some extent it's a Central Intelligence Agency matter and I'm sure you know how jealous they are of information—they don't share it with State unless they're forced to. I don't have the clout to force them. It's possible they know things we don't know but there's nothing I can do about that."

"Just tell me what you do know."

"Well it's our best judgment that the terrorists probably are Cuban exiles. We don't know who they are, actually, but the circumstantial evidence points to that conclusion. This morning a ransom demand, a penciled note, was received through the mail slot of a Venezuelan newspaper in Caracas."

"Howard, I know that much. I've heard the radio. What did the ransom note *say*?"

"They want ten million dollars. In cash. American dollars. Small bills, unmarked. And they want eleven political prisoners released from jails in Latin America."

"What prisoners?"

"Five in Venezuelan prisons, four in Colombia, two in Mexico. They were convicted of various guerrilla crimes—hijacking, violating gun laws, murdering Cuban communist rebel organizers, so forth. What they have in common is that all eleven are anti-Castro people. They're not all Cubans but they're all rightwing. Two of them are Germans from Paraguay. Therefore we're assuming the people who kidnaped Harrison Gordon and Robert must be anti-Castro Cuban exiles who want to get their leaders out of jail and raise money to finance guerrilla action against Cuba."

"What's being done to rescue the hostages?"

"Very little, I imagine. It's not like Entebbe, you know. Nobody knows where the hostages are. How can you mount a rescue expedition if you don't know where to send it?"

She said, "Will the ransom be paid?"

"I don't know. And I don't know whether the eleven prisoners will be released. It's not up to me, Carole."

"What's Washington doing about it?"

"I don't know what pressures are being applied. This thing's in the laps of the governments of Mexico and Venezuela and Colombia. It's up to them to decide whether to meet the demands or not. They're the ones against whom the demands were levied. Officially it's not Washington's problem—only indirectly, since some of the hostages are Americans.''

"Including a United States Ambassador. Doesn't that mean anything?''

"Of course it does. But it's an awkward situation—''

"Awkward situation. Good Christ.''

"Carole, there simply isn't a hell of a lot we can do about it right now. Our hands are tied, on top of which we're blindfolded.''

He stubbed out the cigarette and looked at his watch again, strapped it to his wrist, and collected the shirt from its hanger. Howard's once athletic physique had been worn down by an unstable and lazy personality; he was no longer trim but neither was he a wreck.

He buttoned it, top to bottom, and reached for his tie. "I don't know what else to tell you. Does any of this help? I don't see how it could. I don't know about you but I feel just as much in the dark as I did this morning.''

She realized the extent of the difficulty with which he was keeping up the calm front. He had to knot the tie three times before he got it right; by the end of the performance he was reduced to oaths and savage jerks at the fabric.

She felt a residue of affection toward him. It was not any wish for reconciliation—too much blood had flowed under the bridge—but she felt sorrow for him and it made her soften her tone when she spoke. "Of course there's one thing you haven't told me.''

He was distributing things in his pockets. "Don't be silly.''

"Of course there is, Howard. I'm not an absolute fool. You don't kidnap people for ransom and leave the delivery date wide open. There's a deadline, isn't there?''

His hands became still. His eyes closed briefly, his lips worked and finally he said, "Today's Tuesday. They want the money and the release of the eleven political prisoners by Friday noon. Two and a half days from now.''

"Thank you,'' she said quietly. She got up to leave. "I do wish you'd make some attempt to make things a bit easier for me. Do you think I enjoy prying things from you with a crowbar?''

"I didn't want to upset you—''

"Upset me? As if I weren't already distraught, you mean? Didn't it occur to you that knowing there's a finite limit to this suspense might be preferable to dragging out the agony indefinitely?''

"I'm sorry.'' He actually sounded miserable. "I'm truly sorry. I didn't think.''

"Please think next time. Don't keep things from me—it's cruel.''

His hands gestured—helpless, apologetic.

"I won't keep you,'' she said. "You'll miss your plane.''

"I'll keep you posted.''

"Will you,'' she said drily. "I'll be in Washington tomorrow afternoon—at the Hay-Adams if they're not booked up.''

"There's no need for that.''

"Isn't there? I don't see where I've got much choice, do you?''

"I don't suppose there'd be any point in my asking you to trust me.''

"It's a little late for that.''

It made him wince. "I deserved that, I guess. All right. Do you want to stay at the house—would it be more comfortable than a hotel?''

"God no.'' She went.

The stewardess came down the aisle looking at laps to make certain of the fastenings of seat belts; a man's twangy voice scratched from the loudspeakers, something about cruising altitude and the landmarks over which they were destined to pass—landmarks that doubtless would be invisible through the clouds below. A junior stewardess who looked no more than sixteen was demonstrating the use of a yellow oxygen mask and the lap-belt inspector was asking if Carole wanted a drink after take-off—Carole had to ask her to repeat the question.

She hated planes: the stale air redolent of tobacco

smoke and kerosene, the immobile imprisonment at six hundred miles an hour, the way even first-class seats had been designed with not quite enough leg room.

With her eyes shut and her head vibrating against the white paper antimacassar she sipped Dewar's and drifted in thought. The mad hurry of the morning recycled itself through her mind—Mort Kyle walking her to her car at noon: "Don't feel you have to rush back for God's sake. If you're still in Washington I'll ship the final cut there and you can screen it at the AFI."

At the car she had stopped to fish for her keys, only half listening to him; she'd said abruptly, "How do you make contact with gangsters?"

He was taken aback. She said, "I'm serious."

It made him show his teeth. "You walk into any studio in town and ask to see the head man."

"You've dealt with the Mafia, I know you have. Nobody can produce pictures in this industry without knowing them."

"What are you after?"

"I don't know. Desperation, I suppose. I want to hire a tarnished knight to go into the jungle and rescue my son. Does it sound imbecilic?"

"To tell the truth yes, it does, if only because you don't even know what jungle to look in."

"There was that private eye who rescued Marlon's son. . . ."

"I know what he'd tell you. He'd tell you to forget it."

"I've got to do *some*thing."

"There's nothing. You're doing all you can. As for gangsters, I know some of the union people. They'd hardly do you any good."

It had been a far-fetched impulse—a fantasy of panic. Now she remembered it with rue.

Warren would have known what to do. She thought of him infrequently now—he'd died more than two years ago trying to rescue a charred Rhodesian family from a napalmed hut. Her brother had been as quixotic as her son was; she thought it must be something in the genes. She wondered if she had it too.

He'd had a great importance in her life. She'd relied on her brother although it was quite possible he'd never known of it. It was a thing of the spirit—merely knowing Warren was alive, knowing he was her brother, knowing he'd come if she needed him: There'd been equilibrium in that.

Warren the intellectual adventurer: Right now he'd have been hiring a helicopter or galvanizing forces or interviewing jungle natives to find the terrorists' hideout. He'd have known where to look, whom to recruit, how to handle it. Warren Marchand—brilliant journalist, compassionate missionary of the spirit, troubled activist. For months she'd grieved his passing. She'd kept a scrapbook of his dispatches from Beirut and Saigon and Johannesburg and Salisbury and Belfast—Warren the eclectic adventurer. Her inscribed copy of his first book was nearly worn off its bindings: Published in 1965 and nearly everything he'd predicted for Viet Nam had come to pass.

He'd free-lanced for the high-paying magazines; not a reporter really—it was his observations for which they'd paid him. You read a Marchand article not for facts but for truths: He showed you the flavor and the significance of things.

Every six months or so he'd appear on her doorstep—the quick Marchand grip and she'd drop anything, cancel any date, to go out to dinner with him and catch up on the latest chapter of his picaresque life. He'd been Robert's favorite, of course; possibly it was Warren's example that had inspired Robert to join the Peace Corps.

The genes, she thought. The same good genes in Robert had overcome the rotten upbringing. The custody fight had ended in uneasy truce after the ludicrous kidnappings and spiritings about; A split-custody agreement by which Robert spent much of the year in boarding school and divided his vacations scrupulously between them.

Robert. Not Bob, never Bobby, but Robert. Robert Lundquist. Robert Warren Lundquist. She was still counting on him. He'd have to get out of it, she needed him too much for him to let her down.

Thursday she haunted the telephones and spent half the afternoon sitting stonily before Howard's desk browbeating him with silent baleful looks. She badgered him into making constant phone calls: State Intelligence, the CIA, even someone at the White House.

There was nothing. No one knew whether the Latin American governments planned to accede or hang tough. No one knew who the guerrillas were or where the hostages were held. There was no further ransom demand; no word at all from the terrorists.

"The deadline," she kept saying, "is noon tomorrow," and watched it annoy him.

Midafternoon—the Latin American desks began to send copies of reports into Howard's office. There were rivalries among Mexico, Venezuela and Colombia; things were bogged down in maddeningly trivial disputes; it looked as if the three governments might fail to reach agreement on a policy of dealing with the demands. Mexico and Colombia favored paying the ransom; Venezuela, taking a hard line, looked as if it would refuse to negotiate, let alone pay.

She screamed at him and he bolted upright from his chair, shouting at her: "Do you think I'm any less frustrated than you are? Do you think I like feeling impotent to do anything about it?"

She waited for him to breathe; she said with dead calm, "I want to see somebody in the CIA. Somebody high up. You can arrange it."

"If you think those guys will tell you a damn thing you're out of your mind."

"You make the appointment. I'll do the interviewing."

"I'll see what I can do."

"Now, Howard. Do it now." She was unrelenting.

He sat severely behind a desk beneath the official photographic portrait of the President. The desk looked to be mahogany. The man wore a checked bow tie on a starched white shirt and wore his salt-and-pepper hair in sleek fingerwaves; his glasses had rectangular lenses and thin white-gold frames and he had the look of an aging matinee idol with a second-string touring road-company. His name was O'Hillary.

She knew how she must appear to him—a slender woman, very tense with eyes hungry for information; and rather a bit helpless. She was not above lying, not above playing a role; she was not above anything.

She said, "I had an appointment with a Mr. Ryerson but they told me he'd been taken suddenly busy and couldn't see me."

"I know. A harmless lie. Sit down, Mrs. Lundquist. Actually, George Ryerson farmed you out to me because I'm dealing with this Mexican mess. By coming here you've avoided the middleman, so it's not really a runaround we've given you."

She said, "What's being done about my son?"

The man ran a palm over his head carefully, not dislodging the neat wave in his hair. "I'm sure your ex-husband's told you everything he could."

"Howard's part of this bureaucracy of yours and possibly that explains why he has faith that everything possible is being done. I'm sorry to be blunt but I want to know what's going on."

"We're doing all we can. Surely you must believe that."

"Specifically what does that consist of?"

"At the moment it consists of a massive attempt on numerous different fronts to acquire information. We can't make any moves while we're blind. You can understand that."

"Do you know where they are? The hostages?"

"No. No idea."

"Do you know who the terrorists are?"

"We have suspicions but not facts. We believe they may be a splinter group of anti-Castro Cuban exiles—left over, so to speak, from the Bay of Pigs days. Determined to foment the overthrow of the Castro government. We've sent investigators—most of them from the Federal Bureau of Investigation—into south Florida to find out what they can from the members of the Cuban community there. At this point in time they've been able to shed no light on this. I can't really tell you any more than that.''

"What do the governments plan to do—the Mexicans and the others?"

"About meeting the demands? They're still arguing the point among themselves.''

"And Washington has nothing to say about this?"

"I'm sure the normal pressures have been applied, Mrs. Lundquist. That's out of my department.''

He made a point of looking at his watch.

She said, "It's kind of you to grant me this time. I realize you've only done it because somebody somewhere must owe a favor to my ex-husband, but I appreciate it all the same.''

"Please feel free to call on me at any time.''

She didn't rise from the chair. "Mr. O'Hillary. I know you've been less than candid with me. I know it's inevitable—it's the way you are, the way you operate, it's ingrained. Information is doled out on a need-to-know basis and I, as a sideline noncombatant, don't need to know anything at all from the official point of view. But I think you know a great deal that you haven't told me and if I find out later that this was the case I intend to make a noise. I have a certain amount of clout myself, particularly with the press, and I'm capable of making a rather loud noise. It seems to me your agency is under quite a cloud already these days—I'm sure you want to avoid any further embarrassments if you can. Am I making some sort of sense to you?"

"What do you want? Truth or pretense? The truth is we don't know where those people are, Mrs. Lundquist.''

"The truth but not the whole truth. Tell me this: If you did know where they were, what would you be doing about it?"

Her statement dangled like a baited hook. She saw O'Hillary begin to smile; she'd caught him out—he hadn't credited her with enough cleverness.

She said after a moment, "You probably wouldn't do

a damn thing. Very possibly you know exactly who these Cubans are and where they're hiding. *But they're on our side, aren't they?*"

O'Hillary cocked his head a bit to one side; the quizzical hint of a smile didn't change. He seemed to be waiting for a rider to her statement.

She said, "For all I know they have your tacit support. Even possibly your active support."

"Kidnaping an American Ambassador? Hardly." O'Hillary folded his arms across his chest—a blatant indication of rejection, both of the accusation and of Carole. "You're quite wrong."

"If this were a scenario for a Hollywood movie," she said, "and I were reading it as the director, I'd have to ask the screenwriter why the secret agents aren't doing the standard secret-agent things. Why haven't you made it clear to these terrorists that if any harm befalls these important American hostages, then the CIA will spare no expense to track down these animals, wherever in the world they may choose to hide, and exterminate them?"

"Gunboat diplomacy of that sort went out quite a while ago, Mrs. Lundquist. I understand your feelings very well. One of the hostages in that party happens to be a fairly good friend of mine. I'm keenly concerned for him, just as you are for your son. But I've had to learn, painfully over the years, that indignation is a pointless response to terrorism."

"Is it? I'm not sure of that. Maybe I'm not jaded enough."

"This would hardly be an appropriate time to beat our breasts and thunder threats of retribution against these Cubans. They'd only laugh at us—at best—or start murdering hostages to prove their seriousness. That's what we're trying to avoid. We're keeping a very low profile on this, but it's not for lack of keen concern."

His unflappability unnerved her; she controlled herself rigidly, realizing that her anger put her at a disadvantage against O'Hillary's cool dispassion. She knew there had to be a better way to handle this. Warren would have known how. She said, "Don't you people keep tabs on these Cuban counterrevolutionary groups?''

"That's classified.''

"Of course you do. And if you've been keeping tabs on them you must have known something was in the wind. Possibly even known about this kidnaping before it took place. And if you knew about it why didn't you put a stop to it?''

"How?''

The single word seemed to reveal the extent of O'Hillary's knowledge. She hated him then.

He stood up. "I really must get back to work, Mrs. Lundquist. The minute anything breaks we'll be in touch with your ex-husband. I'm afraid there's nothing further I can tell you. Except perhaps this. I think you credit us with far more power in the world than we possess. We're talking about Cuban terrorists who committed a crime in Mexico, managed to involve two other Latin American governments, and probably are hiding out somewhere between Durango and Rio de Janeiro. Only in the most indirect sense is this an American affair. We can't dictate policy to the government of Venezuela, no matter what the pundits may suggest—anyone who follows the ups and downs of OPEC policies knows that much. We simply don't rule the world. You need to understand that. Even if we did, as long as totalitarian solutions are unacceptable, then problems like this one will not be solved.''

He held out his hand to shake hers; he said with a smooth smile and a soft cadence in his voice, " 'Be wary of what you desire—you'll get it.' Emerson, I believe.''

It was one of those impressive curtain lines you spoke as you went out the door; O'Hillary wasn't leaving, but he turned away from her and walked toward a filing cabinet.

There was nothing left to be said and she saw no point in spoiling his contrived finale. She left his office and, on her way past the secretary's desk, glanced at the girl's intercom. The *On* button was depressed. Either the secretary had taken the conversation down or she'd taped it.

Carole, unsurprised, waited for the guard to escort her to the elevator. She felt neither anger nor disappointment; she felt drained.

She awoke conscious of having dreamed—something fearful that left her short of breath—but she could not recover it.

She'd left a wake-up call for eight; it was seven-twenty. Friday.

Sitting bolt upright she said, "Robert?"

She arrived ahead of public visiting hours and was forced to wait on the Twenty-first Street entrance, fuming while she cooled her heels on the sidewalk. The State Department building was modern and massive, seven stories, heavy with import but not with style. After two minutes of it she could stand it no longer. She found a public phone.

Despite everything the telephone company could do she finally reached Howard. "Tell the bastards to let me in."

Thus armed she got past the guard. The receptionist signed her in; she made her way to the familiar cubicle. It wasn't much—a partitioned roomlet in government green.

She said, "Stand up when a lady comes into your office, you son of a bitch."

He gave her an anemic grin. "Come on in."

She deposited her handbag, sat down, watched him light up a cigarette. "Did you sleep?"

"Not much."

"Neither did I."

He said, "There's been some movement. Mexico and Colombia have put up the ransom between them. They've agreed to release the six prisoners in their jails. They've broadcast it—I don't know if you heard the news?"

"I listened to it. I'm not sure I heard it."

"Venezuela's balking. The money's been raised without them but five of the political prisoners are in Caracas and the Venezuelans insist they aren't going to release them. It's the standard hang-tough policy."

"Are they that heartless?"

"The only way to survive this kind of terrorism is to have a firm policy for dealing with it and to stick to that policy. The only real surprise has been the willingness of the other two countries to knuckle under. Venezuela's posture is, diplomatically speaking, the correct one. Of course usually you negotiate with the terrorists while you're hanging tough. In this case there's nobody to negotiate with. Appeals have been broadcast on the radio in Latin America but it's been a one-sided conversation."

"Hasn't there been any word from them at all?"

"Yes. A note last night to a newspaper in Mexico City. Giving details of where and how the ransom was to be paid. A helicopter drop over a fairly remote forest area on the Yucatan Peninsula."

"Are they sure it's genuine? I mean, couldn't anybody take advantage of a situation like this and deliver a ransom note?"

"It appears to be genuine. It's been examined. It matches the earlier note—the one that turned up in Caracas. Half a page of anti-Castro propaganda, same as before."

"Is anybody searching that Yucatan area?"

"In a way."

"What's that supposed to mean?"

"You can't send troops crashing around in the forest. They'd give themselves away instantly. And you can't use planes or helicopters for the same reason."

"Then nothing's being done. That's what you're telling me."

"Not quite. The helicopter that delivers the ransom will photograph every foot of the ground under it. Both standard film and infrared. There'll also be—I shouldn't tell you this, it's top secret—an overflight by extreme high-altitude reconnaissance aircraft using that James Bondish sort of high-resolution telescopic photography. There's a fair chance they'll spot the pickup of the ransom and be able to trail it back to its destination. Also of course there's a radio transmitter concealed in the container but that probably won't help—usually they're smart enough to take the money out of the container and put it in duffel bags before they move it. Still, you have to try."

She said, "They won't be released right away, will they? Even if they get the ransom."

"They'll want some assurance the political prisoners have been freed and flown to Argentina."

"Argentina? Do you mean to tell me the Argentine government has agreed to give them asylum?"

"Not exactly. They've agreed to keep hands off until Gordon and the other hostages have been released. Which means, probably, that the terrorists must have set up some clandestine escape route to get their people out of Argentina. Probably across Paraguay or something. It can be done—it's easy to disappear down there."

"Then it doesn't end at noon today, does it?"

"Did you ever think it would?"

Noon came and went. She sat listless, her eyes drowsy with memories. Robert's nine-year-old feud with the piano; his erratic career in college; his positive mania for justice.

Howard was on the phone. "There's no movement at all? . . . Very well. Thanks, I'm sorry to keep bothering you."

Carole said, "If I had charge of the assembled might of this technocracy I don't imagine I'd be sitting on my ass the way these people are doing. I'd have had those hostages out of there."

"You and Moshe Dayan."

"It's not possible that an organization as powerful as the United States government can fail to locate and rescue its own Ambassador. This whole system is rotten with the most suicidal and hysterical incompetence I've ever seen. Somebody should fold, spindle and mutilate the whole bureaucratic population of this town."

"Do sit down, for God's sake."

She paced back and forth—four steps, turn, four steps.

"How naïve you are," Howard said. "It's strange how familiar your tune sounds. You can't understand how the most powerful government on earth can fail to lick a handful of scruffy terrorists. Don't you remember hawks saying exactly the same thing about Viet Nam?"

She professed not to hear him. "What's the CIA doing?"

"How do I know?"

She advanced upon the desk. "What's that man's number—what's his name, O'Hillary."

"He won't give you the time of day after the way you iced him yesterday."

"Then you call him."

"It's pointless."

"Call him anyway."

"What for?" He met her eyes. "Carole, it's no good browbeating me any more. It won't accomplish anything. We're both upset as it is—what's the point of henpecking each other to distraction?"

She studied his face. His eyes were raw and pouched; there was a red spot on his lip where he'd chewed the chapped flesh. She said, "The conventional wisdom on the left is that the Department of State is nothing more than an arm of the Pentagon and the CIA. How much truth is there in that?"

"Some." She was surprised by his candor. "It depends who's in the White House. Right now we're better off than we used to be."

"If these terrorists were left-wing radicals, would this thing be handled the same way?"

"Terrorism is equally reprehensible whatever direction it comes from."

"Don't give me the official line."

"I don't think—"

The phone interrupted him. He picked it up and she watched his face change. He was looking straight at her but his eyes lost focus and he shrank.

"All right. Thank you for calling." He cradled it very gently as if he were afraid of disturbing something; from that action she knew what he was going to say before he spoke.

"They have killed him." He uttered the words with great slow precision as if by enunciating them fully he could himself believe in their reality. "They have murdered Robert."

She couldn't breathe. "They haven't—they can't. They mustn't."

He came around the desk blindly, groping for her. "He's dead. My God, he's dead, Carole."

She found herself submitting to his embrace. Her eyes were painfully dry and she seemed incapable of getting oxygen into her lungs. She was aware of the tobacco-stink of his shirt and the tension in his arms. Silent, open-mouthed, trying to hold onto consciousness, she felt him weep.

Then she heard herself say, "Something must be done."

Part Two

Chapter 3

When Glenn Anders entered the Coral Gables office the Deputy Chief told him of the death of Robert Lundquist.

"They dumped the body on the back steps of the police station in Merida, Yucatan. They left all his identification on him so they'd be sure we got the right message. And a note pinned to his shirt. I don't need to tell you what it said." The Deputy Chief—Mackinnon—had a sour jowled face and wisps of black hair across his bald head. "It's a goad, of course. Proof that they mean business. The message is directed mainly at Venezuela. The note said among other things that they'll kill another hostage tomorrow and another the day after that and so on, saving the Ambassador till last, until their demands are met. The idea here, I guess, is that they started with the least prominent of the hostages. The kid was an accidental member of the party."

"This is the Peace Corps boy, I take it? Lundquist?"

"Yes. Poor son of a bitch. At least they did it clean. Shot him in the back of the head. Maybe he never knew it was coming."

"Anything useful in the note?"

"The same anti-Castro propaganda. It's in the lab in Mexico City. Along with the kid's clothes and personals. They're flying him into Houston for the autopsy. Who knows, maybe something will turn up under his fingernails."

"Did they set a new deadline?"

"Noon tomorrow. Predictably."

"Any word from the Venezuelans?"

"Not that I know of. But there'll be a lot more pressure on them now. They're holding out against three countries. A couple of Congressmen are making noises about embargoing oil imports from Venezuela. It wouldn't happen, of course, but the fact that anybody suggests it is pretty hard on the Venezuelan image. Tourists are canceling reservations, that kind of thing. Maybe they'll knuckle under. Personally I wish they wouldn't. The only way to deal with these bastards is to refuse to deal with them. I'm all for the Venezuelans—let 'em stonewall it."

Anders made no reply to that; he rarely believed in certainties or flat statements. If the Venezuelans hadn't stonewalled it, he thought, this Lundquist might not be dead now. But who knows. Everything was caprice.

Mackinnon said, "I take it you didn't turn up anything."

"A couple of names that need checking out. Emilio Ortiz, Guillermo Garza. Mean anything to you?"

"Not especially."

"They're both out of the country on business trips."

"Well maybe they are."

Anders went out to the desk they had lent him and wrote up a report of his day. Then he put through a call to O'Hillary on the scrambler. "Anything new on the Lundquist boy?"

O'Hillary's voice was calm, smooth, avuncular. "No, except that the killing achieved its purpose. The Venezuelans are capitulating. It's not public yet but I have it on good authority. They'll broadcast it tonight—they'll be flying the prisoners out to Buenos Aires in the morning."

"So the bastards get everything they asked for."

"For the moment. Until we find them and take it back. That's still your job, Glenn."

"At the present rate," Anders told him, "I'll probably find them in nineteen ninety-three. Nothing's breaking around here. Anything from air recon?"

"Some marvelous photographs of clouds and trees."

"Shit."

"The beeper in the container hasn't moved since it

was dropped. We don't know if they're leaving it there deliberately or if they've removed the money and left the container behind.''

"Probably the latter," Anders said. "Any instructions?"

"No. Just carry on. We have every confidence in you."

We have every confidence—it made Anders smile when he put down the phone. He was both amused and concerned by the Agency's attitude on this thing. By putting the job in his hands they had revealed a great deal. In the hierarchy of things he was junior-grade. By putting him in charge Washington was going through the motions but it was clear to Anders that nobody was going to be axed if he failed to produce. The whole thing was indicative of the ambivalence with which Washington and Langley regarded this affair. Terrorism must be countered of course—but what if the terrorists weren't quite our enemies?

What a marvelous embarrassment it would be, he thought, if I actually nailed the bastards.

Rosalia came along to his desk. Euphonious Rosalia Rojas. She had the pert eager bounce of an earnest trainee stewardess; certainly she was out of place around here but Mackinnon had called her our best pipeline to the Cuban community. The word that suited her was cute. She had dark tangled hair, cut medium-short, that bounced when she moved. Pug nose, very large black-brown eyes shaped into an expression of astonishment and vulnerability, a short-waisted buxom little body with a nervous brisk way of moving. From the outset she had appealed to him carnally. It had ripened beyond that and beyond anything he'd anticipated: Yet somehow it wasn't alarming.

She had a small steno notebook from which she started reading aloud before she stopped walking. "I checked into those six names. Four of them are here in the Miami area working at their jobs and they haven't been out of town in months except one of them took the wife and kids to Disney World six weeks ago. This leaves two, if the new math hasn't altogether corrupted

my arithmetic, and one of them is definitely in Mobile
on one of those corporation refresher-training courses.
He fixes cars for the Oldsmobile dealer and they've sent
him to GM mechanics' school.''

"Leaving one more.''

"Go to the head of the class,'' she said cheerfully.
"His name is''—just the slightest trace of accent, *hees-
name-ees*, you might miss it if you weren't listening for
it—"Ignacio Gandara, age forty-one, occupation construction worker. At the moment he is laid off and
collecting Unemployment but he didn't pick up the two
most recent checks at the Unemployment office and no
one who knows him has seen him in about three
weeks.''

"Does he have an American passport?''

"Yes.''

"Find out if he's used it, can you?''

She made a note. "How did you do?''

"About the same as you. Five negatives, two pos-
sibles. Guillermo Garza, occupation lawyer—or so it
says on his shingle—and Emilio Ortiz, who's—''

"A construction engineer,'' Rosalia said. "I know
Emilio, he's godfather to one of my sisters. He's been
shuttling back and forth to St. Thomas, working for a
company that's building a condominium over there.''

"That could be a cover, couldn't it? Let's not scratch
Ortiz off the list just yet.''

She said, "Maybe you're right. But I've always liked
him.''

"One of the delights of this business is learning how
little you can trust people.'' He looked at his watch.
"Join me for supper?''

When he looked up he caught the sparkle in her eye.
"I'd love to. I'll be ready in ten minutes—I'll just put
the Gandara inquiry on the wire to Passport Control.''

It was a flat low rectangular building on the Tamiami
Trail, its only distinguishing feature a huge towering
electric sign that looked like something along the Strip
in Las Vegas. The parking lot was the size of a football
field. Rosalia clipped along beside him chattering—her

way of talking, like everything else about her, was quick and cheerful. Inside the place he had to stop to accustom his eyes to the sudden dimness. It was one of those structures that had been built since the invention of central air conditioning; it had no windows at all. The chandeliers were imitation wagonwheels, the decor was ersatz Wild West, the booths were heavy wood lined with padded black leather, the jukebox boomed with Waylon Jennings and Willie Nelson. The menu offered steaks, rib roast and lobster; the drinks came in massive frosted tumblers like the mugs in drive-in root-beer stands. A girl in backless top and a skirt so short it exposed her fanny, and heels so high she tottered, guided them to a booth and, when Anders made a dry remark, guided them to another one farther from the hammering of the jukebox. There was a lousy painting of Custer's Last Stand over the bar and the two bartenders wore handlebar mustaches and ten-gallon hats. Anders detested Florida.

When they slid into the leather banquette he said to his companion, "I was thirty before I ever saw this part of the world. I had friends in Chicago who'd go to Miami Beach every winter—I grew up in that kind of set, lower-middle-class snobs. They kept telling me I had to go to Miami Beach and see all the fabulous hotels. I never intended to go there. I expected sooner or later Miami Beach would come to me, as it does to all men. I was right."

"This isn't Miami Beach. It's Coral Gables."

"Yeah. What'll you have?"

"A hangover." She was studying the menu. "But I think I'll start with a banana daiquiri."

When the tedium of ordering was concluded he gave Rosalia his full attention. In the jaundiced light her skin seemed pale and velvety. She had an emphatic way of returning his gaze. Then she screwed up her nose at him. "You're a big shambling teddy bear, aren't you."

That made him laugh. "I think I'm falling in love with you." Immediately it sounded lame; he'd meant it to be light, but not facetious: a joke to cover the fact that he meant it.

"Shucks, all the guys say that."

"I believe that," he agreed. "A backtrail crowded with broken hearts."

She said, "I broke up with my boy friend three months ago. I moved out. I cried for a week and went numb for a week but I'm great at bouncing back. I'm telling you that because I didn't want you to waste half an hour groping around for a way to ask me if there were any other serious men in my life. Or men seriously in my life, or whatever—I majored in English lit but it's still my second language. I was going to be a teacher," she explained, "but then I realized I hate teaching. I don't have the patience to deal with people who don't learn everything right the first time. Anyway I'm more useful here, you know. My father was very important in the Cuban exile movement. He died a few years ago but I've still got the family contacts."

"Don't you feel you're selling them out?"

"Sometimes," she conceded. "You have to decide where your loyalties are, don't you. We left Cuba when I was four. I'm a citizen of the United States. I don't picture any scenario in which the exiles will ever recover the properties they lost to Castro, do you?"

"I don't think the restoration of confiscated properties is the motive. I give these folks a bit more credit than that."

"They don't like Castro—they don't like Communism. I don't think much of Castro or Communism either. But then I'm sure I wouldn't have thought much of Batista either. You know it's not easy when you're born into the middle of a squabble like this. Whatever I do, I'm a traitor to somebody. I've spent my whole life arguing these things with my family and friends."

"And?"

"I can't see how war and killing will solve the problem. The counterrevolutionary movements want war. They're wrong. So I'm against them."

He envied her. She'd managed to make clear simple sense out of a complex muddle.

She said, "This Lundquist thing—what do you think will happen?"

"It's foregone. We haven't had a prayer of getting close to these guys in time to do any good. The ransom's been paid, the political prisoners are on their way to B.A. and I expect either the Ambassador will be turned loose in a few days or the bodies will turn up in a common grave in the jungle. Probably they'll turn 'em loose because that way the thing will die down sooner."

"And then?"

"We'll interview the survivors and maybe we'll be able to identify the terrorists from that, but I get a feeling it won't work out that way—they haven't been stupid up to now. I'm not confident. Either way it'll be forgotten. Nothing stays in the headlines. Another crisis will come up."

"They've got ten million dollars for making war."

"The terrorists? Maybe. They can't overthrow Castro with dollar bills. It's got to be a pretty small group."

"They can make a lot of trouble."

"There's always trouble," Anders said.

"Have you had any experience with hijackers before?"

"Sure. That's why I was assigned to this one."

"These are brighter than most, aren't they?"

"Cool and careful. That's worth worrying about. Terrorists are usually neurotic kids without sense—suicidal fanatics. They throw tantrums and smash toys to get attention—they're too immature to think about consequences. Mostly they end up killed. But these guys have kept the rear exit open, nobody's touched them and I won't be surprised if they disappear with the ransom money. We'll pick up a trail somewhere but it may be too cold to do us any good. Here come the lobsters."

His mind had jumped off the straight track and he listened with only half attention to Rosalia's bursts of talk while he pursued this new line of thought. Over coffee he broke into her monologue with an abrupt rhetorical quiestion: "What if the setup was a false front? What if they're a little gang of ingenious crooks who've found a clever way to steal ten million dollars?"

"What?"

"Suppose they're not politicals at all. It fits," he said. "It's starting to look as if they don't belong to the known Cuban exile movements."

"But then why would they bother with the propaganda ransom notes and demanding the release of the political prisoners and all?"

"There'd be reasons enough. A smokescreen to throw us off the track. And everybody knows governments treat political agitators more gingerly than common crooks. And in this case there's the anti-Castro aspect—we'd have committed more resources to the hunt if they'd been Communist terrorists."

"Is that really how you see it?"

"I don't know. The theory fits a lot of the facts. It'd be a daring risky kind of crime but it's not much more dangerous than knocking over a bank and it's a little bit more lucrative. And if they're not politicals that would help explain why we haven't tumbled any leads. For all we know they could be a gang of Mexican bandits out of a Pedro Armendariz movie."

Rosalia had a flat in a two-story apartment court with its own pool and palm trees. The furniture was a reflection of her hectic person: busy fabrics but clean shapes. The Parsons tables were black plastic, the lamps were stark and the end tables were clear lucite cubes. There was a profusion of potted house-plants. On the walls were matted enlargements of high-contrast photographs—winter birch forests, a rocky coast that looked like Maine, something that looked at first like an abstract but turned out to be a shot of wood grain in close-up. When she turned on the stereo he was surprised by the selection: a jazz quintet coolly psychoanalyzing *Don't Get Around Much Anymore*.

She said, "Drinkie?"

"Got any rum?"

"That's very diplomatic."

"Not really. I like it."

"It's not Cuban," she said drily and went clipping

into the kitchenette, speedy and practical and sure of herself.

He liked her. He thought perhaps he loved her but he had thought that a few times before and his ex had crashed into an overpass abutment at eighty miles an hour with a blood-alcohol content later measured at near comatose levels; now he was wary because he felt he'd driven her to it. In any case he wasn't sure what women saw in him. He'd always been just a little over-weight; he had the square face of a vacuum-cleaner salesman; and the Anders hair, a product of Danish genes, was pale and thin—it flowed in the air like seaweed, he thought. He had confidence in one thing: He did his work well. That was a reason to feel close to Rosalia. She understood the work. But then it didn't make sense looking for reasons for such things.

She said, "What's on for tomorrow?"

"I'd better get down to Mexico."

"Oh."

He said, "Your Spanish is better than mine."

"Anybody's is. Yours is atrocious." Her eyes wandered away.

"Look," he said, "how would you like to fly down to Mexico with me?"

Her smile was as good as a kiss.

Chapter 4

A fish jumped through the surface of the river: broached, shook foam, dived. Cielo watched for a while but it didn't leap again. He listened to the birds and then finally went back along the riverbank reluctantly; it was time to put things in motion.

There were clouds; steam in the air; soon there'd be rain. It was what he had waited for—a safe time to move the hostages out. Later if someone tried to backtrack them with dogs or infrared the rain would protect them by washing away clues between the camp and the dock. The whole thing, he thought, was a quixotic farce; but one might as well maintain security. He slapped at a mosquito.

Cielo wasn't the name he'd been born with; the *nom de guerre* had been chosen mainly for its meaninglessness. *Cielo:* sky. Only two of the nine men in his band knew his real name, not that it mattered; Rodriquez was not so astonishing a surname.

No one was in sight; that was in obeisance to the discipline of the camp—there was no knowing what sort of high-altitude equipment might be in search of them; the rule was to stay under cover at all times. Cielo entered the camp from tree to tree until he reached the covered walkway.

The camp had been built long ago by a Dutch oil company as quarters for its men during an exploration for petroleum in the river delta. When they found no oil they'd floated their rigs away to try again farther down the coast; they'd left the camp behind, as they usually did—it was cheaper to prefabricate a new one than to dismantle the old one and haul it away.

Cielo had left it all untouched; when he was gone he wanted to leave behind no sign of his presence. Nothing had been disturbed; machetes were forbidden—not even twigs were allowed to be broken.

He found Vargas and the big Draga boy in the money hut standing well away from the cage and looking expectantly toward him; he had interrupted their colloquy, startled them, and there was no way for Cielo to know whether they had been discussing the weather, the subject of sex, or the possibility of stealing the ten million dollars from Cielo.

He said, "It'll rain soon."

Vargas had a terrifying smile; it went with his size. It was said Vargas had broken a man's back with his hands but Cielo knew the story to be false. Vargas was as gentle as he was massive; a man that big rarely needed to lose his temper. Cielo had known him twenty years. That was part of the trouble, he thought: *We're too old to believe in this nonsense. It takes children.*

No, the money wouldn't tempt Vargas; and as for the Draga boy, the idea might amuse him but in the end he would not steal because he did not need to steal. Emil Draga was the heir to his grandfather's fortune, which would be enough to discourage him from taking suicidal risks. The lad wasn't in this for money. He was in it, in an atavistic sense, for the adventure—he was a clever youth, big and muscular, ugly, stuffed with Draga legends of *machismo* and arrogance and financial bucaneering: Through determined rapacity the Dragas had acquired empires of cane and rum. Left to himself the hard and ruthless young Emil probably would become a corporate-takeover pirate, a Wall Street raider; if and when the old man died, Emil probably would move instantly to New York. Cielo had no illusions that The Movement could survive old Draga.

For the moment Emil would stay at Cielo's right hand until the old man ordered him elsewhere or he saw an opportunity to flex his brutal muscles again.

In the cage with the money the squirrel and the parakeet showed no signs of illness. It had been long enough. Cielo said, "You can pack up the money and give their freedom back to the bird and the squirrel.''

Vargas showed his chilling smile. ''It's our day for being magnanimous. Today we give freedom back to everybody.''

''Don't forget your hoods.'' Cielo went toward the door wondering if he'd neglected anything. The parakeet and the squirrel had been caged forty-eight hours with the ransom money because Cielo had heard once about a rigged payment of money that had been radioactively treated so as to infect anyone who handled it. During the past days they also had studied the money under infrared and ultraviolet lights to make sure it hadn't been dyed; they had sifted laboriously through the $50 and $100 notes looking for evidences of serial-number sequences or counterfeiting; they had subjected the money to every test they could think of. So far as Cielo could determine, it was clean. No doubt there'd been giveaway devices attached to the canister in which the money had been dropped from the helicopter, but they hadn't even bothered to search it for transmitters. They'd left it where it had fallen until fourteen hours after the drop, when they'd moved it under cover of rain and transferred the money into the canvas sacks and gone out the way they'd come in—by canoe part of the way, outboard motorboat the rest.

He always preferred boats when it was possible. He was an island man, that was part of it, but also there was the fact that a boat left no footprints.

He said, ''We'll go in half an hour,'' and left the hut.

He pushed the camouflage net aside and went aboard the ketch, stooping to clear his head when he went below. He cranked up the receiver and put on the headphones and consulted the dashboard chronograph; Julio was due to broadcast in three minutes. He waited with relaxed patience. He had learned patience long ago and practiced it all his life. In Sierra Maestra of the Cuban civil war, on the beaches of the Bay of Pigs waiting for the air cover that didn't come, in Castro's prison, in all the slow years since his escape from Cuba in 1964—the nondescript demeaning jobs, the secrecy,

the undercover work for old Draga. The slow acqui-
sition and equally slow disintegration of the hard tight
determined cell of Free Cubans. After the Bay of Pigs
and the softening of U.S. relations with the Castro
regime old Draga had lost any trust he might have had
in the American government; he had gone it alone,
trusting no one outside his own household and Cielo's
tight little band. They had practiced a conscious and
businesslike paranoia—Cielo's, alone among the movements, had successfully avoided infiltration by agents of
Washington and Langley. Draga kept them isolated
from all the other exile armies; Cielo had admitted to
membership no new recruits—the *commando* was
manned entirely by those with whom he had done time
in the dripping Havana cells.

Until now. Emil Draga; he couldn't be certain of
Emil. The hothead had already exploded once. It was,
he felt, another sign of the rot that had infected the
group surreptitiously for years.

The radio crackled in his earphones. Good de-
pendable Julio, the best of all possible brothers: mer-
curial, given to fits of gloom and sunshine, *macho* spirit
and great lusty laughter and deep brooding sorrows.
The loves of Cielo's life were few: his three daughters,
his wife, his brother. He cherished them—there was
nothing else. The dream of glory had faded beyond
recall.

"Merida to Constellation Three. Merida to Constellation Three." Julio's big voice, its boom thinned by
static. "Message follows. Consignment arrived safely in
Buenos Aires. All shipments on course and on schedule.
Weather forecast light rain for eighteen hours. Have a
good voyage. Merida out."

Cielo switched it off. *We've succeeded, then,* he
thought. The irony of it: empty gestures to placate a rich
old man's obsessions.

For a time it had been all right. He hadn't minded; it
was something to do. But no one was supposed to have
been killed.

In his quarters he packed everything neatly into the

B-4 bag, set it by the door and went around
meticulously wiping everything with a damp towel to
obscure prints, searching and searching again: Nothing
must be left behind.

He went outside with the bag and set it on the pile of
satchels and valises and knapsacks. Luz was there, his
face an utter blank. "Put your mask on," Cielo said,
and went along under the covered walkway to the third
hut. The last thing he did before reaching for the door's
latch was to press the heavy beard against his cheeks to
make sure it was fixed in place. By now he was used to
the pillow-stuffing under his belt. They'd remember him
as a big man with a soft belly and all sorts of beard. It
was what he wanted them to remember.

He unlocked the big padlock and put it in his pocket;
it wouldn't be needed again and he could not leave it
here—it was remotely possible it might be traced: Locks
had serial numbers.

Inside the windowless Quonset the air was stale with
sweat. The Ambassador was in the middle of the floor
doggedly doing push-ups; from the beginning he had
put Cielo in mind of Alec Guinness in *Bridge on the
River Kwai*—stuffy, blimpish, courageous. Cielo
couldn't picture himself ever trusting the man but he
rather liked him and was pleased no harm had come to
him.

Cielo spoke in English because he knew the Mexicans
among the hostages understood it. He was not so sure of
the Ambassador's Spanish.

"We're going to blindfold you. Don't be frightened—you're going to be set free in less than twelve
hours. Our ransom demands have been met and we
intend to honor our part of the bargain."

He watched their reactions. Vacuous slow gapes;
tears; explosions of relief; glares of disbelieving suspicion. One of the Agriculture Ministry men beamed
gratefully at Cielo.

It was his first experience in the management of
hostages but he had heard that they sometimes became
sycophantically dependent on their captors. The

friendliness with which most of them stared at him did not surprise him.

He said without conviction, "You're close to freedom now. Please don't risk it by foolish behavior. If anyone tries to run for it we'll shoot without hesitation. If you co-operate you'll be free by morning."

They watched him expectantly. The Ambassador, on his feet now, tried to squint defiantly but his relief was too evident; finally he turned toward the others to hide his involuntary smile from Cielo.

He fingered the submachine gun absently. "In a moment we'll blindfold you. You'll be taken out of here and down the same path by which we arrived. We're going to take you back aboard the same boat as before and you'll be locked in the crew's quarters forward. As you recall there are six bunks and a toilet. It will be cramped but it's only for a few hours. Before daylight you'll be set ashore and you'll see the last of us."

One of the American Marines glared at him, filled with distrust. That one had been a troublemaker from the beginning; in retrospect Cielo wistfully wished that if someone had had to be killed it could have been the Marine rather than the Peace Corps youth. The youth had made trouble with his mouth and drawn attention to himself but this Marine was far more dangerous in his silent scheming ways. Two nights ago he'd tried to organize an escape by digging out under the back wall. Vargas had heard the noise and they'd put a stop to it, bloodying the Marine's nose as a lesson, but it hadn't put a stop to the Marine's brain. The Marine was dogged—a good soldier; Cielo didn't lack admiration for him.

"When you're set ashore you'll find a burro trail leading into the forest. Follow the burro trail for several hours. It will be morning by then, you'll have no trouble. By noon you'll come to a paved highway. After that you'll make your own fate. A car or a truck will come along, you'll make your own decisions. By tomorrow night you'll be home with your families. So please be patient just a little longer."

He addressed this last directly to the Marine because he understood the Marine to be susceptible to reason. Threats would not dissuade the Marine from resistance or rebellion; reason might. It all depended whether he could convince the Marine that he actually meant to set them free. If the Marine believed he was destined for murder then no amount of logic would calm him.

The Marine's thoughts were not readable. He met Cielo's stare without guile, reserving judgment.

Cielo said, "It is, you see, in our own interests now that you all be released unharmed. It proves to the world that we are men of our word, and also in a practical sense it will help to calm the rage of your governments. If we were to murder you we'd become hunted outcasts everywhere. If we keep our word and release you, we are heroes—at least to those who agree with our purpose. I therefore beg your co-operation for a few more hours."

He was thinking, *To them I must be a terrifying apparition*—the size of him, the beard, the machine gun, the unnaturally gruff rasp he used for a voice in their presence. It was a good thing they couldn't see the fraud underneath. He was searching his brain: Was there anything else he ought to say to them? He couldn't think of anything. It would have to do.

He backed toward the door. "In just a little while now," he told them, and left. At the moment of going through the door he realized that if Soledad could see him now she would laugh at him.

He imagined the bubbling caress of her voice and thought, *I am truly a figure of ridicule*. The thought put him in a better frame of mind until he went into the big hut and crossed glances with young Emil. The youth gave him a rakishly defiant look, brimming with sullen resistance. That one had made a murderer of Cielo and the thing had gone altogether sour then; Cielo was in command and could not absolve himself of the responsibility but it was Emil who had killed the American boy, without orders, and thus put an end to Cielo's plan that no one be injured. From that moment it had no longer been a bluff; up to then Cielo had been prepared

to give it up if the target governments had refused the
ransom demands but after Emil's act there had been no
choice. Once the American was dead it would have been
foolhardy not to make use of the corpse so he had ordered it dumped in the town.

The American's jiggling earnestness, his ceaseless
talk, had irritated them all but in truth the American
had meant no harm and done none, except to their
nerves. Cielo thought, *I had better light candles for him.*

He'd already reprimanded Emil harshly but beyond
that did it matter? It wasn't Emil's fault that nobody
had told him the whole exercise was a sham, a bit of
theater, a command performance for the entertainment
of old man Draga. Emil, in committing them to the
irrevocability of their course, had merely shown that he
believed it wasn't a lark; it was war. Well it was war
only in Draga's withered mind but Emil didn't know
that because there was no way for anyone to explain it
to him. And maybe Emil was right. You had to do this
sort of thing believing in it; otherwise you were worse
than a fool.

Emil had served in the American Army toward the
end of the Viet Nam absurdity; there he had learned to
kill dispassionately and casually. Perhaps he had murdered the American boy to remind his older companions
of what he thought they were up to. Cielo remembered
the sullen contempt in Emil's eyes when he'd ad-
monished them beforehand. *There's to be no killing.*

Such a stupid farce, he thought. The old man would
have done better to entrust his job to Emil. For purposes of revolution you needed kids. People too young
to have grown inhibitions.

Cielo fingered the submachine gun again. At least he
could finish the job; that much he could do. Get the
money back to Draga and make sure it wasn't hijacked
along the way by outsiders. But one thing was sure. No
more hostages were going to be murdered. He'd shoot
Emil before he'd let him kill another innocent.

The others in the room came forward slowly, sweep-
ing the walls and the cot frames with damp toweling,
preparing to quit the hut. Cielo drew back the cuff of

his fatigue jacket to examine his watch. Just right. Any minute now the rain would begin and daylight would drain away. Soon they'd be on the river bound for the sea. Ghosts in a rainy night; no one would catch them now.

Chapter 5

When Carole emerged into the steamy Houston heat there was a ravening mob of journalists on the concrete steps and Howard took her arm, leading the way, trying to drive a wedge through them. Strobes half-blinded her and there was the flicker of lenses. One of the bayonet microphones almost took her jaw off. The reporters were all talking at once and she couldn't understand a word; she cringed, shaded her eyes, got behind Howard and pressed forward, using him as a ram. "Get me out of this."

Can you tell us how it feels. . . . Have you been told if anything has been learned. . . . What sort of boy was he. . . . Your reaction to the Venezuelan delay that may have cost your son his life. . . . How does it feel?

She screamed. "You fucking hyenas!" knowing the obscenity would render their films and recordings useless.

Howard was booming calmly, "Give us a break, this is no time. . . ." His voice was lost in the babble.

He fed her into the car; she punched the lock button down and stared ahead stonily. Like slavering kids at a candy store window they pressed up against the windshield. She held herself rigid. Flashbulbs exploded. One of the reporters stumbled against the car, making it rock. Howard fought his way around and squeezed into the driver's seat. When he turned the key in the ignition she said, "Run them down."

"Take it easy. We'll be out of this in a minute." He gunned the engine in neutral, making a noise. It drove the pack into retreat and he pulled it gently away from the curb. When she looked back she saw the red light still winking above a TV camera's zoom lens. Then they were around the corner and she slumped. "Ghouls."

"I know. I know." He pulled up at a red light. "Look, we'd better drive up to Beaumont and catch a plane there. They might be covering the airport here."

"You go ahead. Drop me by a taxi. I'll check into a motel."

"What's the point of hanging on here?"

"I'm going to wait and fly back to Virginia with the body when they're finished with it."

"That's morbid."

"One of us has to do it."

"They'll send it on. We've got to get back to Alexandria—the funeral arrangements have to be made. . . ."

"You go ahead then."

"It's something else, isn't it?"

She said, "In all the madness I didn't really get a chance to talk to that Marine."

"You won't get a crack at him for weeks, Carole. He'll be closeted in debriefing sessions with the others. They won't let him talk to outsiders until they've squeezed him dry—they may not even let him talk afterward."

"I have to know," she said.

"There's a better chance of that in Washington than there is here. At least we may be able to squeeze some information out of O'Hillary."

"There's a taxi. Pull over."

"Nonsense," he said. "If you're determined I'll take you to a hotel. Any preference?"

"I've never been in Houston in my life. How do I know?"

The car's air conditioner blew a dry chill against her face. The street was a wide boulevard lined with structures that looked tentative and temporary; it might have been Los Angeles. Traffic endlessly streaming. *Life goes on*, she thought with bitter banality.

At the first motor hotel she said, "That one will do," not caring; Howard pulled in under the porte-cochere and opened the trunk to get out her overnight bag. The heat was close and depressingly heavy.

By the room, key in hand, she said, "Go ahead. I'll be all right. I've got phone calls to make." She opened it and pushed inside.

"I don't like leaving you just now."

She turned, lurching; walked blindly toward a door.

"Where are you going?"

"The bathroom," she said. "Don't worry, I'm all right."

"Don't go. Stay here."

"Howard, I'm going to make a fool of myself and cry."

"Fine. I'd rather you cried here with me than by yourself in there."

She sat down. "I'm sorry to be such a fool. I'll get over it in a minute."

"Suppose I stay on a while. I can take a late-night flight. Let's have dinner before I go."

"I'm afraid I can't. I've just remembered I have a terrible headache."

He pressed his hands together until she heard the knuckles crack. "I wish I knew what to do for you."

"Nothing. I'll be all right. You can depart with a clear conscience."

"Please don't be like that."

"I'm sorry." She was too exhausted to argue.

"Look, if there's anything—"

"The fact is right now at the moment I'm unable to meet the emotional demands of this and I need to be left alone to collect myself. If you stay much longer we'll start degrading each other."

After he left she went to the window and watched his car until he got into it and drove away into the traffic. Failing to collect her thoughts she attempted to rest but her eyes wouldn't stay shut and finally she made a number of phone calls trying to arrange a meeting with the Marine but everything was shut to her.

Then she had a half-formed idea. There'd been a dimly familiar face in that mob of journalists on the steps. She went back to the phone. It required three calls. One to Los Angeles Information; armed with the number she called the L.A. paper; armed by the

Examiner with a Houston number she called Dwiggins' hotel.

Dwiggins arrived in something under twenty minutes and gave her a baffled smile.

"Come in," she said, "I'm unarmed."

"Why me?"

"Because I want something from you."

"Quid pro quo?"

"Yes. You can have an interview if you think it's worth it."

"You're front-page copy right now. Celebrity mother of terrorist victim." He came in but seemed hesitant about shutting the door. She made a vague gesture and he closed it and crossed gingerly to a chair where he sat up on the edge like an expectant pupil.

Dwiggins was fortyish and quite fat, his hair prematurely white and wispy; he had a journalistically bibulous nose and wry eyes that had seen everything.

She said, "I noticed you in that lynch mob but it didn't register until afterward."

"I'm flattered you remember me at all."

"Your column on me wasn't particularly friendly, as I recall—something about me being the apostate leader of a new wave of sentimentality and cornball trash—but you did me the extraordinary courtesy of printing what I'd actually said in the interview. I find that unique."

He dipped his head an inch. "Thank you."

"Are you also old-fashioned enough to honor an agreement to keep something off the record?"

"If the agreement is made beforehand. I won't print anything without your permission."

"You won't even discuss it among your friends. Fair enough?"

"All right. But—"

"The quid pro quo, I know. I'll give you an interview you can print. This is something else."

Dwiggins acceded with a dip of his broad face.

"I'll make it as painless for you as possible." She nodded toward the tape recorder, granting permission. "You want to know how I feel about the death of my son. I feel every which way—like a kaleidoscope. Right at this moment I have an acute desire never to feel anything again."

"Sure."

"I'm sure you don't need remarks from me about the senselessness of this tragedy. Of course it's arbitrary, it's a grisly waste of a brilliant human life, it's pointless and maddening."

He said quietly, "Have you cried much?"

"Yes, I have tears but I don't let them blur my vision. Mainly right now I feel rage. I want revenge, you see. I can't help it, I can't rationalize it away. It's intensely personal and I'm sure that's a useless response to such an impersonal attack but that's how I feel. I want these terrorists punished."

"Brought to justice."

"Justice," she said, "doesn't come into it. I'm talking about emotions now. Justice is an abstract concept." She made a loose fist and contemplated it; she looked up at the reporter. "I want to be there, physically present, the day these animals are destroyed. I'll get satisfaction from it—I know, nothing can bring my son back. But all the same. It's what I feel."

Dwiggins said, "Tell me about Robert."

At one point he stopped her to flip the tape cassette over to Side Two. They kept talking and it was unreal to her: Two people conversing normally as if the world still were the same as it had been a week ago. She tried to be candid and articulate. She tried to listen carefully to his questions and respond appropriately. But the words— both Dwiggins' and her own—broke up in her mind. Half the time she was not aware of what she was saying, although a canny part of her mind kept hold of the secrets that had to remain off the tape and off the record; she talked automatically but not carelessly.

When the tape was finished Carole said, "Thank you. You could have made it much harder for me."

"I promise you there won't be any snide asides about cornball trash." He had relaxed during the interview, slumping back in the chair, crossing his legs, watching her amiably while she spoke. He was not a threatening figure. She sensed a great deal of sadness in him but had no clue to its source.

She asked if he wanted to drink and he declined, surprising her. "I'm a bit of a lush," he confided, "but I keep it under control and I don't drink when I'm working."

"Do you mind if I have one?"

"Not at all."

It was a two-ounce screw-top bottle of Scotch she'd dropped in her handbag on the airplane. She sucked it straight from the nipple of the bottle. "We go off the record now," she said. "All the way off the record. This is exclusively between you and me and it goes no farther."

"Fair enough. What do you want me to do?"

"Did you ever know my brother?"

"Warren Marchand? No, not personally. I admired his work a great deal. He was a hell of a writer."

"I thought you might have known him. That series you did for the *Examiner* about the CIA mercenaries in the Montagnard country."

"That was years ago. I'm astonished you'd remember it."

"I remember it because it was the kind of thing my brother would have done."

"I take that as a considerable compliment."

"It was meant as one," she said. "Is that the only time you've departed from your usual Hollywood beat?"

"No. I did a series on the Alaska pipeline a few years ago. And I was in Angola a while during that mess. I covered the aftermath of the Allende assassination in Chile, too. Once in a while I ask for a hard-news assignment. It reminds me of the real world out there beyond the tinsel."

"Do you still keep in touch with any of the people you interviewed on those stories?"

"Which people?"

"Mercenaries."

His eyelids dropped; he gave her a long scrutiny before he replied. "This is hardly the century for that kind of romantic gesture, you know.''

"Maybe it's a good idea whose time has come back. I'm descended from good solid Norman stock. People whose record of violence and rapacity would make Caligula look like Shirley Temple. If you look at it that way it would be completely out of character for me to sit by and do nothing in the face of this—this, what can I call it? Obscenity? Affront?''

"You're being irrational, you know.''

"Of course I am. If God had wanted us to be entirely reasonable he'd have made us in the image of a Univac computer.''

Dwiggins said, "Forgive me if I pick this up as if it were ticking.''

"It won't be any risk for you, whatever happens.''

"I don't want to be the one to send you into the jungle.''

"You're a good guy, Dwiggins.''

He said, "What do you know about terrorists?''

"Not much.''

"I've made a few observations over the years. Want to hear them?''

"Certainly.''

"The terrorist is a juvenile delinquent, whatever his age. He's not much different from a kid who gets into drugs or joins the Moonies or makes his bedroom into a shrine to some rock group. Does that surprise you? He senses misplaced feelings all around him, and inside him. The terrorist can't stand the idea of being an ordinary person like anybody else. And he can't stand the idea that ordinary people may actually enjoy their lives. In a sense he has an amazing affinity for the banal—violence, I think, is one of the stupidest but most natural responses to frustration, and what's the real difference between terrorism and football? The problem isn't terrorists, the problem's the world that creates them. When things get so big and complex and impersonal that no individual feels he can affect anything around him, he becomes sullen and apathetic and he resents his impotence and sooner or later he explodes. One way or another. We all have our own private explosions. We're all caught up in the obsession with novelty—marching to ever new tunes, excited by ever new fads of salvation—astrology, drugs, gurus, revolutions. One man's 'est' is another man's terrorism. Do you see what I'm saying to you? I think you seem to have managed to convince yourself that the people who killed your boy aren't human. It's the key psychosis of warfare. The enemy isn't human because he's the enemy.''

"Dwiggins," she said with a tight little smile, "you can take your social theories and wrap them in sandpaper and shove them all the way up."

He professed not to hear her. "I'm not excusing them. God knows they're more to be censured than pitied. But look, when children drop and smash their toys you don't murder them, you just clean up the mess as best you can."

"These are not infants. They're responsible for their acts."

Dwiggins sighed. "You're convinced they're not going to be apprehended?"

"I have no doubt of it."

"You may be right. If they're half clever they'll stay out of reach until the world loses interest in them. There won't be any extended outcry for their capture. The people—including politicians—the people get exercised but they never get concerned. The voice of the people is mainly an indifferent groan."

She let him run on. He was talking himself into it; she didn't need to prompt him.

He made a last-ditch effort at resistance. "You don't like to feel that you're an ordinary person who can be pushed around by these events. That's something you have in common with the terrorists—your motives aren't much different from theirs and now you're proposing to use their methods, too. Does that leave any difference between you and them?"

"I never aspired to the sainthood."

"It's a *kamikaze* idea." Dwiggins' elbows were on his knees. He exposed his palms to her. "You are nuts, you know that?"

"I grant the possibility."

"Certifiable," he said. "It costs money, I expect, and nobody could make any promises."

"I know. I have some money and I don't expect promises."

He said, "I want to cover this story."

"Let's see how it works out first. I may let you know how things go. Then again—"

"That's not good enough."

"I did you a favor," she told him, "and I asked you one in return. If you want to renege I'll try someone else, but—"

"What do you want? A private army?"

"I want one man. Someone who can find them—someone who knows that part of the shadows."

He brooded at her and she met his glance. She was tired of his evasions and admonishments; apparently he saw that, for he gave a quick little nod. "I'll ask around. Where will you be?"

She felt at the same time relieved, satisfied, and all at once frightened—as if a door were slowly closing, shutting her into a private hell.

Chapter 6

In the fading September light the trees were heavy with dark leafery and she walked heavily. The funeral was still an open wound and she had no idea when it might begin to heal; she anticipated nothing.

O'Hillary in his office was as before: all plastic surface, running his hand through that wavy hair of his. A quick pleasant smile and cold eyes. Smooth, cynical and adept; earnest and compassionate, without an ounce of feeling in it. He probably made love as if he were dictating a memo. According to the white-gold ring he was married and she found this astonishing.

"I appreciate your coming," he said. He pronounced "appreciate" with a very precise "c." "We've debriefed Ambassador Gordon and some of the other hostages. I thought you might like to know the results. I'm afraid for the most part they're negative. We know there were at least seven terrorists. The leader was a big man with a bushy beard. The beard may have been false, of course. The others wore masks or hoods at all times. They spoke with Spanish accents. At least one or two of them have some background in seamanship—they transported the hostages in a sailing boat. Now as to the death of, ah, Robert Lundquist, I'm afraid we've learned less than we'd have liked to learn by this time. As you know, one of the Marines on the security detail had been struck a severe blow on the head, and evidently your son was concerned there might be concussion—he badgered the terrorists to get medical attention for the Marine. After a while your son was taken out of the hut. The others thought he was being taken to see the leader so he could press his request for medical attention for the Marine. That was the last any of them saw of him. They didn't see the murder take place, so I'm afraid his murderer won't be identified until we've apprehended the terrorists and interrogated them.''

"You've found the hiding place, haven't you?''

"It's being searched. Every lead is being pursued.'' Something—possibly the coldness of her face—prompted him to add, "This gang seems to be some sort of wild-card outfit. None of the known Cuban exile groups knows anything about them. We'll come up with results, I think I can promise you that, but it's going to take time.''

"If a crime isn't solved in the first forty-eight hours it probably never will be solved. Statistical fact, Mr. O'Hillary.'' One of Robert's statistical facts. "I'm not a supplicant begging for scraps. I'm a citizen. I'm the one who pays your salary.''

O'Hillary's face colored a bit. "Of course I understand how upset you are. But we're on the same side, aren't we?''

"I don't think we are.''

"Isn't that a bit—well, paranoid?''

"It's consistent with the facts.''

"Consistent? You could say that about a cathartic. We're doing our jobs, Mrs. Marchand, as best we know how to do them. There's no massive conspiracy to cover up the facts about your son's death. I think you must be careful to make sure your anxieties don't drive you into emotional difficulties. I know this is an excruciating cliché, but nothing any of us can do about this can bring your son back or make up for your loss.''

"I haven't entirely taken leave of my senses,'' she said. "I simply want to be able to face myself when I think of my son. Never mind, Mr. O'Hillary.'' She saw it was no good; there was no getting through to the *apparatchiks*; she got up and left.

It wasn't much of a walk back to the hotel. An old woman went by walking an infinitesimal dog, and somewhere a siren shrieked; a young man came along bearing cut flowers in white tissue wrappings, beamed at her and went on by with a spring in his step. She nearly snarled at him. She knew she was going to have to do something about this rage before it destroyed her.

At the desk she found a message from Dwiggins; in the room she dialed with the eraser end of a pencil and sat tapping the pencil against her teeth, listening to it ring. Dwiggins answered on the fifth ring and said, "Call me matchmaker. Have I got a boy for you."

"Good grief. You're drunk."

"Do you want to hear this or not? You'll love the guy. He's this big lug, got his nose right next to his ear, hairy all over. Just like a movie star."

"Yeah," she said. "King Kong."

Dwiggins laughed uproariously.

"All right," she said. "Who and what is he?"

"Crobey. Harry Crobey. I knew him in the highlands. Listen, the guy's a creature of clandestine warfare the way a tiger's a creature of the jungle. He's the kind of guy you're looking for." She heard the sound of ice in a glass.

She said impatiently, "Tell me about him."

"Who?"

"Crobey. Harry Crobey. For God's sake."

"Oh yeah, him." The phone seemed to drop from Dwiggins' mouth. She vaguely heard him muttering, then after a moment his voice came back on the line. "Sorry, I dropped the phone. You still there?"

"I'm still here."

"Tell you about Crobey," he said. "He used to fly in and out of the highlands on this old Air America plane, DC-3. I went in with him a couple times."

"He's a pilot?"

"Yeah, he was then. He'd take off with a six-pack of beer by the seat. Drink the beer, refill the empties by urinating in them, drop them out the window on Cong villages. I mean the guy's beautiful. A top-grade infidel."

"You do make him sound attractive," she said.

Dwiggins' belch sounded cavernous. "I talked to him. He's between jobs right now. He's willing to listen to your proposition."

"Where and when?"

"Nassau. If you want to talk to him you have to go there. He can't come to Washington right now."

"Why not?"

"Maybe he ought to tell you that. I don't like telling tales out of school. You haven't had second thoughts, have you?"

"No."

She heard him drink—sucking swallows. "I hope they don't write this up as Dwiggins' folly," he said. "I hope you don't get killed or something."

"Tell me about this Crobey person."

"Well there are people who like him. And then there are people who find him a thoroughly poisonous creep. You mustn't trust any of these guys. They can be trusted to obey the laws of their own existence—they'd never walk into a potential trap without reconnoitering the exits first, they'd never rape a woman if they thought her husband could do them any harm, they'd never shove a stack of chips out to the middle of the table if they didn't think they could beat the other guy. But dope, extortion, murder, any of the really vile crimes—those are paper laws to these guys. I'm not trying to impugn Crobey particularly. I'm just telling you about these people as a class. They don't operate according to the inhibitions you're used to. They're pretty wild."

"All right, you've forewarned me. What about Crobey?"

"You ask him. He'll tell you whatever he wants you to know about himself. It's better that way."

Hooting pedestrians out of the way, the taxi carried her along a stifling narrow passage. Black people occasionally stooped to peer at her through the open window of the cab. Their faces were sullen like thunderheads.

The driver kept up a running tourist-folder commentary and she didn't quite have the nerve to shut him up. Finally the machine stopped abruptly, almost pitching her out of her seat, and the driver said cheerfully, "We

here, miss,'' pointing up through the windshield toward
a ramshackle stoop, a collapsing porch roof and the
dismal coorless doorway under it. *Rooms to Let.*

She paid him twelve dollars: the fare from the airport—exorbitant but not worth a quarrel. She slung the
overnight bag by its strap over her shoulder and clipped
up the worn steps. Hunks of stucco had peeled off the
walls leaving concave gray scars. Once there'd been a
front door but the powdered remains of its frame
testified to the earnestness of the termites that had
demolished it. A child startled her, bursting out of the
darkness and rushing past her with a leap to clear the
steps; another child followed, giving chase, whooping in
mock anger. Urchins, both of them in rags. She might
have been in Harlem.

A wooden sign hung on chains from the corridor
ceiling above a door on the right, letters painted in a
fading crescent legend: *Manager—Ring Bell.* She rang.

A black woman opened it. Very fat and, from the
smell and the eyes, a little drunk—cheerfully high: She
smiled beatifically in Carole's face. ''Yes mom?''

''I'm looking for Harry Crobey.''

''Oh, you the lady from the States. Crobey expecting
you. He gone down Paradise Bar.'' The fat woman
squeezed past her and waddled to the porch. She wore a
sleeveless dress, patterns of red and gold; when she
pointed up the street the flab dangled under her arm and
billowed like a sail. ''You go up that corner and turn the
left, mom, you see Paradise Bar up there.''

''Thank you.''

''Yes mom.'' The woman grinned again and stumbled
back into the darkness.

Walking around the corner she felt dark eyes on her
and was unnerved, too conscious of her whiteness. In
skirt and flimsy blouse she felt unclothed. Traffic
darted through the streets, old cars stinking of badly
tuned exhausts, and there were dozens of blacks and
whites and it was broad daylight but just the same she
was uneasy with fear. Impatiently she chastised herself
for being racist; she turned the corner briskly and found
the Paradise Bar a block away on the waterfront, the

Paradise Island bridge looming in graceful arc beyond it. Pretty little boats zigzagged through the Nassau passage and off to the left she saw the stack of a cruise liner. The heat dissipated remarkably in the length of that single block; a breeze came off the water, cool and dry.

The bar was vast and low-ceilinged, stinking of beer and pounding with jukebox regurgitations of steel-drum band music. A group of young men in T-shirts stood at a pin-bowling table sliding the chuck around with boisterous violence; five or six men were ranged along the bar and the only white in the place was a man at a tiny three-legged table by the wall. He watched her with no expression until she walked toward him. Then he stood up. Not excessively tall; not King Kong at all. He looked as if he had once been presentable enough but had gone a bit to seed. He had a lot of sable hair thatched over his forehead; his white shirt, open down to the third button and with the sleeves rolled up, was clean enough but needed ironing—perhaps it had been too long in a suitcase. She put him at more than forty but the more defeated her.

She said with a trace of uncertainty, "Mr. Crobey?"

"Yeah, Harry Crobey." English accent—that or South African or Australian.

"Carole Marchand." She thrust out her hand. He took it with a bit of a smile. His hand was coarse but he wasn't a knuckle-crusher.

"Have a seat. What can I get you?" He had a harsh deep voice.

"Fruit juice, a soft drink, I don't mind. I think alcohol would give me a headache in this heat."

"If you're not used to the heat you'll get the headache with or without booze. But whatever you want."

"All right. Would they have Dewar's here?"

"I doubt it. They'll have something that passes for Scotch whisky. On the rocks?"

She watched him walk to the bar. He had a bit of a sailor's roll to his walk. The big head was set square on a size-seventeen neck and his biceps were hard beneath the rolled-up sleeves. Very narrow hips like a horseman.

When he returned from the bar bearing drinks she saw why he rolled his walk: He had a very slight limp and the roll almost concealed it.

He showed that he could smile. She felt she could have lit a match on his jaw. She said, "You're not exactly what I'd expected."

"What did you expect?"

"Three hundred pounds, a brush crew cut and a loud brutal voice."

"A thug."

"Maybe. Dwiggins was a little vague."

"Probably drunk," Crobey said.

"You *are* a mercenary, aren't you?"

"Honey, I'm Harry Crobey. Also I mercenare."

"Why?"

If he was surprised by the question he didn't show it. "It's a living," he replied.

She had wanted to shake him a bit, find out what was under the facade of easy self-confidence; it hadn't worked and she was momentarily nonplussed. She looked about the cavernous barroom. The jukebox had gone silent. The place seemed to extend away into an infinity of darknesses. She said, "Where do they keep the caskets?"

He didn't chuckle or smile. "You want to make small talk all afternoon?"

"Look, I suppose you've done this lots of times. I'm new to it."

"Okay. The first thing is, most of the people in my trade don't like to be called mercenaries. It's like calling a Japanese a Nip. Personally I don't mind it, I know what I am. But keep it in mind for future reference."

"I wasn't planning to make it a habit."

"Hiring yourself a mercenary? I guess not—you don't look the type. But soldier-of-fortune has a better ring to it."

"That sounds like something out of a cheap men's magazine."

"What kind of literature did you think these guys read?"

"But you're different, is that it?"

"You're a little abrasive, you know that? What's your first name again?"

"Carole," she said. "You can call me Miss Marchand."

"More like Mizz Marchand from the look of things." He waved his glass toward her shoulder. "There's the door, right there, behind you. Any time you want to excuse yourself." He was chewing up an ice cube the way a dog would grind up a bone—with loud sharp crunching noises.

She said, "I thought you needed a job."

"You can look at that one of two ways. Either I'm unemployed or I'm free."

"From the looks of your boarding house—"

"I eat."

She said abruptly, "Why couldn't you come to Washington to discuss this? Dwiggins offered you the fare money, didn't he?"

"I've temporarily exiled myself from the States. To avoid alimony jail. Next question?"

"You're married to an American?"

"I used to be. The answer to your next question is Liverpool. But I left there when I was fourteen. My passport's American. Naturalized. I mention that in case you're leery of foreigners." He was studying the plunge of her neckline. Then his eyes lifted and he smiled with cool insincerity—the polite wintry insolence of a clerk in an exclusive shop. Belatedly she saw the extent to which he was putting her on.

She said, "As long as we're inventorying your personnel file, what's the limp? A battle injury?"

"Sometimes when I'm drunk with a pretty lady I claim that's what it was. Actually the ankle got busted by a bouncer in Macao—a bar that looked kind of like this one. It wouldn't have caused any trouble but it was set by some virgin surgeon who didn't know an ankle bone from a hole in the ground. I can still run as fast as I need to. If that enters into your considerations."

"Dwiggins told you the nature of the job."

"Sort of. Your kid was killed by the people who snatched the Ambassador in Mexico. You're not the type to go lying down on the tracks. That's what he said. I see he had a point. You want them tracked down.''

"I want them to hang."

His laugh was a bit cruel. "Here I'm the one who's supposed to be the nihilistic professional but that's as cold-blooded as anything I've heard in a while. What do you do for a living again? Produce films?"

"I don't produce them. I direct them. Sometimes I write them."

"Same difference. I don't go to the cinema much. I think the last one I saw was *My Fair Lady*. Not counting some Roy Rogers movies on black-and-white TV sets dubbed into Portuguese." He picked up her empty glass and went to the bar. She tried to compose herself. She'd expected a crude simple tough who would take her money and obey orders without questions. But on reflection she realized that type wouldn't have been very useful to her. The thought startled her: Had her intentions been that unrealistic? Was she in fact merely going through the motions of something she didn't really mean to carry through? Was her passion already cooling?

He settled into his chair. The table was hardly big enough for two glasses and four elbows. Crobey said, "Tell me about yourself, then," contriving to look interested.

"What for?"

"I'm having a little trouble sizing you up. You're a product of that lofty bit of WASP society where they take charm and wit for granted and that doesn't sit too easy with the image of somebody who travels two thousand miles to sit in a grungy saloon hiring a middle-aged gunslinger."

Middle-aged gunslinger. He had a curious way of regarding himself simultaneously as a romantic hero and a worn-out loser. In an odd way he reminded her of New York and the unwashed tramps who sat in Washington Square Park playing chess: at once quaint and repellent. Crobey was clean enough in the hygienic sense—he was close-shaven, he'd had a haircut recently, there wasn't any grime under his fingernails—but he exuded the shabbiness of a well-worn coat, expensive once but gone green with too much use.

The jukebox began to thunder again. Crobey bellowed at the bartender: "Turn that thing down."

The bartender's black startled scowl came around to their table; after a moment Crobey's expression impelled the man to go around to the end of the bar and reach behind the jukebox. The volume dropped to half its former decibels. The bartender returned to his slot without looking at Crobey again. It made Carole look at her companion in a new way: Something in him had terrified the bartender.

Apparently struck by the edge of the same reaction, the four black youths at the pin-bowl table strolled insolently out of the bar, one of them looking back over his shoulder, staring at Crobey.

She said, "I had a brother, a reporter—Warren Marchand. Did you know him?"

"Yes. He was all right. Kind of stupid to go in there and get killed the way he did, but I liked him. His stuff was good." He pushed the tumbler of whisky toward her. "Now drink up and tell me everything you know about this situation."

He took her to a fish place for dinner. The decor was primitive and most of the clientele was black. It wasn't on the tourist maps, she was sure of that. But the sea bass was edible. Crobey pumped her for details and she found herself remembering trivial things she'd have forgotten if he hadn't goaded her into retrieving them: the hint, from Dwiggins, that the Mexican reporter (Ochoa? Ortega?) thought he'd recognized the leader; the mention, from Howard who'd got it from O'Hillary, that the leader had a Spanish accent but not Cuban—possibly Puerto Rican. Things like that. Crobey grilled her for hours, going back over the same things until she was sick of it. Finally she said, "Have you made up your mind yet?"

"I'll have a crack at it."

"Mind if I ask why?"

"The only suitable reward for a spy is money. Napoleon said that. I expect to charge you a lot of money. In return for which I offer the possibility, but not the guarantee, that I may be able to dig these guys up for you."

"How much money? I'm not the Federal Reserve Bank."

"A thousand a week, American. A bonus of twenty thousand if I find them. And don't bargain with me. It's firm."

"All right. You're hired," she said. "You've worked for the CIA, I gather. Who else?"

"People who paid me to fly for them or fight for them. You can ask around if you want—a few of them might give me references. You want some names? A lot of them are dead by now, of course. Assassinated in one coup or another. Most recently I was over in Ethiopia but I got sick of it."

"So you just bugged out?"

"I served out the contract. I don't just bug out. I've done contract work in Rhodesia and back in the old days over in the Congo and some other places. A few years ago I was down in Angola. I never sign on for more than six months. You get tired of places."

"Do you still fly a plane?"

"When I can get one. I've still got my ticket, AFT license, but I don't do it for fun. I'm not a Sunday warrior."

"You always fight on the same side?"

"What do you mean?"

"Anti-Communist, I suppose."

He said, "Not always."

It was the sum of his answer. She smiled a bit. "You're as free with information as a gaffer in a poker game."

"What do you want to know? My ideology? I haven't got one. Zealots bore the hell out of me. I hang around revolutions because that's where the work is. You ever read a writer named Ambrose Bierce? I had a long stint in a Montagnard village once, the only book in a language I could read being *The Devil's Dictionary*. I committed a couple of his definitions to memory. One of them sums it all up. Revolution is an abrupt change in the form of misgovernment.''

Her eyes puckered with suspicion. She had a feeling he probably had committed a lot of things to memory. She was puzzled by the mask he wore.

As if reading her thoughts he said, "Some people are satisfied with make-believe, or spectator sports or maybe playing a tough game of handball or squash. I'm not the vicarious type, that's all. Look, we belong to a race that reaches for the moon and then plays golf on its surface. Why get worked up over what this species does to itself? Maybe when I was a lot fresher and greener I had a small capacity for sustained indignation against social injustice but you find it dwindles quickly with age.''

"You're peculiar," she said.

"I had a traumatic childhood you see. When I was three years old my father was taller than me. I never got over it.''

"How can you find these Cubans, or whoever, if you don't even know their names?''

"If I start to look like a proper nuisance they may come after me. Anyhow it's worth a try. It can't be done too obviously, of course—if they think I'm advertising for attention they'll pull back.''

"Isn't that risky? What happens if they catch you?''

"I'll be dead and you'll be shocked.''

"Do you need to be so cold-blooded?''

"You're pretty defensive, aren't you? No need to feel guilty, ducks. I'm volunteering, remember? I wouldn't be much use to you if I was the sort that went all a-twitter every time somebody threatened to cut a sunroof in my skull.''

Carole grunted dubiously: Now he was flexing his muscles again.

He said, "Have you given any thought to what happens if I find this lot for you?''

"I'm not asking you to kill them. Just find them.''

"You needn't worry. I don't go around killing people where there may be witnesses afterward. I don't know of any country where you can defend yourself for murdering a man by producing written instructions from a woman ordering you to kill him.''

She said, "I want them exposed. Tried and convicted and executed. I've got to force Washington's hand because, to mix a mean metaphor, they're dragging their feet. Not to mention that exposing the terrorists is a good way to guarantee their failure.''

Crobey studied her. He mused. "You're a lady who's lived her whole life in a neat plastic-wrapped civilization where people think there's a difference between the politician in column A and the politician in column B. Somewhere along the line something blows up and you make the amazing discovery that the world contains hate and violence and injustice. Most civilized folks respond forthrightly to that shocking discovery by sulking and whining and complaining. Ducks, I admire you a little because you've got the gumption to do something about it, but let's not pretend that exposing this handful of clowns is going to effect much improvement in the situation. You want revenge, fine, I'll do what I can for my thousand a week, but let's not pretty it up with talk about justice and that rot.''

"Where did you pick up that speech? Humphrey Bogart?''

"I'm trying to make a point,'' Crobey said, not without a bit of a smile. "My getting hanged or put away in Ures prison forty years isn't included in the price of your ticket. If it gets dicey I'll shoot to kill—and so will they. This isn't an exercise in schoolbook justice. You want to understand that right up front, ducks.''

"I gave up believing in the tooth fairy a while ago, Crobey. I don't really need your sermons on disillusionment—all I'm asking you to do is find them for me. Now shall we talk about the down payment?''

Part Three

Chapter 7

They made the transfer uncomfortably in a heavy chop forty miles off San Juan. A line came across from the catamaran weighted by a small grappling hook; Cielo's crew drew the two boats together and with great care they cabled the money sacks across by a breeches-buoy system. Then they used the dinghy and everyone got soaking wet.

When the ketch turned about and headed back into the Gulf toward the Mexican town from which it had been rented, the three men aboard her were newcomers to her deck. Cielo and his entourage ensconced themselves along the rails of the catamaran and watched her go. The ketch slid quickly into the darkness, running without lights. A good vessel; they'd never see it again.

It wasn't a storm, just a wind; the men stood on the open decks drying out in the warm breeze. Someone revved the engines and the catamaran's stern went down as she wheeled toward home. Cielo with his head thrown back counted stars and felt gloomy. Before sunrise they'd arrive on the coast; the boat had only left port a half day earlier and this was its home registry so there would be no customs inspection, not for a brief fishing foray. The ransom would go ashore without trouble.

Julio was on the half-rotted little dock to greet him: a bear's embrace. "*Hermano*—I meant to be aboard the catamaran to meet you but my plane from Mexico was late."

"No harm." Cielo batted his brother about the shoulders and they watched the men file ashore. The money sacks went into the station wagon; two other cars stood aslant on the coast road and there wasn't any traffic at this hour—it wasn't yet daylight. The catamaran's captain, who was Vargas' cousin, shook Cielo's hand and exposed his teeth in a piratical grin and went away to drive his boat back to San Juan. On the lonely coast Cielo studied the sea and the sky and the mountains; then he spoke to his men. "You know where to wait. Don't show yourselves. I'll be along by noon."

The men—Vargas, young Emil Draga, Luz, the rest—climbed into the two sedans and Cielo watched them draw away. Beside him Julio hocked and spat. "The old man is worked up."

"I'm not surprised."

"He's angry, I mean."

Cielo opened the car door and noticed approvingly that the interior dome light didn't go on. Disconnected. Julio was good at that sort of detail.

The money was heavy. There was so much of it in the back of the station wagon that the car bottomed on the ruts. Julio drove very slowly and without lights until they got onto the paved surface. Then he turned it east, built up the speed and switched on the headlamps in a hollow. The Michelins hissed metallically.

Cielo leaned back against the headrest and rolled his head to the left to watch his brother's profile. Julio just now was possessed of a sort of Wagnerian sadness. It meant very little; in a moment he might be bursting with laughter. Cielo watched him squint against the oncoming headlights of a truck. Julio had skin like rough concrete, large greasy pores on his nose, a drooping mustache like a Mexican bandit's. He'd gone mostly bald; there was a black monk's fringe around the back of his head. He was two years Cielo's senior but had always deferred to Cielo's intellect, even when they were children.

"How did the old man's grandson behave?"

"He went wild once—killing the American boy."

"Perhaps it was for the best." Abruptly Julio glanced at him and smiled. He had a very good smile: It changed his face radically, surprising strangers, often changing their minds about his character. "Is it really that much money?"

"We counted it."

"*Dios*. Hard to believe."

"It's not as if it's ours to piddle with."

"No. Not yet, anyway."

Julio wrenched the wheel and a battered car shot past on the left, going too fast for the curves. "Christ. Puerto Ricans make the worst drivers in the world. It's a wonder they're not all dead."

Cielo had been watching the overtaking car but it shot on out of sight and he relaxed. He was thinking how ironic it would be to be hijacked here on the highway by petty robbers. What a surprise they'd get when they went into the back of the wagon.

Every security precaution was laid on, no matter how redundant. Julio drove clear into Rio Piedras and eased the wagon into the down ramp of an office building's garage; stopped at the automatic lift-bar, extracted the computer ticket from the machine, waited for the bar to rise, drove in and parked in a vacant slot. Then Cielo waited by the wagon, a bit unnerved, while his brother walked among the parked cars in the dim silent cavern and disappeared beyond a thick pillar. Shortly thereafter a four-door Mercedes slid forward through the gloom and stopped in the aisle just behind the parked wagon. Julio unlocked the trunk, throwing the lid open. They had a look around to make sure they were unobserved; then with a good deal of grunting and whooshing they transferred the money sacks into the trunk of the Mercedes. It made a tight squeeze and the sedan went right down on its springs. Julio slammed the trunk lid, tested it and grinned. They drove out of the garage at dawn, paying at the booth, merging into the light early traffic. They ran westward, retracing their route as far as the Dorado turnoff; Julio turned toward the sea, driving with one eye on the mirror. No one followed. Julio said, "No trouble besides the American boy?"

"One of the Marines wanted to be difficult. We had to keep reins on him. But he wasn't hurt. I'm amazed how well it all went. I mean, one or two got dysentery—that's unavoidable. I don't like to think about how their families suffered. But it's over now, for them.''

Cielo picked at a fingernail, squinting through the windshield. Everything was murky in the half light. A tentative drizzle misted the glass. They drove through the palm forest and up past the private airfield and the entrance to the Dorado Beach resort; on along a rutted dirt side track, several miles looping toward the cliffs—undergrowth scratched the sides of the car and Julio said, ''Maybe someone forgot something, left a clue behind. We won't know that for a while. The old man's plans remind me of those guaranteed roulette systems, you know? The roulette wheel never heard of them. . . . I'm just nervous, pay me no attention. The boy shouldn't have died, but . . .''

''No,'' Cielo agreed, ''the boy shouldn't have died. We'll all do some time in Purgatory for that.''

''But tactically it may have been right.''

''Maybe we should tell the old man to his face that he's dreaming.''

''We can't do that.''

Cielo changed the subject. ''Have you seen Soledad?''

''No, I told you, I just got in from Mexico. I did talk to her on the telephone. She's anxious about you. I told her you'd see her today.''

''I wonder if Elena got rid of her cold.''

''You'd better stop in town and buy presents for them.''

''You're right, I'll do that. Thanks.''

''I know,'' Julio said. ''You've had a lot on your mind.''

The gate guard recognized the car of course but it didn't cause him visibly to relax; he wasn't paid to take things for granted. Julio rolled the window down and the guard stooped to search their faces. No words were exchanged. The guard merely retreated to his post out of the rain. There was the noise of electric motors, gears gnashing; the iron gates swung open with stately slow ease and Julio steered the stocky car through them, up the winding drive amid oleanders and bougainvillea, palms and cacti, the oversized rock garden that served, as if by coincidence, to screen the house from the view of anyone on the landward side of it. A man in a gray uniform and black Sam Browne was walking two Dobermans on leashes. He watched the car go by and dipped his head an inch and a half to Julio, who said, "You'd think the old man was already in Batista's palace."

"He never will be," Cielo said.

"You think we should tell him that, don't you?"

"Somebody ought to."

"He wouldn't listen."

Cielo got out of the car and looked up at the house. It wasn't excessive or even prepossessing; whitewashed stucco, curved red tiles on the low roof.

The old man came out to meet them. Julio opened the deck lid and the three of them contemplated the money. The old man opened one of the sacks and fingered a few banknotes. Then his eyes flicked at Cielo like a lizard's tongue. "Well done." Then he turned away—he'd seen money before. "Come inside. Have you had breakfast?"

They ate on the terrace overlooking the sea. The veranda roof and the screen kept the rain out. The breakfast came in courses; with rigid Old World courtesy the old man refrained from discussing affairs of importance until the dishes had been cleared away and the second coffees served.

The old man, Jorge Felipe Vandermeer Draga-Ruiz, was a sly figure, full of calculation and insinuation. He was gaunt and had once been quite tall; now he stooped. The backs of his hands were flecked with cyanotic age spots and his flesh hung a little loose. His hair was a bit thin but hadn't receded and he kept it dyed black. He had a ropy chicken neck and a querulous way of thrusting his jaw forward and chewing on his teeth. An engaging grin and an archaic manner of gallantry; pride, and a capacity for cruelty, and the vanity of polished shoes and good clothes and cared-for fingernails.

"It was Emil who disrupted the plan? Tell me the truth."

"It was Emil."

The old man snarled. "What, have the termites got at his brain?"

A woman with a well-developed mustache came out of the house with a pot of coffee and warmed their cups. Cielo had never seen her before; the old man had a staff as big as a hotel's. Three quarters of the house was underground, buried back in the cliff, and there were coach houses and servants' quarters scattered around the property—the place was like an iceberg, you didn't see much but there was a lot of it.

When the woman departed Julio said, "A man who disobeys one order will disobey another." He stared at the old man contentiously.

"This isn't the Wehrmacht," Cielo said, trying to placate them. "And Emil, Jr., didn't train with us. He's young."

"What you're saying is it's my fault this happened. I saddled you with him. Well I thought he might learn something about manhood from you. I meant you no disservice."

"The American's dead," Cielo put in. "Whipping Emil won't revise that."

"Whipping," the old man said, "doesn't come into it. No one is going to whip Emil."

Julio stroked his bandit's mustache and watched Cielo ingenuously, eyes like black olives. Abruptly and brashly Julio said, "If we punish him we make him our enemy, he'll come at our kidneys one night with a knife. But if we don't punish him we'll only encourage his contempt for what he believes is our weakness. Either way he'll betray us sooner or later. I don't give a damn whose blood relation he is." And his eyes rolled back to the old man again.

Cielo sucked in his breath. It wasn't the proper time for such a confrontation.

The old man took it calmly enough. "What, did you expect we could retake Havana without firing a shot? Don't tell me after all the blood that's been shed you're

turning into mangy intellectuals, you two. Pacifists, is
it?''

"No, we're soldiers," said Cielo. "But we weren't at
war with the American Peace Corpsman."

"Emil won't betray his own family." Cunning thinned the old man's eyes. "The two of you would
welcome an excuse to ease him out, wouldn't you. His
presence threatens your authority."

Cielo felt a twinge of disembodied pain. He felt
trapped between his brother and the old man. He was
losing ground, as he always did before the old man:
Draga might as well have been his father, he always
made Cielo feel eleven years old. He was like a
Renaissance cardinal.

He made a feeble attempt: "We must do something,
you know."

"Leave my grandson to me. I'll make sure he understands."

Julio spoke up resolutely: "We must take a position,
that's all there is to it."

Draga frowned at Julio, then turned to his brother.

"What do you say, Cielo? You know I've always
trusted you."

"With all due respect, sir. We believe we are the ones
to settle the matter."

"You have the floor."

Cielo drew a breath deep inside, expanding with
reluctant resolve. He knew he must step in, if only to
protect his older brother. The old man would accept it
from Cielo—he must have sensed Cielo's lack of ambition. Julio was another case and his presence at this
meeting goaded Cielo into taking a stronger position.
"You'll recall none of the hostages was to be killed," he
said finally.

"There was an excellent reason for that. One can't
very well litter the landscape with American corpses and
expect the Americans to reconfirm their neutrality afterward. I don't expect support from Washington but
we must have their assurance that they will keep hands
off. That's why this crime distresses me so deeply."

And never mind that an innocent boy died, Cielo

thought sorrowfully. To the old man the boy was a casualty of war. He could hear himself thinking: *Why don't we tell him the truth?* He looked at his brother, expecting a mocking expression; fortunately Julio had put his nose in his coffee cup.

Cielo said, "The thing would have worked out according to plan if I hadn't been saddled with your grandson."

The old man went very calm. "Yes?"

"From here on I'll move only with my own people. Not your grandson, not anybody from this villa. I know this deprives you of eyes and ears—I'll keep you abreast. But I must maintain absolute discipline and I can only do it by excluding outsiders."

"Emil is hardly an outsider."

"He is to us. He wasn't in the Sierra Maestra—he didn't fester in Fidel's prisons."

He heard the breath sawing through Julio's nostrils, saw the encouragement and surprise in Julio's eyes.

The silence stretched until he thought his nerves would crack. Then the old man put on a brittle smile. "This demand—is it non-negotiable, as they say? Or may I have a moment for rebuttal?"

Cielo sagged back. It hadn't worked.

The old man pushed both palms against the table, rising to his feet. He began to pace, chewing on his teeth, emitting hard little bursts of dogmatic thought:

"The organism's a fragile thing. I should have checked into a hospital long ago. They tell me I've got to have surgery for this and that—hernia, prostate, whatever. We're all dying, aren't we? I'm sure I shall be forced to settle for the limited satisfaction of having set things in motion. I won't live long enough to see these efforts come to fruition. I envy you—you've both got so much more future than I have."

Cielo had heard it before. He didn't dare look at his watch.

"That a man like me should have instigated this movement is peculiar, isn't it? I never took much interest in politics. I've no desire to correct injustices or reform the world. In fact I've never viewed the human plight as anything one ought to improve—as Léautaud said, I'd like to be a lover of mankind but unfortunately I have a good memory. . . . This started with me because I wanted to redeem the family name by recovering our lost properties. The arrogance of that snaggle-bearded jackass, expropriating things he'd never have the ability to build. . . . I suppose they've learned their lesson under Castro—they're far worse off now than they were before, they've got no shred of dignity left but they brought it on themselves. You know, I begin to see as I approach the grave that I never honestly cared whether I reoccupied the mansion in Havana. Cuba wasn't my home, it was our family's corporate headquarters. Even if we win this fight in my lifetime I'll have no wish to leave this house. Yet I've gone on with the fight. Do you know why? It's a matter of challenge. It's not very different from raiding a corporation—you don't need the money, you do it to prove yourself.''

The old man paused at the screen. "The rain's stopped.'' Then he swiveled slowly and paced again, hands in his pockets. "I could have paid for this operation out of my pocket. The kidnappings were necessary not to raise money but to legitimize the raising of money. The question would have been raised as to who was financing our movement. There'd have been inquiries—that might have led them here. After all, how many expatriate Cubans are wealthy enough to mount the operation we're planning? But now we have ten million in cash and they know where it came from, so it won't occur to them to seek its source. If necessary we'll be able to spend twenty million. Spread it around and no one will notice the discrepancy. Clever, isn't it?''

Momentarily pleased with himself, he walked out to the corner and pressed a switch. The screens slid up into the veranda roof—a soft humming of motors. The old man hunched his shoulders in the breeze and stared down at the sea. "I won't live to see it finished. Emil will.''

Cielo glanced at his brother. Julio rolled his eyes toward Heaven and shook his head.

The old man turned to face them. "My blood is in

him. I want him to be there. To see it when that infamous regime of thieves and pimps is brought down. My satisfaction, you see, is in knowing Emil will be there—to slap Fidel Castro in the face with the name of Draga.''

Such foolishness, Cielo thought sadly.

''You will keep him by your side. Discipline him if you must. But you haven't the authority to dismiss him. I don't grant it to you. Understood?''

Cielo said, ''We had to try. You can see why.''

''Your positions are threatened by his presence.''

''No,'' Julio replied. ''It is our discipline that is threatened.''

''Nonsense. Discipline him. I'll help—I'll remind him he is under your orders and can expect no protection from me.''

''You're protecting him right now,'' Cielo pointed out.

''Don't split hairs.''

Julio made a face but held his tongue. Julio had dreams of political power—and of course Emil was a threat to that.

The old man approached. He stood before Cielo and addressed him directly, excluding Julio. ''I trust *you*.''

''Thank you.'' He felt miserable but he met Draga's watery eyes. By playing along with the farce he was, in an ironic way, betraying the old man. It filled him with guilt.

''I trust you,'' the old man said, ''not to try to circumvent Emil after my death.''

''And what if *he* turns against *us*?''

''Then you'll do what you must. I'm not an oracle, nor a psychiatrist. I think he has it in him to be a leader but he wants more training, more discipline, more experience. These things you can give him.''

Emil might have the makings of a tyrant, Cielo thought, but he didn't have it in him to be a leader. The old man was wrong—blinded by the sentimentality of blood relation. But no purpose would be served by arguing the point now. Familial prejudice was stronger than reason.

I'll have to give him my word now—and break it later. Dismally Cielo said, "All right."

The old man straightened—now he was brusque: "The next step is the acquisitions. You know enough to be circumspect. You've got my list of dealers? Yes, of course—you wouldn't have misplaced those. Very well, I hope to hear from you."

Cielo stood up with Julio at his side. The old man gravely shook their hands; Cielo saw a wistful sadness in Draga's eyes when they withdrew.

At the front of the house a Volkswagen was drawn up, keys in the ignition. They settled into it and when Julio put it in gear he said, "The old man's still quite an adventurer."

"I suppose we'll just have to string him along." Cielo fastened his shoulder belt. "We'll buy the ammunition and the ordnance. After all, we've got the money. We may as well go through the motions—it'll please him."

"Do we owe him so much?"

"We owe him everything," Cielo said, "beginning with our lives. Take me home first, then we'll go on to meet the others."

He wanted to see Soledad first—he needed to draw strength from her.

The smell of Soledad's talc was thick in the room. He called out and heard her answer, faint in the back of the house; he went through and found her waiting for him, combing her fingers into her long dark hair and lifting it loosely, high above her head. She gave him a blinding smile and it immediately lifted his spirits.

"You see? I'm home unharmed. You can release the hostages." He made a joke of it but after she kissed him, running her tongue around his mouth, she stepped back out of his grasp and hugged herself.

"What's wrong?"

"You were gone so long," she said.

"I'm back now."

"For how long?"

"Who can say. What difference does it make? Let's take what we have."

Her smile, then, was sweet and shy. Fourteen years,

three children, and she still had the slender quickness of
a fawn doe. She took his hand and led him to the
bedroom.

He sat at the kitchen table with both hands wrapped
around the coffee cup and his eyes returned at intervals
to the clock. When Soledad came into the room she
made a face. "I wish you'd learn to put the toilet seat
down."

"Did Elena get over her cold?"

"Sure. It's been *weeks*. She has a new boy friend.
Very rich and fourteen years old."

"I hope he doesn't keep her out at night. At fourteen
these days they're more worldly than we were at
twenty."

"She has a head on her shoulders," Soledad said.
"She inherits that from—well, God knows not from
you." She wrinkled her nose at him. "I don't care if she
retains her virginity—"

"At *thirteen*?" He was shocked.

"—but I do care that she not give it away too cheaply.
I've told her that. She knows what I meant."

"Por Dios."

"Well it's not the same world anymore, *querido*."

"I feel old."

"Not in bed, thank God."

She was going past the table; he arrested her, reaching
out for her hand, pulling her into his lap. Her arms slid
around his neck and he tasted her mouth. The hoot of
the VW's horn outraged him. Soledad looked toward
the window. "Julio?"

"Yes. I asked him in but he preferred to wait in the
car. He's reading a science fiction."

"How long will you be?"

"I'll be home tonight. Fairly late."

"What's wrong?"

"It's something I have to do."

"Something you don't want to do."

"Well it's got to be taken care of."

"Let someone else do it. Julio, Vargas."

"It's not something I could shift onto someone else."

"Then I'm sorry, *querido*. I'll go out and buy a bottle of bourbon for tonight."

"Two bottles," he said on his way out the door.

Julio shifted down into second and made an abrupt unsignaled turn into a one-way street and stopped the VW almost immediately at the curb. Cielo twisted around in the seat to watch the boulevard. Traffic streamed past. No cars turned into the one-way street. If any had, Julio would have backed out into the boulevard and gone on his way, leaving the tail stranded halfway down the one-way street. It was a simple device designed to prevent pursuit, one of many in Julio's bag of tricks. He was always the one who took the wheel; Cielo was a mediocre driver.

They went along Highway Three to the east, bottled in by heavy traffic as far as the El Verde turnoff where Julio turned south and picked up speed. In town they doubled back on several packed-earth streets; there was no tail and they emerged from the town with church bells ringing noon behind them. On the country road a horseman drove a bunch of cattle across, delaying them five minutes, and then they caught up with a farm tractor and couldn't get past it until they were over a hill. The mountains ranged up ahead of them, tier upon tier, shades of pastel green. Sugar cane on the right, pasture on the left; Julio turned the VW into a narrow driveway between fences. There was the smell of manure.

Vargas and two others ranged along the porch of the farmhouse trying not to resemble lookouts. No weapons were in evidence but they were near at hand out of sight. Cielo walked along to the end of the porch. Julio sat down on the wooden bench, pressing back the dog ear on the page of his paperback galactic-empire saga. Vargas turned to go into the house and Cielo said, "Ask Kruger to come outside." Old Draga had infected him with a paranoia about indoor microphones.

When Kruger came out Cielo said, "Any problems?"

"Luz was complaining there's no television set. When do we go up to the camp?"

"Maybe tomorrow. Julio and Vargas will scout it

first. We want to know if anybody's been there.''

"Nobody's likely to find it unless they know where to look. And the guards we left there—''

"The guards could be dead or in jail and there could be an ambush waiting for us," Cielo said. "Let Julio scout it first—he knows how to go in for a look without being spotted.''

"You have a good head for security," the German admitted. Kruger was slight, almost delicate with a little round head and wide thin lips that gave him an ascetic appearance. He talked with a Bavarian hiss. He was forty-six, much too young to have been a Nazi, but some of the others joshed him by greeting him with stiff-armed Heils and addressing him as Mein Führer. Kruger didn't seem put off by it; he had a healthy sense of humor. At first he'd been a mercenary but the Bay of Pigs had made a believer of him.

Cielo said, "Keep your eye on Emil. I want him here at nightfall.''

"I understand.''

Darkness came. A light from the porch fell obliquely through the window bars, painting stripes across the floor. Emil stood at a cracked mirror in the hallway. A sprig of hair stood up disobediently at the back of his head, glistening with the water he'd used to try and stick it down. He was hacking at it with his palm.

Julio moved toward the door and Cielo faced Emil. The others had gone back to the kitchen; it was only the three of them, and Kruger who stood at the far end of the hall blocking it, his back to them and his shoulder propped casually against the doorframe. Emil at the mirror finally got his hair stuck down and turned to glance at Cielo. Something in Cielo's expression betrayed him and Emil went rigid. His face, almost always studiedly calm, went slack and his thief's eyes went restlessly around the room. Julio lifted the .44 Magnum revolver into sight and made a show of cocking it, the noise quite loud in the room. "Stand still now.''

Cielo walked toward Emil, a gun in his fist. He felt

foolishly melodramatic. Emil flattened himself back against the wall. "What's this? What's this?"

Julio said, "I guess nobody trusts you, Emil. I'm sorry."

The flash in Emil's eyes, Cielo thought, was that of someone in the climax of orgasm.

They went out to the yard. "Bring his car around."

Emil's car was a sporty little Mustang convertible, dented here and there, the paint flaking off; it had seen better days. Kruger got in behind the wheel and Cielo pushed Emil into the back seat, feeling foolish with a gun in his hand.

Julio stood outside the car. "All right?"

Cielo nodded to him and Julio walked away to get into the VW. It followed the Mustang down the driveway and they went in convoy up the El Verde road through the town onto Highway Three; then a few miles of divided road and another turnoff to the seacoast road, passing through villages. The morning's rain had left puddles in the chuckholes. They went out into the banana farms and Kruger stopped the car at the verge when Cielo tapped his shoulder. Kruger got out of the car; Julio's VW stopped alongside and Kruger got into it and the VW drove away leaving Cielo alone in the Mustang with Emil. The keys dangled in the ignition. Cielo climbed out and reached for the keys, put them in his pocket and spoke. "Stay there. We'll talk a minute." Through the open door he kept the revolver pointed at Emil.

Emil, breathing through his open mouth, stared at him without blinking.

Cielo said, "Other people's lives don't seem to mean much to you but I wonder how you feel about your own."

Emil's mouth snapped shut. "I came here to get killed, not to listen to a speech."

"Listen to this one and maybe you won't get killed." He studied his revolver. "So?"

"So I'll listen."

"I brought you out here as a favor to your grandfather. Otherwise I'd have had to shoot you in front of the others. You understand? It's nothing to do with you—I don't care if the others see this or not—but I prefer not to offend the old man."

"That's smart."

"Don't sneer, Emil. The order not to harm the hostages came from your grandfather, not from me. You knew that. It was your grandfather you disobeyed. He's run out of patience with you. Just the same I owe him something—I'd rather not be the instrument of murder against his family, but he's told me he won't stand in the way of my disciplining you."

"What do you want?" Emil feigned disinterest.

"I want you to remember that Julio and I are the *padrones* and that you are with us by our sufferance. I want you to learn, and never forget, who runs this outfit."

"I believe my grandfather runs it." Emil had a hot kind of courage and this icy calm was unlike him; Cielo stepped back a pace to keep his revolver out of Emil's reach.

"Your grandfather is the President, so to speak, but I am the General. I give the orders in the field and he doesn't countermand them. Am I getting through to you? When you volunteer to serve with an army you take orders from its generals, no matter who your grandfather is. Your grandfather understands that. I understand it. Now it's time for you to understand it."

Emil considered the Magnum. "You can't teach a man much by killing him. Now it seems to me either you're going to shoot me or you're not. Which is it?"

"If you turn on us, sooner or later one of us will finish you. If that happens you won't have an easy death. What if Julio gets at you, or Vargas? Vargas, for example, has a thing about pouring boiling water into a traitor's ear through a funnel," he lied. "You look unimpressed. All right—I'll impress you." And he clubbed Emil across the side of the head with the revolver.

It wasn't a very hard blow but Emil fell back with a grunt and it dazed him enough so that he didn't put up effective resistance when Cielo proceeded methodically to batter him with his boots, cracking a rib and bruising a kidney but not doing anything that would leave visible scars. A man of Emil's vanity wouldn't be able to live with that; he'd have to come back for revenge. This way perhaps Emil would get over the rage and chalk it up to lessons learned.

He nudged Emil to make sure he was awake. Emil uttered a sound and blinked up at him. "The point is," Cielo said, "I can be just as hard as you when I need to be. And I'm a kitten beside Julio or Vargas."

He tossed the car keys on Emil's chest and walked away.

A few hundred yards round the bend he reached the Volkswagen. Julio, in the back seat, leaned forward to open the door for him. Cielo got in and they drove off. Kruger said, "All right?"

"Yes."

Julio was dour. "What if he learns nothing from it?"

"Those who do not learn from history," Cielo said airily, "are doomed to die from it."

Kruger said, "I don't trust Emil. I never will."

"He understands power," Cielo said, "and he understands fear. In any case, as long as the old man is alive we're saddled with Emil."

"And afterward?"

"Emil's the sort who'll destroy himself, I think. He may not even need any help from us." Cielo sank back in melancholia. "The old man won't live forever. Neither will any of us."

Chapter 8

Glenn Anders unpacked his suitcase with the efficiency of long practice. It wasn't merely his suitcase; it was, largely, his home.

At the bedside desk he swept aside the fan display of tourist folders and local guides—*This Week in Mexico*—and reached for the phone to buzz Rosalia's room but before he touched it the instrument rang. Disquieted by the coincidence he picked it up tentatively. "Hello?"

"Anders?"

"Yes."

"Wilkins."

"Hello, George."

"How're they hangin', old buddy?"

"All right."

"O'Hillary asked me to brief you. Right now all right? I'm in the lobby."

"Come on up." Anders pushed the cradle down to break the connection. Then he dialed Rosalia's number. "If you're all beautiful and your pantyhose are on straight, come on down to my room. Bring your notebook. We're getting a briefing from the station chief." He hung up and glanced around the room. No possibility of its being bugged; he'd booked it at random. That was the best kind of security. He had no reason to suspect anyone might be interested in his conversations but when you went into any foreign country where you were known as an agent of the U.S. government you had to expect counterintelligence types to keep an eye on you as a matter of drill.

Rosalia's tap; and as he opened the door to her he saw George Wilkins tramping forward in the corridor.

Wilkins' high long face developed a funereal smile as he followed the girl into the room.

Rosalia perched by the desk with her notebook, looking efficient, but the soft smile in her eyes betrayed something else and Wilkins seemed wise enough to spot it and cosmopolitan enough to refrain from comment.

"Welcome to the pits," Wilkins said. "I suppose I should say something like that. By way of official greeting and all."

"How're things?"

"Tedium, ever tedium. I wish somebody would try to overthrow the government around here. At least it would give us something to take an interest in."

Anders said, "Did you know this Lundquist kid?"

"No."

"Who did?"

"Allerton did, I think. Over at the consulate."

"We'll talk to him. What have we got?"

"Not much since we sent the last report to O'Hillary. They haven't turned up but one or two items out of that old oil camp." Wilkins talked with a slow prairie twang. Kansas? "A Gauloise butt, for instance, and a corner of a page out of a paperbook book. Been dog-eared a few times and broke off, you know how they do. A whole gang of bright scholars are trying to find out what book it's from. Only got about four complete words on it and bits of a few others so it may take them a while and then I expect they'll come up with something like *Gone with the Wind* or *How to Have a Happier Sex Life*."

"It's in English?"

"Yeah. We already knew they spoke English, didn't we. Let's see, what else. Oh yes—debriefing on Velez, he came up with an item—"

Rosalia looked up from her notebook. "Velez who?"

"Juan-Pedro Velez. Mexican Ministry of Agriculture. One of the hostages, you know. The one that had to go into the hospital with dysentery."

"Coals to Newcastle," Anders observed.

"He's all right now. They turned him loose yesterday and we interrogated him. Anyhow he seems to remember one of the gang talked Spanish with a German ac-

cent. Thin guy, he says. Not very big." Wilkins blinked
slowly; he looked tired. "They're scraps but it's the best
we can do right now. Any of it help you?"

"Who knows," Anders said.

He told Rosalia to go around and see the consulate at-
taché who'd known Robert Lundquist. Nothing would
come of that but he wanted to accrete more of an impression of the dead boy. Why had Lundquist been
chosen as the exemplary victim? Was it simply because
he'd been the least important of the hostages or had
there been something abrasive about him that might
have provoked them to kill him? If the later, would this
tell him anything about the nature of the terrorists? He
doubted it but believed in thoroughness.

She was putting on wraparound sunglasses. Anders
glanced at her notebook. "Your handwriting's an
atrocity."

"I can read it," she said defiantly. She slipped the
notebook into her shiny red plastic handbag.

"They used to teach us that penmanship was a matter
of communication, not self-expression. But I guess that
was back in the days when you still hadn't grown a
chest."

"Yes, you're so old you're creaking with age." With
her hand at the doorknob she said, "If I get drunk
tonight will you promise to take advantage of me?"

He spent a largely fruitless afternoon shambling
around Mexico City interviewing informants he'd cul-
tivated over the years. He hadn't expected anything to
come of it. He had nothing like the network of contacts
that the local station personnel had developed. Anders
had a few people in each of most of the Third World
capitals—acquaintances rather than agents; they
weren't spies but favors were exchanged and Anders
had built up a rudimentary list. One of the men he went
to see was an export broker of the kind who admitted to
a degree of knowledge about the traffic in arms and
narcotics. Another was a printer who vehemently
claimed he did not deal in false passports and identity

papers. Neither of them purported to know anything about the terrorists.

At four he went around to the Federal Police barracks and was granted an audience with Chief Inspector Ainsa who was burly and sly—he might have been assigned to his role by Central Casting. Ainsa had charge of Mexico's harbor police activities. Glenn Anders had not known him before so there was the monotony of establishing credentials and exchanging amenities; then Anders said, "Ambassador Gordon's a yachtsman. He had a feeling the boat was a ketch. They were blindfolded but I suppose sailors have intuitions for these things. I don't know much about it myself—a ketch is usually what, a forty- or fifty-foot sailboat?"

"They vary in size," Ainsa said. "It's a two-masted design with the taller mast forward and the rear mast above the rudder. In English *cómo se dice*—mizzenmast. Quite graceful. Usually there is a low cabin amidships. They tend to be long and narrow, being designed for speed and sport rather than capacity."

"This one must have been big enough to accommodate about twenty people."

"That's possible. With some crowding below decks."

"It occurred to me," Anders said, treading gingerly because it wouldn't do to get the policeman's back up, "that perhaps the boat was stolen or hired."

"Hired? Ah, you mean rented. Yes, I see."

"It's hard to picture a terrorist group owning a sporty sailboat."

"Yes."

"There can't be too many vessels of that size stolen or available for hire in the Gulf of Mexico."

Ainsa's smile was indicative of low cunning. It was a pose, for nothing he said was suggestive of stupidity. "Especially," he said, "ketches stolen or rented during, say, the month of August?"

"That would be the framework," Anders agreed. "I've already asked the United States police to check around the Texas and Louisiana ports."

"Honduras, Guatemala, Nicaragua, Costa Rica, Panama, Colombia . . ."

"We're checking them all."

"Leave it to me. I'll put out the word immediately."
Ainsa stood up and pressed against the desk to reach
across for Anders' hand.

He called Rosalia from a pay phone. "What did
Allerton tell you?"

"He only met Lundquist once or twice. Sorting out
his papers when he first arrived for the Peace Corps. He
couldn't tell me anything we didn't already know. I'll
type up the notes for you but I certainly didn't see
anything in it. Incidentally Mr. Wilkins says they've
identified that torn page from the paperback book. It's
a science-fiction novel."

"Good grief."

"One of those adventures about intergalactic wars or
something."

It came as no particular surprise to Anders. Once in
Nam he'd dived into a bunker and thrown himself flat,
terrified by the exploding rockets and bullets cracking
everywhere; he'd looked up and discovered a grunt
who, in the midst of that madness, was reading a paperback Western shoot-'em-up, enthralled.

Rosalia on the telephone said, "I've got it all doped
out. The whole thing. You know what we're up against,
don't you?"

"No. What?"

"A nest of aliens. Martian invaders."

"Right," he said. "I'm on my way to Wilkins' office.
Meet me there in an hour. Stop by the newspaper on
your way and see if they'll let you have another photo-
copy of that ransom note."

He went along toward the embassy on foot; it was
rush hour and he made better progress that way. Traffic
was clotted in the boulevards and there was a dry chill in
the thin air. Two blocks short of the embassy he espied
Harry Crobey.

He wouldn't have noticed Crobey in the throng of
commuters but for the peculiar roll of Crobey's limp. It
gave him a swaying gait that made him noticeable

because he didn't move with the same rhythm as the others in the crowd.

"Harry."

Crobey gave him a startled glance; a bit furtive, Anders thought. A quick distracted smile twitched back and forth across Crobey's lips. Crobey shook his hand; the crowd milled past, jostling them both.

"Let's get out of this jam." Anders selected the empty pocket beside an office building's revolving door and pried his way toward the opening. The building was emptying out and people eddied past them into the stream.

Crobey seemed to have gone a bit to seed but then, Anders recalled, Crobey had always managed to look that way. "What're you doing here, Harry?"

"You know. This and that. You look good—lost some weight."

"Not as much as I ought to." Anders looked at his watch. "They told me you'd signed on in Ethiopia."

"Contract ran out. So did I."

"You never did have much of an attention span." Anders studied the hard face. "I didn't know Mexico was at war with anybody."

"Somebody told me it was a nice place for a holiday." Far back around the edges of Crobey's accent you could detect a residue of sooty Liverpudlian squalor.

Suspicion ran high in Anders. He did not buy coincidences right off the shelf. "I want to talk to you."

"Sure, Glenn."

"I'm on my way to the embassy. Keep me company."

"Can't," Crobey said, "I've got an appointment. Where are you staying?"

He felt a keen reluctance to let Crobey out of his sight but he had no weapon with which to hold the man. Anders considered the options and conceded. "The Hilton."

It provoked Crobey's caustic smile. Everybody in the trade knew the stale joke—two secret agents meet by chance in the lobby: "I say, old chap, this is frightfully

embarrassing but can you tell me, is this the Tel Aviv
Hilton or the Cairo Hilton?''

Crobey said, ''Drinks then. What time will you be
free? I'll come by the Hilton.''

''Make it nine.'' •

''See you.'' Crobey thrust his prow into the crowd.
Anders watched him sway out of sight.

Wilkins said, ''I just got off the scrambler with Sturdevant in Buenos Aires.''

Anders sat down. His feet were tired. ''Anything?''

''The politicals seem to be coalescing toward Paraguay. It looks like they'll be taken in by one of
those Bund groups on the Pampas. You know. Bunch
of senile characters with brown pasts. We've had taps
on their phones for years but the Bundists know it. They
don't use the phones for much except ordering groceries
and selling their beef cattle. But there's no sign of
unusual activity there. We'd know it if they were planning to start World War Three.''

''Doddering Nazis in their seventies or eighties.'' Anders shook his head. ''They're just waiting to die.
They've got no wars left in them.''

Wilkins' smile agreed with him, rueful and doleful as
always—the man lived under a cloud of wry gloom.
''Sturdevant asked me if you want him to bring one of
the politicals in for questioning.''

''No. O'Hillary's orders—we shadow them but keep
hands off.'' Anders resented having to wear reins and
blinders but you didn't kick up a nest until you found
out how many and how virulent the hornets were.

Anders unfolded his copy of the list of the eleven
politicals who'd been released from prisons at the
terrorists' behest. They were old-timers, most of them.
Leaders from the early 1960s. One of them had tried to
lead a commando force into Cuba to assassinate Castro
in 1961; another had gone around systematically
executing people who were suspected of having been
followers of Ché Guevara in Bolivia and Ecuador. Some
of them probably didn't even know one another; the
thing they had in common was their anti-Castro

fanaticism. Now they'd been turned loose but apparently no one had made contact with them except the old Germans in Paraguay who were offering them not armies but refuges.

The only geographic spot all eleven politicals had in common was the airport at Buenos Aires to which, on the terrorists' instructions, the politicals had been delivered at various times during the day following the murder of Robert Lundquist. But the airport had been covered by surveillance platoons and no one had spotted anything. The politicals came in, they were processed through, they were followed when they left. No one saw any of them make contact with anyone except the aged chauffeur who had collected all of them; the chauffeur was a deaf ex-Wehrmacht colonel who, under questioning, showed no reluctance to reveal his instructions. He'd been sent to B.A. by his employers in Paraquay who felt the politicals would need a hand of friendship and who had dispatched the chauffeur with small amounts of money to be given to each of the politicals along with an open invitation to join the German hosts on their Paraguayan estates. The way in which it was all done, openly and cynically, suggested that the German invitation was a matter of sympathy more than conspiracy. Two of the eleven politicals were themselves German; that probably contributed to the Bundists' decision to offer a haven to the ex-prisoners.

"It's one of two things," Anders said. "Either it was a propaganda gesture or it was a smoke screen. If it was a propaganda gesture it was designed to show the world that the anti-Castro people still have friends. That would have some value, I guess, if it encouraged other people to get on the bandwagon. It's the only political purpose I can see in this business because it's becoming obvious the terrorists don't have any real practical use for these eleven politicals. Most of them are has-beens anyway. Relics of the sixties."

"That's the way I see it," Wilkins agreed.

"Or it could be a smoke screen. Maybe these guys are simply a little team of crooks who figured out a handy way to earn ten million dollars tax free."

Bemusement seeped into Wilkins' dewlappy eyes. "Now that would be funny. You think that's what they are?"

"I don't know. In any case I don't think these eleven are going to lead us anywhere. Probably they don't know any more than we do. But I guess we've got to maintain surveillance on them. It'll be a waste of time but you have to go through the motions. Right now I imagine they're sitting around a German ranch swapping yarns about the good old days."

"Speaking of the good old days, guess who dropped in a little while ago?"

"Harry Crobey."

"You saw him, then. Good. He was looking for you."

"Was he now?"

Wilkins said, "You think he's got anything to do with this?" He looked honestly surprised. "Crobey? Terrorists?"

"He's a hired gun. He works for just about anybody."

"These guys are circumspect. They wouldn't hire a known mercenary."

"Maybe that's just why they would," Anders said. "He agreed to meet me for a drink tonight. If he keeps the appointment I'd like to have him shadowed when he leaves the Hilton. Can you spare a few men and a couple of cars for a day or two? They'll have to be good at it—Crobey's not a fool."

Wilkins scratched his throat and blinked dismally. "Crobey? No, I can't see him tying up with that kind. He's arrogant, he wouldn't hire out to a gang of off-the-wall crazies."

"Then what's he doing here?"

"Maybe he came to get laid. Who knows. But I can let you have a surveillance team for a little while." He picked up a letter opener and made a dour stab at a fingernail.

Rosalia was cross when he refused to take her with him. She wanted to meet Crobey because she'd heard some of the legends about him. Finally Anders compromised. She could wander into the bar at 9:45 and he'd introduce her. But he wanted time alone with the Englishman.

Crobey was more than punctual. When Anders arrived Crobey was already there in a corner banquette; probably he'd been here twenty minutes trying to spot ambushes or eavesdroppers before they could get set. A bit amused Anders said, "Been here long?"

"Just got here. How've you been?"

"Busy. You know how it goes." Anders sat.

"Getting anywhere on this terrorist thing?"

"That's pretty blunt, even for you."

Crobey said, "I'm working on the same job. Let's help each other."

"This afternoon you pretended you didn't want me to see you. What's the game?"

"No game. You startled me on the street—I hadn't expected to run into you there. I had something on my mind. But I wanted to see you."

"You didn't say so."

"I hadn't decided how to play it yet," Crobey conceded.

That was plausible enough but Anders reserved judgment. Crobey was too good at looking you in the eye.

Crobey grinned. "I could ooze a little guile. Would that make you more comfortable?"

"Probably."

"How far have you got?"

"It's no good pumping me, Harry, I haven't got any secrets for sale."

"I was thinking more about the lines of barter."

"What are you offering to swap?"

"I just had a talk with Ortega. He was helpful. You ought to go see him."

"The *Times* reporter?"

"Yeah, him. You remember he said he thought he recognized something familiar about the big guy with the beard—the terrorist leader."

"We sat him through two days with the mug books.

He didn't come up with anything.''

"You didn't ask him the right questions," Crobey said quietly.

"And you did?"

"Yes. I know who the bearded guy is now."

It extracted Anders' slow smile. "That's quite a teaser."

"Isn't it."

"And you'll give me the name if I'll divulge what I know."

"That's the idea, Glenn."

"If Ortega remembered something for you he can remember it for me. What if I just ask him?"

"He doesn't know the name. He only knows the face." Crobey lifted his glass, an ironic toast. "Ask him. He's probably home, you've got his number. You want me to order you something while you're on the phone?"

It couldn't be a bluff; too easy to call. Anders subsided in the seat. "You're cute, Harry. All right. Who is he?"

"Scratch my back first. Then I'll scratch yours."

"Who are you working for?"

"That would be telling."

"Then we haven't got much to talk about."

"You don't want the name of the terrorist, then?"

"Look at it from my point of view. I have to calculate the possibility that you're working for the terrorists. Maybe they sent you here to find out how close I am to getting my hands on them. Maybe you're supposed to send me on a wild goose chase?"

Crobey said, "Give me a minute, I'll think out a way around that."

"Do that."

Crobey tipped his head back and closed his eyes.

Crobey was getting a bit long in the tooth, Anders thought. How old was Crobey now? Late forties anyhow; Crobey had flown combat in Korea.

Crobey had flown P-51 Mustangs. He had peculiarly rigid prejudices—he hated jets and when they'd transferred him to Sabers he'd turned in a wretched performance, a kind of protest, cracking up two planes on the runway. The Air Force had yanked him out of the combat zone and set him to training young pilots on piston-engine planes at Edwards Air Force Base. Crobey, fuming, had served out the rest of the Korean War there.

At the first opportunity he'd resigned his commission and gone mercenary, flying any kind of old crate so long as it had propellers. He wouldn't touch jets. But that was all right because most of the Third World air forces were too poor to equip themselves with jets. Whole generations of African and Latin American military pilots had been trained by Harry Crobey. Most of them probably still remembered the first time he had sent them out to find a skyhook or a bucket of prop-wash. Crobey's pranks were like the bad jokes of vaudeville comedians.

Anders' first meeting with Crobey had been on a field in Alabama, the property of one of the Agency's innumerable civil-air front companies; Crobey had been brought in to teach Cuban exile pilots how to avoid flying their B-26 bombers into chimneys, mountains and power lines. That had been 1961; Crobey already trailed a legend—the Congo, Indonesia, the Dominican Republic. He didn't limp then and his hair was a bit darker and his face had been almost cherubically naïve. Those who knew him insisted he had an aging portrait in his attic but in truth Crobey was only in his thirties then and it was pre-Bay of Pigs and pre-Kennedy assassination— life was still a wild sort of fun for men like Crobey: *The world is my whorehouse.*

In Djakarta they said Crobey had screwed his way systematically through every brothel, working north to south, until the government had tied a can to his tail: Everybody knew that half the whores in Djakarta were Communist spies. Crobey's retort made its way into the Agency's folklore. He said it wasn't his mouth he exercised in bed. Anders had never found the story particularly uproarious but the line—"Don't exercise your mouth on her"—had worked its way into company jargon until it became a shorthand notation of the fact that a woman didn't have a security clearance.

The Crobey myth was Bunyonesque among the young Turks in the Agency, of whom in those days Anders had been one. Crobey was a free-lance and didn't have to take jobs he didn't like—that alone made him the envy of every civil servant but beyond that was Crobey's *panache*, his Scarlet Pimpernel *insouciance*, his way of greeting the world with a distended middle finger and a cheerful *"Merde."*

Anders had met him fairly frequently during the late 1960s and early '70s; their paths had crossed at intervals in Laos and Chile and Viet Nam, Crobey flying surplus Spitfires or rattling DC-3s or wornout B-24 Liberators; as long as it wasn't a jet Crobey would fly it. Anders had formed an acquaintance with him, something short of friendship; it had lasted with a reasonable lack of abrasion over a decade but he'd lost touch with Crobey after the fall of Saigon. At first he had enjoyed Crobey's cut-ups; they'd got drunk together and wasted several bars in their time but Anders had outgrown that. After a while it had begun to occur to him that Crobey wasn't dashing; his jokes were crude and sometimes cruel, his personality often offensive—he had a rude way of rebuffing ordinary politeness, a contempt for normal people. "There are only three hundred real people in the world," Crobey used to say, "and we all know each other. The rest are farmers and shop-keepers and politicians—otherwise known as the gutless rabble."

Crobey opened his eyes and fixed them on Anders. A waitress, unbidden, took their empties and placed a second round of drinks on the table; it was that kind of bar—you spent money or you left.

In the depths of Crobey's glance was something Anders hadn't found there before. Maybe it was the birth of maturity or a belated sense of mortality or the beginnings of the hangover from twenty-five years' irreverence; maybe it was simply sham—Crobey was something of an actor.

"Phomh Penh," Crobey said. "Remember? Those Cambode MPs wanted to put some welts in our skulls."

"We had it coming."

"If I hadn't dragged you out of there—"

Anders had to smile. "I owe you that one."

"Then there was the time you tried to decapitate yourself on that chopper's rotor blades because you forgot to duck going in—"

Anders nodded; he'd forgotten that one. Now it came back—the shock of being tackled from behind, Crobey's weight slamming him down.

Crobey said, "Beirut, now, that was interesting, too. Kalashnikov slugs going every which way." Then his brazen smile. "But there's no need to keep books on it, is there?"

"Are you fishing for references?"

Crobey tapped a finger on the tabletop. "I'm not asking you to fall on a grenade. I'm only asking you to trust me with information. I'm asking you to go first because I'm not bound by oaths of secrecy and you are—you've got orders to keep your trap shut and you're a fairly good German; I need the leverage to shake you loose from that position. That's why you have to go first. You can refuse me—it depends how much you want the name of this joker."

"I could haul you in for interrogation."

"Debriefing with scopalomine and rubber hoses? No, you won't do that. I came to you voluntarily."

"Who are you working for?"

"No signatures. I get paid in cash. But I'll go this far—you and I are on the same side. We both want to nail these guys."

There was a glint of forlorn doubt in Crobey's eyes as if he saw he'd shot his bolt. Anders felt disquieted. He studied it briefly but there was no need to dissect it; the impasse was still there. He squeezed his lips together and shook his head back and forth just slightly. "Can't do it," he said. "If I knew who your clients were—"

"The client is no threat to you."

"I don't know that, do I?"

"You do now. I just told you."

"Come off it, Harry. I was born a little earlier than that." Anders began to slide over. "I'm going to assume you're bluffing. If I assume you don't really know anything then I don't have to file a report that would get you hauled in for questioning.''

"In Mexico? You guys are damned arrogant.'' Crobey leaned across the table and touched his arm, arresting him. "Sit still a minute. I'll tell you who the client is if I have your guarantee it goes no farther than this table. You don't report it back to Langley and nobody harasses the client.''

"How can I sign a blank check like that?''

"The client's an individual. Not a government, not a terrorist gang, not a corporation. One person. Vulnerable. Now you see the point?''

"A Cuban?''

"No. If you want I'll try to set up a meeting—just you and me and the client, no minions. Fair enough?''

Anders bit into it and began to chew; and Crobey said harshly, "It's farther than I intended to go. It's more than I owe you. And I'll tell you this—if you turn it down I'll rub your fucking nose in it. I promise you I'll make it a point to find those guys before you do and then I'll make sure O'Hillary hears about it. Your ass will be grass.''

"Don't threaten me, you cheeky bastard.'' Anders grinned at him. "I don't scare, remember?''

"That's because you're a bloody fool.''

Anders said, "At last we understand each other.''

"Right.''

He extended his hand; Crobey grasped it. Anders said, "All right. Who's the client?''

"Carole Marchand.''

"Who?''

"The Lundquist boy's mother.''

In astonishment Anders sagged back in his seat. He must have been gaping; Crobey leered at him.

Then Crobey said, "Your turn at the wicket now. I want to know everything you've got.''

Crobey's claim was too wild to be disbelieved. Still Anders said, "I'll want to talk to her.''

"I told you, I'll arrange it.''

"All right." He bought it. Time might prove him an imbecile but he had to take the chance.

He began to talk, keeping back nothing of consequence; Crobey was a good listener, he didn't interrupt. After a little while Rosalia came into the bar expectantly eager but Anders, after curtly introducing Crobey to her, shooed her away; the girl looked so crestfallen it made Crobey laugh. When she was gone Anders resumed his litany.

Afterward Crobey squinted shrewdly. "Most of it won't get you anywhere. You'll find the guy they hired the ketch from but he won't know anything—they'll have used a blind front for that, a cut-out, some guy without a face. Boats don't leave tracks. The eleven politicals, they're a dead end, too—likely they don't know who rescued them. But then you'd already discounted that. Your theory about it being a caper strictly for the ten million bucks—that's cute but I don't buy it. I think they're in it for nationalist reasons; they're not just thieves."

"Why?"

"Because—I told you—I know who the head man is."

"It's time you gave me the name."

"If I give you the name, what will you do with it?"

"What do you think?"

"I don't know. My client thinks your people are determined to sweep the whole thing under the rug."

"Your client's wrong, as far as I know."

"As far as you know?"

"I can't read minds," Anders said. "Who's the terrorist?"

"He used to go by the name of Rodrigo Rodriguez, believe it or not."

"Never heard of him."

"He was one of the pilots who washed out of that Cuban flight school I ran in Alabama. I think he was kicked out before you got there."

"Rodrigo Rodriquez? What kind of name is that?"

"Far as I know it's the name his parents gave him.

But I'm sure he's got something else in his passport by now. I've already checked out the Rodriguez angles. All blind alleys. He's covered his tracks beautifully."

"That's why you came to me?"

"There's a limit to how much legwork can be done by one man with a sore leg. You've got armies—your people can sift a thousand leads through the strainer and come up with a clue. Give me that clue and I'll find the guy for you. I know him a little, I know how he thinks."

"What makes you connect this Rodriguez with the terrorists?"

"He was a kid then, it was long before the Bay of Pigs and I don't know what happened to him afterward, but in those days he had what your military types like to call leadership qualifications. Tough, bright and blokes liked him."

"But he washed out of pilot training."

"You don't have to be an expert sharpshooter to be a good general, do you?"

"All right."

"I got onto the idea because of the report that was filtered back from Ortega—something about the guerrilla leader wearing a beard and a big belly. It put me in mind of Rodrigo Rodriguez in his Santa Claus suit at the Christmas party in 1960."

"You're kidding."

"Well it wouldn't have occurred to me if that was all I'd had. But I started from the obvious premise that the beard was phony. If that was phony then maybe the belly was phony. Then we got the interesting tidbit from one of the Mexican hostages that the leader had a Puerto Rican accent. Rodrigo has a Puerto Rican accent—he's Cuban by birth but his family ran a business in Puerto Rico. They were in the rum trade in a minor way. Rodriguez and his brother went to school in Mayaguez. Which brings us to another point, the brother. I think his name was Julio. Actually there were three of them, like musketeers, inseparable—the two Rodriguez brothers and a young brute by the name of

Vargas. Now Vargas used to smoke Gauloises. And Julio Rodriguez used to read pulp magazines all the time. Science-fiction pulp magazines. You see where it all points?''

"Flimsy," Anders said. "Flimsy as hell."

"It was," Crobey agreed, "until I showed Ortega an old photograph of Rodrigo."

"Ah."

"Ah indeed. I didn't tell Ortega the name of the guy in the photograph but he identified it." Crobey's hand came out of his pocket with a two-by-three glossy. "Keep it, I've got a bunch of them."

"From where?"

"Florida. I went through the files of the old Free Cuba outfit. Hardly more than a shell nowadays but they've still got a secretary and an office. She remembered me from Alabama."

The face in the photograph was striking enough. Enormous square cheekbones and bleak eyes overhung by great ramparts of bone. Hard, but you sensed the capacity for compassion—that must be the aspect that invited people to like him. There was intelligence in it, and stubborn boldness.

Crobey said, "You wouldn't have tumbled him. He hasn't been affiliated with any of the organized exile groups since sixty-three. As far as I know there's no record of his escaping from prison in Havana but he must have. He was one of the troops captured at the Pigs."

"What rank?" Anders was businesslike when he needed to be.

"Second lieutenant I guess. Platoon leader, or that's what I heard. It's a long time ago. I think he was one of the ones on Red Beach. Lucky he didn't get shrapnel up his ass."

"I see the problem. He's had fifteen years to establish a new identity."

Crobey said, "You can probably get your hands on his fingerprints from some file or other. That might help a little."

Anders doubted it; he knew of no case in which a fugitive had been found on the basis of fingerprints. But he had to try.

Anders said, "For all practical purposes you're simply handing him over to me. Why?"

"I'll reach him before you do, Glenn. Don't worry about it."

"I don't see how. Not with what you've given me."

"We'll see. Do you still want to talk to the client?"

"What does she want?"

"She wants a little justice. Just a little justice."

"Vengeance is mine."

"You ever read Francis Bacon?"

"Maybe in high school. I don't remember."

"Revenge," Crobey quoted, "is a kind of wild justice. Bacon."

"The lady's angry then."

"You could say that," Crobey agreed. Then he got up to go. "I'll be in touch."

Anders watched him beat a path among the tables. Highly puzzled, Anders finally slid out of the booth and went toward a phone.

Chapter 9

Cielo had tumbled asleep like a weary peon who had shaken off his load but when he awoke he found evidence in the tumbled bed of a difficult night; nor did he feel rested.

After a while he went along to the kitchen ramming his shirttails into his pants. Soledad stood over the ironing board looking cross, her hair tied in a horsetail with a small ribbon; he thought she was breathtakingly beautiful.

She said, "You were impossible. I had to sleep on the couch in the end. I don't know what the children must think."

"I'm sorry. It must have been bad dreams or something."

"And now you have to go out again?"

"Si."

"For how long this time?"

"I can't say. You realize I should be up there with them all the time—I'm shirking my duty, laying so much onto Vargas and my brother."

"When will this madness stop?"

"When the old man dies, I suppose."

"The Dragas are long-lived—his uncle lived to ninety-four."

"But blind and senile the last few years, wasn't he?"

"Old Draga isn't blind or senile."

"Don't nag me," Cielo said, "you won't change anything."

She said, "It takes young men to do this sort of thing. He should know that. Your heart isn't in this."

"No, most of the time it's not. Once in a while I try to

remind myself. You know I talked to Ortiz yesterday? Raoul Ortiz?''

"You didn't mention it."

"Ortiz was in Cuba just a few months ago. Running guns to people in the mountains. He said it is even worse than before. The squalor and all. The despair.''

"You're trying to pump yourself up but it all keeps leaking out again, doesn't it.''

"Well I'd like to do something for them. You know.''

She said, "Surely, but this way? Who are you—Don Quixote?''

Cielo watched her push the iron back and forth across his black chinos. "It's not that bad, you know. I don't mind what we're doing now. One day these weapons will be used.''

"But not by you.''

"No, I'm too old. I've turned cautious.''

"Someone will confiscate the weapons before anyone can use them. How do you expect to keep them hidden for years?''

"Bury them. Nobody looks in El Yunque.''

"It takes a big hole to bury cannons and machine guns.''

"We've got plenty of time to dig it.''

"Not really. The old man, Draga, he'll get impatient soon.''

"I'll tell him the time isn't right yet.''

"And he'll believe it just because you say so?''

"He trusts me.'' The statement came out like a confession, shaming him.

She said, "Rodrigo—talk to me about it.''

"How can I talk about things for which there aren't any words? Feelings—''

She smiled mournfully. "You poor thing. You hang onto this nonsense as if it was the first woman's breast you ever sucked. You've even forgotten why you're doing it.''

"I know why it's done. But it's just that it's no longer fashionable to spend one's life discussing the ultimates of good and evil. That's for university students. The advocates of revolution.''

She said, "I remember the days when even villainy was innocent."

"You know the CIA has received orders from the White House to stop all secret anti-Castro exile activities. We must be circumspect. Old Draga understands that—he'll curb his impatience."

"Those orders were issued more than a year ago, *querido*. Nobody paid much attention to them."

"Just the same."

"Is it the old Draga who worries you—or the young one?"

"Emil." He only sighed.

"That one is trouble, since he was little."

"You know the expression 'trapped between a rock and a hard place,' *querida*? Well the old man is the rock. All the same, I think we can control Emil. I think we've thrown a little respect into him. His ribs are still taped up, though he doesn't want anyone to know it."

Suddenly he could feel the air whistling through his own nose. He unraveled the handkerchief from his hip pocket and blew his nose.

She sighed with infinite tolerance. "Put it there with the laundry and get a clean one. *Por Dios*, you can't even get out of the house in the morning without soiling another bit of cloth."

"When the girls come home from school I want you to have a talk with them about this TV business. We should ration their hours—there are things in life besides television."

"They would listen more closely to you than to me. It's something you ought to take care of."

"I probably won't be here tonight."

"Then it can wait until you come back. Tomorrow maybe?"

"Maybe. I can't promise."

"It's a good thing I know you. Otherwise I'd think you had a woman squirreled away."

He reached out for her hand, took the iron from it and stood it up on the metal pan; he put his hands on her shoulders and uttered each word as if he had coined it on the spot: "I adore you with all my heart and soul. I always will—to the end of my life.''

The liveliness came back into his eyes. She walked into his embrace.

He went out the back way across the rear neighbor's yard and skirted trash cans on his way past a carport. He'd left the car two blocks away for reasons of security. When he reached it he was already sweating—the humidity was shocking, the sun ablaze; the faded stucco houses seemed to cringe. An infant was tumbling on a parched lawn watched by an old woman who sat shriveled in the shade fanning herself with a magazine. Two cats pursued each other comically up the alley and Cielo opened the deck of the Volkswagen. Last night he'd removed the rotor from the distributor and walked away knowing the car would still be there when he needed it. Now he replaced the rotor from his pocket, snapped the clips onto the distributor and unlocked the door.

Ernesto Mendez—the name on his mailbox—might be a tame lower-class surburban but *Cielo* had been trained in the guerrilla arts. It was this training that alerted him to the presence of a man standing in a doorway half a block distant. The man wasn't watching him but Cielo knew the neighborhood and the man didn't belong there: poplin suit, tie, the sun glinting on polished cordovan. Standing in the doorway, Cielo thought, was foolish: It only framed the man, focusing attention on him as if he were a portrait. A smart one would have strolled in the open, looking as if he had business.

Possibly it had nothing to do with him but he was troubled. He made a U turn in the potholed street and drove away watching the mirror. His alarm increased tenfold when the man turned and went inside the house whose doorway had framed him. If the man was going to a phone. . . .

Driving into Hato Rey he was remembering his introduction to the heroic arts: the Sierra Maestra, 1958, nothing more than a skirmish really—the rebels under Ché Guevara had ambushed the trucks and Cielo had

dived out into the ditch along with the other soldiers.
The rebels had used mortars and Brownings and grenades; the noise of battle had confounded and in-
furiated Cielo. Finally—to stop the noise—he had per-
formed heroically. Madly. Afterward six rebels were
dead and Batista himself pinned the medal on Cielo. It
was all so comical. He'd had no thought of earning
medals; he'd only wanted to stop the noise.

But after that he was a hero and they promoted him
and he was looked to as a leader and he was too young
to know better than to play along with it. The attention
was too flattering to be rebuffed.

An accidental moment of madness, but it had
changed and colored everything in his life since then. He
had never confided this to anyone but Soledad; no one
but Soledad would understand. Not even his own
brother.

Still troubled by the man in the doorway, he pulled
around behind an open-front cantina and parked the
Volkswagen in the dust where it was hidden from the
street. He went to the public kiosk and Luz answered
the old man's phone. He exchanged counterproposals
with Luz and then cradled the phone and walked
away—walking up the alley past the Volkswagen and on
past the back doors of several seedy shops. At the
corner of Avenida Hostos he turned north and walked
at a steady pace, using the side mirrors of parked vans
to examine his backtrail. No one was following him; he
was positive of that after ten minutes. At the corner of
the Calle Eleanor Roosevelt he waited in the shade until
a bus came by. He rode it across the causeway into San
Juan and dropped off at the edge of Santurce. He went
around the block twice on foot, picked up no tail, and
was waiting by the curb when the Pinto drew up. Cielo
got in and the car started moving before he'd pulled the
door shut. Luz, at the wheel, said, "Señor Draga is
anxious to know what this is about."

"Maybe nothing—maybe it means nothing."

"But if it does. What would they be?"

"Police. CIA. Castro's men. Who can say?"

"But they were not watching your house?"

"No, I'd left the car away from my house and that was where I saw the man. Near the car."

"Where were you yesterday that someone might have noticed you and taken down the license number of the Volkswagen?"

"The old man knows where I was. I reported to him last night by phone."

Luz's voice had the quality of a rusty hinge in motion. "You'll have to stay out of sight for a while. Don't go back to your home."

"I know that, you don't have to tell me."

"And don't telephone the house again."

"He gets upset if I don't report to him."

"We'll have to find a way to do it without telephones. *El viejo* no longer trusts their security."

Luz drove east toward the airport. Cielo had never quite comprehended Luz's exact place in the Draga scheme of things; Luz apparently was something between bodyguard and secretary, with a bit of valet thrown in, but the old man had secretaries and bodyguards and a valet besides Luz. There wasn't much likelihood that Luz was of any importance in the management of the Draga businesses—Luz wasn't a businessman, he was too coarse, he was nearly a thug. He was a Cuban mountain peasant whose parents had worked for the Draga interests in some capacity.

Luz was low-profile; he usually didn't appear in public at Draga's side and most of the world didn't associate him with Draga, which gave him a certain freedom of movement; Cielo suspected that Luz perhaps acted as a sort of bagman in Draga's dealings with officials and police and the Jews and Italians from Florida with whom the old man did certain kinds of business. It was old man Draga who in 1963 had acted as intermediary between the Free Cuba movements and the Santos Trega group of Sicilians; the Sicilians had made six separate attempts on Castro's life. Santos Trega himself was Cuban, a former criminal boss in Havana, imprisoned in '61–'62 by Castro, then deported—after a substantial *sub-rosa* payment to Castro—to Miami and New Orleans. Jack Ruby, who had shot Lee Oswald in Dallas, had been one of Trega's associates; Cielo had heard rumors that Sam Giancana and Johnny Rosselli were part of it as well. In subsequent years old man Draga had withdrawn from most of his contacts with Trega and Lansky, mostly because he disapproved pragmatically of their ethics but also because he came to regard them as bunglers.

It was taken for granted by Draga and those around him that the assassination of John F. Kennedy had been formulated in Havana and dictated by Castro because Castro knew that the CIA had employed the Mafia to try to assassinate Castro: The killing of the President had been a retaliatory hit. Cielo had believed in these conspiratorial complexities for a long time but just recently he had begun to question them; he no longer knew what to believe—he no longer was sure he cared.

Along the service road beside the airport Luz slowed the Pinto. Its air conditioner blew a chill draft against Cielo's throat and he reached out to change the direction of the vent ribs. By the side of the road a small station wagon was parked, a man in the front seat; its sun visors were lowered to indicate all clear. Luz drew past the station wagon and touched the brake pedal—three taps, to signal the station wagon—and drove on toward the big hangars that butted up against the chain fence. Cielo glanced back and saw that the station wagon was following. He hadn't recognized its driver.

He began to think about the niceties of his situation: Was this an execution ride? But he knew better; he was relaxed when Luz stopped the car behind one of the hangars. "Is there anything you want me to relay to the old man?"

"No. Tell him I'll be in touch." Cielo pushed the door open and got out.

The station wagon drew up and its driver left the door open when he walked forward. The driver nodded civilly enough and went past him. Cielo recognized him now—he'd seen the man around Draga's place a few times walking the dogs on leashes. He'd never seen the man out of uniform before; that was what had thrown him.

The dog handler got into the Pinto, the seat Cielo had just vacated; the Pinto drove away.

It was so hot there didn't seem to be any air. Cielo went squinting to the station wagon and shut himself in, grateful for the air conditioning.

He had a look around the car's interior and opened the glove compartment to see if anything had been left for him—an envelope or whatever. There was nothing, only a flashlight and the car's registration papers made out to somebody named Juan D. Ruiz at an address in Ponce—he was sure it was phony although it looked good enough to his untrained eye; Cielo had no talent for forgery.

He put it in drive and pointed it out toward the highway, thinking now of the old man up there possibly sitting over iced tea on his veranda overlooking the Cerromar golf course and all the tourists getting their exercise in electric carts: The old man sitting on his wealth and still deluding himself into the belief that he was the power behind the operation that would liberate Cuba.

The farm was deserted except for one man whom Julio had left on guard: Stefano—small, ruddy, quick, with an incipient potbelly and under his mustache a set of buck teeth like a steam engine's cowcatcher. Stefano had a disconcerting wart at the corner of his lower lip. Stefano greeted him with a casual remark and an easy smile, and it struck Cielo suddenly how old Stefano looked—how old they all were getting.

Cielo sent out a three-second radio signal; then he popped the tab of an aluminum can and sat down on the porch trying to find the breeze; he tasted the thin Puerto Rican beer and thought how egotistical their dreams had been, how pathetically comic and how posturingly tragic. They had been blind to the realities of power. The old man and the other zealous exiles believed, against all evidence, that they needed merely to provide the spark and that the tinder would burst into flame immediately, fueled by a popular will that would sweep away the Castro commissars. It amazed him now how

long he had been able to sustain his own belief in that
scenario.

After about three hours the Land Cruiser appeared at
the head of the cornfield and came forward along the
furrows, Vargas at the wheel. Vargas' big lips went all
shapes when he smiled. Cielo dropped off the porch and
tossed his bags in back and climbed into the passenger
seat and Vargas turned the Land Cruiser around to head
back up into the hills. Cielo looked back—Stefano
waved to him. Stefano's chest had caved in with age; his
clothes looked as if they hung on a hanger that was too
small. *My God*, Cielo thought, *how ridiculous we are.*

Vargas said, "Julio's run out of books."

"Hell. I forgot to bring more." The damned science
fiction. How did Julio tell them apart? They all had the
same covers. Byzantine creatures with all sorts of eyes
and arms.

"How goes the cave?"

"It goes. Not very fast."

"That's all right, there's plenty of time. Everything's
out of sight?"

"We're very careful," Vargas said. "Enrique's very
stern, he doesn't let anybody make mistakes." Kruger's
first name was Heinrich but they'd called him Enrique
for nearly twenty years—it hadn't made a Latin of him.

"Did you see the old man?"

"A couple of days ago. In his counting house." Cielo
grinned a bit maliciously; it pleased him to think of
Draga as a miserly Scrooge. The vault in Draga's
basement was truly formidable. Cielo had watched in
amazement while the old man unhooked alarms,
inserted keys, dialed combinations and turned handles
up instead of down. "If a man turns it down," the old
man had told him with ferocious satisfaction, "he gets a
squirt of disabling gas in the face."

Cielo was bemused that after so many years the old
man would entrust him with such a secret. It was
because the old man wanted his confidence, of course;
the old man was thirsty for information—he'd wanted
every detail no matter how trivial. How much was this
dealer charging for Kalashnikovs? Couldn't they have

got a better price in Algiers? What was the exact range
of the rocket launchers? How many rockets? Which
model of flame thrower had been settled on? How much
was being paid per thousand rounds of rifle ammunition? It all went into the ledger in the old man's head.
Cielo remembered thinking, *You won't make a profit*
on these transactions no matter how you bargain the
prices down. But it was in the old man's blood.

The Land Cruiser bumped painfully into the woods.
The trail lifted them at a grinding deliberate pace
toward the Cordillera—green peaks rising in a thin mist
that the heat never quite seemed to dissipate. After a
little while it dipped into a wide cañon and Vargas
guided the wheels carefully up onto a vast shelf of rock
that was tipped just enough off the horizontal to give
Cielo a queasy feeling—one day, he thought, the Land
Cruiser would tip right over on its side along this
stretch.

Off to the right the tire-truck ruts resumed at the edge
of the rock; in plain sight they stretched up into the
woods toward the southeast. Julio and Vargas had spent
half a day making that false trail.

Vargas put the Land Cruiser down the slope toward
the creek that made its shallow way along the bottom of
the rock slab. Driving slowly in the water with white
froth birling off the hubcaps they spent a difficult five
minutes pushing uphill in the streambed. This part
always troubled Cielo because the rock supported no
growth at all and this meant they would be visible from
the air for the duration of this stretch. Ground trackers
would lose them at this point but all it needed was one
helicopter or a light plane passing over at the wrong
moment.

Zigzagging from one side to another Vargas wrestled
the Land Cruiser toward the head of the canyon. Eventually the bottom changed from solid rock to gravel; the
walls began to narrow and the trees to press down; here
Vargas and Cielo had to get out and unwind the cable
from the winch. Hooking it to an enormous banyan
they hauled the Land Cruiser up over a slumping
shoulder of rock, after which Vargas reeled in the cable

and they drove on through the trees.

This was the edge of El Yunque—the Luquillo Caribbean National Forest, the only tropical rain forest on U.S. soil—the Puerto Rican mountain jungle. In his odd-job days as a tour guide in the late 1960s he had recited by rote that the El Yunque Forest covered nearly thirty thousand acres, climbed to an altitude of thirty-five hundred feet and absorbed an annual rainfall of more than one hundred billion gallons. The figures were impressive in the abstract; when you got down to a personal level what was more impressive was the sense of utter isolation that cloaked him every time he penetrated the jungle. Once inside the towering shade of El Yunque he no longer had any confidence he was on the same planet.

A paved road of narrow hairpin bends and frequent washouts bisected the forest to the east, going right over the central pass between the peaks of El Toro and El Yunque; that was the tourist route and if you were on it you could be back in the fleshpots of San Juan in less than an hour—it was only twenty-five miles away. But on these outer slopes there were no roads, no farms, no evidence that humans had ever passed this way.

Overhead the sun flickered like a moving signal lamp among the interlaced branches of sierras and tree ferns, colorados and palms, clumps of bamboo a hundred feet high, dotted bromiliads and orchids below; a rotting rich thickness of life.

Bugs buzzed. Parrots, macaws—flashes of color. And always the chirping of tiny coqui frogs like cicadas in the branches. The air was damp but not unpleasant; thinner here than at sea level and the smell was rain-clean.

Even to cut their basic primitive pioneer road they'd had to spend months chopping their way through coagulated undergrowth and laying stones across watercourses; at frequent intervals the rains washed these away and there was never a trip without having to stop and replace them. And still the pitch of the ground was so steep they had to use the winch several times each way.

It made for a long difficult trek despite the fact that the distance between the lowland farm where he'd left Stefano and the El Yunque camp was not more than seven miles as the buzzard flies and perhaps sixteen miles by pioneer track: They'd never done it in less than two and a half hours.

Twice after the rock slab they covered their trail again—made as if to strike out along false roads they'd prepared; then doubled back through water or rock.

A determined *Indio* tracker with dogs might find the camp eventually but he'd need to have a good idea where to look and he'd take so long about it that they'd have considerable warning of his approach. As added security they'd laid tripwires across the path on the high ridges nearing the camp. Driving in, Cielo had to dismount twice from the Land Cruiser to disconnect the wires while Vargas drove across them; then he hooked them up again and they rolled on into the camp. The tripwires were connected to cowbells in the cave—a rudimentary device but adequate.

The roadway entered the camp by way of a narrow gap—bamboo on one side, a sheer drop on the other: The path rode along this brief shelf and tipped down toward the camp of huts. Nothing short of a wrecking ball could make headway through the thickness of high bamboo that screened it. This was the only way in—easy to command, easy to defend; conceivably a man or two could deny passage to a battalion.

It wasn't going to come to that. Cielo had no ambition to hold out heroically against an armed assault. Discovery here would mean surrender; he wasn't prepared to sacrifice his men for nothing. The chief weapons in his arsenals were secrecy and concealment and deception.

There was a man on guard at the gap; there always was; this one waved his hand lazily and didn't bother to unsling his submachine gun and Cielo reminded himself to have a talk with the man later—they all were slipping toward apathy, taking things for granted, depending on tripwired cowbells in place of vigilance.

Past the gap the road dipped toward the huts. It was a

compact area with its back to the cliff, screened by thick growths of high bamboo and trees that soared to vertiginous heights; the cliff was a jagged upheaval of faults and abutments on top of which was a flat granite promontory, an open field beyond which another tier of jungle sloped up steeply toward the heights. The promontory overhung the camp and it was his plan to use it as a helicopter landing pad from which heavy equipment could be winched down and rolled into the cave behind the camp.

When he stepped out of the Land Cruiser he found Julio waiting for him.

"Did you bring me a few books?"

"I'm sorry, I forgot."

"Damn."

"Read the old ones again. What difference does it make? You can't tell them apart."

"The hell I can't. A man gets bored up here. Did you give the girls a kiss from their uncle?"

"Sure—sure."

Cielo went into the command hut with his brother; Vargas and Kruger drifted in and Cielo made his report to them—it contained no surprises except for the possibility that the man in the doorway had been spying on him. This disquieted Kruger more than the others; he was volatile and tended to fret about things. Kruger's Spanish was even worse than his English, even after all the years, and in his presence they all tended to speak English although their conversation was peppered with common Spanish words and phrases. Druger said, "If someone's onto us, who?"

"I'll consult the tea leaves and let you know," Cielo said, making light of it.

"Have you no idea at all?"

"None, nor do I care very much. Whoever he is he didn't follow me up here, did he? Let's have a look at the cave."

They all trooped out to the foot of the cliff like an inspector general's party, everyone suitably deferential. The cave was natural—a fault in the rock cleft by some disturbance aeons ago. It was nearly thirty feet high and

extended well back into the mountain to a depth of a
city block or more. Its width varied considerably from
point to point. The floor sloped up from the mouth
toward the back, which was a good thing because it
meant rainwater didn't run into the cave. When they'd
first discovered it they'd known it was the best they were
going to find. You could crowd quite a lot of heavy
military equipment in here. Nothing like airplanes or
helicopters, nor would it accommodate more than a few
tanks, but they weren't acquiring anything that heavy
anyway. The planes wouldn't be needed until the very
end—and Cielo believed the very end would never
come. In the meantime there was room for field mortars
and rocket launchers and flame throwers, machine guns
and small arms and grenades and a few Jeeps that could
be winched down or driven up the pioneer road.

The floor of the cave was dusty with debris. Several
men were hammering rock drills into uneven lumps;
small explosive charges would be set into them. The
floor of the cave in its natural state had been jagged and
useless; they were flattening it as best they could and
knocking protrusions off the walls at the same time.

He vaguely hoped all this violence wasn't going to
bring the whole thing crashing down. There didn't seem
too much likelihood of that—the cliff was so massive,
the cave so small in relation—but Cielo didn't know
much geology and thought perhaps there might be
cracks that would be widened by the dynamite. It wasn't
anything he intended to lose sleep over.

He said, "Satisfactory, I think. You'll be finished in a
day or so?"

"As near finished as we need to be," Julio replied.
"We've already begun clearing the junk off the floor as
you can see. It'll be ready to receive the *armas* by
tomorrow."

Kruger said, "Are they delivering so soon?"

"Some of the things will be available tomorrow
night," Cielo said. "Some others will take several
weeks."

They were walking back out onto the open ground.
Kruger twisted his head far back on his neck to peer up

through the interknotted treetops. It was not possible to see properly the promontory above; the outcrop was more of a hint—a darker more substantial mass beyond the matted leaves. The occasional thin finger of sunlight probed down through the mist like a laser; other rays flickered on and off as the breeze stirred the trees. The light here was muted and had a greenish tinge. Sound seemed to be absorbed instantly into the damp cushion of the jungle; the quiet was intense and sometimes distressing—the silence, the dampness, the dim light, the invisibility of the outer world, all these conspired to instill the feeling that one's senses had been drugged into half service. Cielo found that he slept longer and more often here than he did anywhere else.

Kruger, looking up toward the top, was saying: "I'm still worried about this helicopter delivery system. It's not secure. A helicopter is so"—he searched for the word—"*visible*. You know? They have ground radar, don't they? And anybody can see it going overhead. And it can be heard for miles."

"I'm not worried about security," Cielo told him. "Aircraft fly around the island all the time. There are helicopters everywhere these days. The radar can't follow the helicopter because of the mountains—radar can't distinguish between one solid object and another. We'll make deliveries only at night when the clouds are down below us. We can guide him to ground with a flashlight or two, it's not as if he needs a whole runway lighting system. It's our good luck Zapatino's a hell of a chopper pilot—he can do everything but fly upside down, you know. The main risk is weather, of course—we'll end up aborting flights because of fog."

Kruger walked away with Vargas; Cielo wasn't sure he'd reassured the German—Kruger was always looking for things that might go wrong.

When the other two had gone beyond earshot Julio said, "Any news from the old man? Has he mentioned what happened to Emil?"

"No, *hermano*. Sometimes I hope I'll never see him again. I wish him to be dead—peacefully—just to have it done with. I don't have the nerve to tell him he's crazy. And in the meantime we go through this farce of bringing in weapons by the helicopterload and caching them in this cave, where we both know they will rust away for five hundred years before anybody touches them again. The waste makes me ashamed.''

Julio looked at him harshly. ''Are you still thinking of going to the old man and telling him he's a blind fool?''

''No, I can't do that. We've worked too hard for him for these fifteen years. We've earned the money he's paid us. And when he dies there won't be any nonsense about waiting for a will to be probated. A man will simply come and give each of us a little booklet containing columns of figures and the numbers of bank accounts in Zurich. Do you think I would jeopardize that? Do you think I want those Zurich bank books burned in his fireplace? We've earned that money—and I don't feel like going back to work guiding tourists or unloading airplane cargos. And I don't guess you feel like driving a taxi again.''

''Just one thing, Rodrigo. Say the old man dies and your man never comes with the bankbooks?''

''Don't worry about that. There are ways I trust the old man completely and that's one of them. He'll cheat in a lot of ways but not that one.''

''Maybe he won't cheat *you*.''

''If you feel that way I'll tell you what I'll do. If when the old man dies and you don't get your share I'll split mine with you. And I'll make you a present of all the arms in the cave.''

''That is a promise, *hermano*?''

''A promise. You can dedicate the rest of your life to seeing that the money doesn't go to waste.''

Julio nodded pensively. ''Or the arms.''

Cielo frowned at him, but he did not want to know any more about his brother's schemes. Then he said, ''Where the hell is Emil?''

''He left this morning for San Juan, so he says.''

''I suppose I should count my blessings.''

''I don't know, Cielo. I don't trust him when I can't see him. Suppose he's hatching something?''

"Hatching what? Do you think he means to hijack this place? Let him—more power to him."

"*Hermano,* don't be facetious. He's dangerous. He sits off by himself too much—he's planning something."

"What? Has he been talking to the others much?"

"He's taken two or three of them aside. One at a time."

"Which ones?"

"Ramirex. Ordovara. Kruger, too, I think, but I saw Kruger give him his back. Maybe others, too, that I haven't seen."

"He's plotting a palace coup," Cielo mused, and smiled when he looked around. "Some palace."

"I'm worried about some of them, brother. Emil is the old man's blood."

"They're loyal, that much we don't have to worry about. Loyal to one another, and loyal to us."

"Or loyal to the Draga name?"

"No, they'd string him along for the amusement but they wouldn't turn on you and me."

"Then why hasn't one of them come forward and told us what he's up to?"

Cielo brooded on that. Cielo said, "I think we'd better have a little talk with Ramirez and Ordovara."

Chapter 10

Toting her overnight case, Howard hurried along ahead of her into National Airport's noisy terminal. By the time she caught up he'd claimed a spot in the ticket-counter queue. She said, "If I'm not back by Thursday, drag the Caribbean."

"I don't see the point of this. There's nothing you can do down there."

"I can't sit on my hands." The line inched forward. She glared at the clock, worried about the time; traffic on the bridge had coagulated around a stalled car and she was late. "Will you do something for me? Will you keep feeding the fire under your friend O'Hillary?"

"Sure—sure."

"Not that it'll do much good. It's a grotesque farce. They're all engaged in this monstrous masquerade."

"You're getting alarmingly paranoid about this, Carole."

"I am? Then why is it, do you suppose, that I could hire one solitary middle-aged man with a limp and no pull at all, and he was able to accomplish in six days what all the forces of the most powerful government on earth failed to do in fifteen?"

"Your man Crobey may think he knows the name one of them used fifteen years ago but that's a far cry from catching them. He's no closer to them than anybody else is. Why persist in this absurd anti-Washington neurosis? You know they're doing everything they can."

The queue crept forward a notch. Howard put the case down to free his hands for a cigarette. Carole said, "Don't you know those things will stunt your growth?'' Agitation made her bounce up and down on the balls of her feet; she kept looking resentfully at the clock above the oblivious ticket clerk. A metallic disembodied voice ran around overhead, half comprehensible—''Mr. Equation Funeral, Mr. Equation Funeral, please report to the American Airlines information desk.''

''You're flagellating yourself,'' Howard told her in an intense hiss. ''Stop building dungeons in the air. No one's conspiring to cover up Robert's murder.''

''Howard, I've never known quite such a round-heeled pushover as you are. Working in the guts of it all this time I'd have thought you'd have learned better. I hold these truths to be self-evident: That irrespective of realities, the deformed indoctrinations of nationalistic stupidities will take precedence every time over basic human morality; that the secret war against Castro is not over just because the President of the United States goes on television and says it's over; and that us niggers are being discriminated against because these terrorists happen to be the right political color—therefore they will be protected whatever their crimes.''

''Carole, your mouth runneth over.'' Howard had gone very pale; he glanced around to see if anyone had overheard.

She slapped her bag down on the counter and demanded her ticket. When that rigamarole was completed—''Aisle or window? . . . Smoking or nonsmoking?''—she snatched up the boarding pass, hiked her bag over her shoulder and turned to Howard to make a grab for the overnight case. Howard kept it, determined to race along with her to the plane. Striding across the terminal he got some of his color back. ''I get awfully tired of banging up against that brittle impregnable wall of your wise-ass cracks,'' he drew a shuddering long breath to continue, ''and I wish that just once in a while you'd give the rest of the world credit for possessing at least a tenth of the lofty moral values that you claim to possess.''

There was another queue at the security funnel. The metal detector kept beeping and several men were emptying out their pockets of coins, keys, cigarette cases, ballpoints. The loudspeaker announced the final boarding call for Carole's flight to San Juan.

She began to push forward, cutting into the line, fuming.

Howard grabbed her sleeve. "Calm down. They won't take off without you—they wouldn't dare." The afterthought amused him; she saw it in his eyes and knew abruptly that he was patronizing her. She couldn't stand it.

She said, "You can still be a master of the gentlemanly shiv when you want to be," and icily put her shoulder to him.

The queue began to move again. Carole placed handbag and overnight case on the moving belt. "Try to keep me posted, will you?"

"Yes, I'll try." He wasn't quite being evasive; he was just staying low-key in order to counterbalance her. She knew he wasn't her enemy. Looking back from beyond the checkpoint she caught the gentle worry in his face. He still had a hopeless remnant of feeling for her.

Howard waved; and she ran to catch her plane.

Incidents could be remembered but it was hard to recall a passion that was dead. She had loved, or been infatuated with, or had fond affection for, or perhaps merely sought refuge in Howard; but what she remembered most vividly from their marriage was the moment in Alexandria when they had looked at each other and realized they were stuck with each other. It was too depressing; not a word had passed between them but after that they had gone about embittering each other's lives until there was no possibility of rewarming the soufflé of pastel dreams with which they had fed their initial illusions. The question of blame didn't come into it: Vindictiveness had consumed them both. Now it was burnt out and she was grateful for that because she was able to view him as human.

Nothing remained between them except a distant fondness, as for a cousin who lived two thousand miles away with whom you exchanged Christmas cards and perhaps a biennial phone call. They were still wired tenuously to each other by memories of the dead child. Robert—*Robert*, she thought, *we owed you a better chance than you got.* She knew in her intellect that nothing she could do would make up for it. But all the same she was on this plane.

Crobey collected her in the midst of a chattering mob. He looked a bit surly. Making no offer to carry her bag he led the way outside into a drizzling rain that matted her hair in seconds. Crobey trudged across the parking lot without talking to her at all and she felt as if she were an errant schoolgirl being tugged along by the ear. He folded himself in behind the wheel of a little bullet-shaped car, not opening the passenger door for her, waiting stone-faced with his hand on the ignition until she pushed her case into the back seat and got in. Then Crobey turned the key; the starter meshed brutally; he jerked the lever into drive and the car lurched forward.

She said, "You're bilious tonight."

"Yeah. I had one of those submarine sandwiches. It keeps surfacing." Finally he came out with it. "I don't recall inviting you."

"I don't recall giving you a choice."

He drove it onto the expressway. An amazing traffic of suicidal imbeciles zigzagged all around them. Carole composed herself. "Do you think you could be an angel and give me a progress report?"

"Not much to report." The wipers batted back and forth. Red tail-lights swam in the windshield. A huge baroque old car fishtailed past, swerving, cutting in too soon, and Crobey had to stab the brake. She warded off the dashboard with her palm. "I made a little progress," he conceded.

She let the silence run until it was clear he wanted prompting. "I'm not just here to feed you lines. What progress?"

"Somebody seems to be interested in me." He had his attention on the rear-view mirror.

"The Rodriguez gang?"

"Or anybody. My ex-wife's private detectives, who knows."

The expressway ended in a muddy rubble of construction. Crobey maneuvered it through the side streets onto Avenida Ashford. The tall beach-front hotels might have been in Miami Beach. Reflected neon colors melted and ran along the wet pavements. A fool blocked Crobey's progress, leaving them stranded at the stoplight. When the light changed Crobey kicked the pedal; the car shot forward half a block and abruptly, without signaling, Crobey turned it into a narrow passage.

Street lights shone pale along the empty alley; at the far corner a traffic light blinked red, on and off. Crobey pulled in to the curb and extinguished the lights.

She reached for the door handle but Crobey stayed her. He kept watch on the mirror. After a while he said, "All right," and switched on the lights and drove on.

"Were we being followed?"

"No."

He was still driving with half his attention on the rear view. She had been in San Juan before but only as a tourist; he was driving through sections she'd never seen—stucco slums, open-front shops blaring an astonishingly loud cacophony of strident recorded music.

They emerged onto a narrow blacktop road that two-laned away to the end of what appeared to be a swamp; then it began to climb into the hills. The rain had stopped. She rolled down the window and heard the pneumatic hiss of the tires on the wet asphalt.

They passed a white paddock fence—horse stables—then ran up along a curling track through a dark tracery of trees. The road had sharp bends and the headlights kept flashing across gnarled tangles of leaves and wood. Sensitive to shadows and compositions, she felt suddenly aware of her position: the dark mysterious hill road, the car in the night, the silence—nothing but the rush of the car—and her companion: half civilized, as coarse-edged as rough hand-hewn woodwork, as secure (she suddenly feared) as a three-legged chair.

"Where are we going, Crobey?"

"Well it ain't the Ritz."

"You could have booked me into a hotel—"

"No," he said, "I couldn't."

They ran slowly through a village: a little row of shops, an intersection. Everything jerry-built and as shabby as the sets for a nonunion movie; corrugated metal roofs, tattered remains of circus posters, here and there a yellow pool under a naked light. A small dog barked at the car. For a little way it chased them, yapping alongside Carole's window; then Crobey accelerated and the dog fell behind and they were out in the lonely darkness again.

"Where are we?"

"The interior. Up-island."

"Specifically."

"Does it matter? You wouldn't find it without a guide." He was slowing, looking for something—he leaned forward to peer out over the wheel. There was a gap in the trees on the left. He turned the car slowly, easing into the narrow opening. A pair of muddy ruts curled into the trees. Crobey hauled the stick down to low and the transmission whined as the car lurched forward.

"Crobey, this is absurd."

He was concentrating only on the driving; he didn't reply. His massive corded forearms fought the wheel. A wet leaf pasted itself to the windshield. Branches scraped alongside, flicking moisture in her face; she rolled up the window. The car pitched and bucketed, the rear wheels spinning at times on the slick mud but momentum carried it through each time and finally they emerged—one last bend and they were in the open, grass on the slopes to either side, dark hulks grazing: cattle or horses, she couldn't tell in the night. Just above the horizon she could see a patch of stars but the sky overhead was dark. She sat rigid with alarm and the uneasy speculation that Crobey might have sold out. Why else would he drive her so secretively into the wilderness? She drew the handbag into her lap—it was heavy enough; perhaps she could club him in the face with it; fling the door open and dive from the car. . . .

A shabby little house loomed in the headlights. Crobey said, "We're here."

She braced her feet against the floorboards, pushing herself back stiffly in the seat as if it were a dentist's chair. Too late to run now. Her eyes went dry and she began to blink rapidly; there was a taste like brass on her tongue.

He ran the car across the grass, around behind the house. When he switched it off there was abrupt silence broken only by the pinging of heat contractions in the engine. The darkness was almost total. She had trouble drawing breath. Then Crobey opened his door and stepped out. "Come on, then."

She let herself out. On rubber knees she lurched a few paces and then waited for him to guide her. He chunked the door shut and took her elbow.

"Crobey—"

"Relax. You're tight as a drumhead."

His grip was light; he didn't squeeze her elbow. She hadn't the presence to pull away. Crobey took her around the house—she had an impression of clumped shadows, a barren yard, another building over to the right (a barn?), the steamy smell of manure and livestock. A cowbell jingled distantly. There was a heavy weight in the air—the rain hadn't refreshed it but only matted it down, like her hair which felt pasted on her skull and wet against the back of her neck.

"Mind the steps." Just the same she nearly tripped; she felt blind—had she ever known such complete darkness outdoors? She felt tentatively with each foot, scraping the rough surface of the steps. Four of them and they were on the porch. Then Crobey's fist was thudding—the rattle of a screen door's frame. Heavy footsteps within. A man's rough voice: *"¿Quien es?"*

"Crobey."

And the door opened, throwing light.

She only saw the man's silhouette—thickset, massive; and the hard outline of a revolver in his hand.

Crobey made an impatient noise in his nose and she felt herself propelled through the door. The man with the gun stepped back, lowering the weapon to his side—an exchange of glances with Crobey; the screen door slapped shut and Crobey leaned back against the solid door to close it.

Crobey said, "Santana—Miss Marchand."

The other man smiled a bit and dipped his head to her. He put the pistol away in a pocket of his baggy pants. She heard him mutter something—*"con mucho gusto"*—and then Crobey walked past to drop her case on a rickety old parson's table.

The room hardly registered on her awareness; it was a basic enclosure—rustic, beaten up, more than lived-in. The air smelled of garlic and sweat. Santana in the light was squat, shorter than she'd thought at first—no neck, jowls, dark unruly hair, a swarthy face. His little eyes kept watching her and she wondered if she was going to scream.

Santana said something in Spanish. Crobey said, "Talk English now."

Santana shrugged and gave an apologetic smile. With a thick accent—*annyWHAN* for *anyone, jew* for *you*—he said, "Did anyone follow you?"

"No. I guess they weren't looking for me at the airport. Well they wouldn't care if I left—it's my staying here that burns them."

Carole drew a ragged shuddering breath. Crobey said to her, "If you want to wash up there's a pump on the kitchen sink. The privy's just outside the back door."

"Talk to me," she said. "Am I your prisoner here?"

"What?"

"Who's your friend?"

"Santana? He used to be my ground-crew mechanic."

Santana beamed at her. "I used to keep Crobey's planes flying." She barely understood him. "Then my brother, he died and I inherited this place."

"I see." She looked at Crobey. "And what do you and your old buddy here have in mind for me?"

"Maybe you'd rather sleep out in the rain?"

"It didn't occur to you they have hotels in Puerto Rico?"

Crobey glanced at Santana, who only grinned infuriatingly; Crobey's eyes rolled toward the ceiling, seeking inspiration from the Almighty.

"Crobey, tell me what's going on."

"We're staying out of sight—I'd have thought that was obvious. It won't kill you to spend the night here. Tomorrow we'll put you back on a plane home." He picked up her case and walked out of the room. She counted four doors: the front one through which they'd entered, one that led into a hallway through which she could see part of a rudimentary kitchen, two others. Crobey went through one of these and she glimpsed a cot before he blocked the view with his body. "This'll be your room for tonight. I'll bunk down on the couch there. Now sit down."

With his gravelly manner Crobey made the most innocuous command sound like a ferocious threat. She backed up to the window and hiked her haunch onto the sill defiantly. She was still trembling slightly.

On his way to the couch Crobey's limp seemed more pronounced; maybe it was the rain. He sat down, gave her a hostile grin and picked up the drink Santana had left on the table. Crobey said, "I've been making waves since I got here. Apparently I splashed the wrong people. I was at the Sheraton like any other tourist until yesterday. Then I went down to breakfast and a cop pulled up a chair at my table. Very polite, very diffident and the personality of a closed door. No threats, but a visit from those folks can be a threat in itself. He asked questions and I told lies, the kind where I know he knows I'm lying—he wanted to know what I was doing in Puerto Rico and I told him I was working for a movie director, which was true, and that I was down here scouting locations for a movie about the Bay of Pigs, which was not true. He wanted to know why I was going around asking peculiar questions and what gave me the idea I could pester citizens without an investigator's license. The hint was that there are people here who can make their wishes known in official circles and that it wouldn't take too long for the order to come down, and when it did I'd probably be collected by the security police and escorted to jail or the airport or something. We're very sorry but you understand, *señor*, an irregularity in your papers. It's funny in a way, if that kind of thing amuses you—I feel like I'm running out of places to hang my hat. Nowadays it seems you can tour all the friendly countries with an overnight bag.''

She had grown impatient with him. ''You had a visit from a policeman and he didn't actually threaten you but you read between the lines and as a result you seem to have spent the past twenty-four hours changing into dry pants, and now you run me through a wringer of mystery and intrigue and when I ask you what it's all about, all you do is stick your jaw out at me and do an impression of Charles Bickford playing a warden who's glaring at the convicts. Let me tell you, Crobey, the acting stops right now.''

She clapped her lips shut and glared.

''Let me remind you,'' he said quietly, ''that I'm not your lackey. For a thousand a week I'm not going to die in the service of the memory of a dead kid I never met. If the precautions seem excessive you'll just have to humor me. Now I'm not entirely as Mongoloid as I look and I do understand a couple of things—I understand that you have this habit, when you get rattled you just tend to keep talking until you think of something to say, and I understand that flip snide insults are to you what fodder is to cannons and I don't expect to break all your unpleasant habits for you overnight but I want you to keep a curb on your tongue because otherwise things could get a little dicey around here. There are people I take insults from but you don't know me well enough to be one of them. You're completely out of your element here and you're scared—you're a city kid out in the wild jungle and every last thing is going to cause fear and trembling until you get used to it. Mostly right now I expect you're scared of me. I don't have a lot of polish, I haven't got any cocktail party chitchat, I'm not the kind of domesticated house-pet you can put in his place with wise-ass remarks.''

His insight startled her—she was, above all, afraid of him. There hung about him a kind of menace; the type of quality that might emanate from a dozing predator.

It wasn't just her private reaction; she saw it as well in the way Santana watched Crobey. And Santana was his *friend*.

Fear was something she wasn't used to. She fought it and this brought out the anger in her. Knowing it was foolish she blurted, "I'd be more impressed with all that if I thought you were doing an acceptable job of chasing the mice. I didn't ask you to lay your life on the line for a thousand a week but I did ask you to do a job. I don't see much sign you've been doing it. For instance maybe you'd better run that Glenn Anders business past me one more time. Maybe you can explain who authorized you to make cozy deals with the CIA."

"Apparently, I was under a misapprehension—I understood I had a free hand."

"Did you honestly think I wanted you to share everything with the CIA?"

"The CIA has facilities that I don't have. It's my intention to use them to provoke Rodriguez. When he learns they're sniffing around his backtrail he'll get nervous and a nervous man makes mistakes. It may provoke him into showing himself and when that happens I plan to be there."

"Even though you've given the CIA the inside track." She snorted theatrically.

"It's no great trick to get there ahead of those jokers," Crobey said mildly. "They move like slugs. Anders is all right by himself but he's lugging all the dead weight of the bureaucracy behind him." Then his voice turned hard. "Did you listen to anything I said before?"

"I heard you talking."

"Right. Look. I can't do a job for you if I'm chained up in a dungeon or thrown out of Puerto Rico. The only way I can make any progress is to go to ground. If they can't find me they can't deport me, you dig? That's why we're out here instead of drinking banana daiquiris at Dorado Beach. I don't know if you were tagged at the airport but we have to assume you were. By coming here you've exposed yourself and that makes my job harder. If they can reach you it's the same thing as reaching me.'' Then Crobey showed anxiety: "You're dealing with terrorists—people who kill people. If Rodriguez gets the idea you're putting him in jeopardy—'' and he shrugged without finishing it. Then: "Maybe it's time you put paid to this thing. Go home to the world you know, don't try to mess about with things you can't handle—you're a guppy trying to swim through a school of piranha. If they're hungry they'll have you for breakfast and they won't even belch afterwards."

"Have they got you scared, Crobey? Is that it? Do you want me to call it off because that way you won't have to think of yourself as a coward?"

"Believe that if it makes you feel better."

"My son isn't any less dead now than he was when I hired you."

"When we get too close to Rodriguez he'll do something about it. You understand that?"

"I understand he'll try. It's your job to make sure he fails, isn't it."

"Given a free hand I'll try. But it means you've got to stay out of it. Go back to the mainland, hide out somewhere, hire a bodyguard if you can, wait it out."

"No. I'm staying, and I'm setting the rules. For a thousand a week you can play it by my rules."

"Rules? Do you think there are rules in this game?"

"I want every scrap of information you get—whether it's useful or negative or just immaterial. When decisions are made I'll discuss them but I'm in charge and I don't put things to a vote. If I want you to divulge anything else to Mr. Anders or the police I'll let you know but until then you'll keep your lip buttoned and say nothing to anyone."

Santana gaped at her—he'd never heard a woman talk to a man that way, let alone to a man like Crobey.

"I hear you," said Crobey, amused, waiting her out.

"I was told in Washington that if they're arrested on American soil they can only be charged with violating the U.S. neutrality laws. Conspiring against a foreign government. That's a slap on the wrist. My son was murdered in Mexico—I want to know what the official Mexican position is. Legally it's their case."

Crobey said, "Forget the Mexicans."

"Why?"

"There's no material evidence he was killed there. The body was dumped there but for all we know he was killed out at sea aboard a boat—and wouldn't *that* be a nicety for a few dozen lawyers. In the second place even if the Mexicans had it airtight they wouldn't touch it with a rake. The rightists would condemn them if they convicted, the leftists would condemn them if they didn't. If you want an opinion, the only way you're going to get revenge on these bastards is to kill them yourself."

"No. I don't just want them punished. I want them punished publicly, in the eyes of the world. I want justice, and I want the world to see it. I'm not about to go to jail for murdering Rodriguez. I don't want it to be a joke, Crobey. I want it to be a memorial to my son."

"You don't get it, ducks." His voice was softer now. "The kind of justice you're asking for is out of stock. It was rendered obsolete by reality. The Mexicans won't touch them. I explained that. And nobody else has jurisdiction."

"You're wrong about that."

"Am I? Show me."

"I've had time to think it out," she said. "There's one government that will be sure to execute them with full-scale publicity. All we have to do is catch them and turn them over."

Crobey looked at her, baffled.

"Castro, Crobey. We deliver them to Fidel Castro."

Crobey scowled. His mouth prepared for a speech but he subsided; finally he cocked his head, reluctantly pleased. "My God. It might work."

"Uh-huh," she said, obviously pleased with herself.

"Anything else up your sleeve?"

"A thought or two. For instance—you must know a few of the black-market arms dealers in this part of the world."

"You want a bazooka for Christmas."

She said, "Suppose you're a terrorist gang and you've

just collected ten million dollars in cash ransom. Where do you spend it?''

Crobey didn't answer for a moment. His face changed a bit. Finally he said, ''I hadn't thought of that one. I wonder if Anders has.''

''A civil-service *apparatchik*? I doubt it.''

''Don't undersell Anders.'' But he was watching her more alertly than he ever had before, as if for the first time he recognized her as something more than an attractive bit player.

Chapter 11

Glenn Anders slouched in an uncomfortable wooden chair while Perez flipped through the photo cards with the repetitive efficiency of a bank teller counting money. Perez had been through mug-shot canvasses before; just the same Anders was dubious—Perez flipped them over so quickly. After a while there was a danger of forgetting what one was looking for. One's eyes began to go out of focus and one might flip right past the vital one.

A girl in an Afro natural hairdo and bone earrings came in. She put a paper bag on the table and smiled brightly and left.

Anders removed two capped Styrofoam cups from the bag.

"Yes. Black please, with two sugars, yes?"

The room was prim and sinister, the windows set high. The tile floor sloped to a center drain and the walls were slick with high-gloss green paint. This was police headquarters: a washable room designed for interrogations.

Anders stirred sugar into the coffee with the wooden tongue-depressor stick and pushed the cup across the table to Perez. "Take a break. Tell me again what he looked like."

Perez—slight, birdy, poplin suit, fake silk tie—had a cocky way of narrowing his eyes and dropping his voice near a whisper, as confidential as a desk clerk pimping for a girl on the third floor. As it happened he was neither pimp nor pusher; Perez was a plainclothes police detective.

Perez said, "I wasn't so close to see him clearly," and

ended the sentence with a nervous meaningless laugh that sounded like a telephone's busy signal. The habit irritated Anders. Perez, proud of his English, said, "I was tired to sit waiting in the car, I was getting out for walk, then I hear the footsteps, yes? In the open he startled me and I went up in a doorway to look like I'm ringing the bell of the house. I am afraid he spotted me. I think so, yes?" And another honk of laughter, this one to cover his shame. It was another point against him that he still hadn't understood Anders' question.

Anders contained his irritation. None of it meant much anyhow. Likely the whole thing was a false lead. The Volkswagen had provoked the attention of the bureaucracy and Anders was obliged to follow up dutifully but he wasn't sure it would take him anywhere.

Reasoning that Rodrigo Rodriguez might spend part of the ten million dollars' ransom on armaments, Anders had activated the clumsy apparatus. Inquiries were made in seventeen ports. The report that flagged Anders' attention came from Fajardo, the port town at the northeast tip of the island of Puerto Rico.

The dealer was a regular police informant who ran a small import business in molasses and wine and occasionally cocaine. He had reported a visit from a Cuban who went by the name of Cielo, was unfamiliar to the dealer and had visited him to inquire obliquely into the possibility of purchasing certain arms—mainly mortars and rocket launchers, not hip-pocket stuff. The dealer informed his visitor that he did not traffic in such items. When the visitor left the dealer made a note of the plate number of the Volkswagen and telephoned to his contact on the police.

It was tenuous but it had drawn Anders' eye because of the locale and the nature of the request. Not just anyone had much interest in mortars and rockets; and Crobey's clue had given him a reason to be interested in Puerto Rico.

Anders had flown into San Juan and exercised a few quiet pressures to set in motion a search for the Volkswagen. The dealer from Fajardo had gone through the same photo files that Perez had before him now; the

dealer hadn't singled out a face but he was an odd vague
sort and a simple experiment had proved he had an
almost nonexistent memory for faces. Under repeated
questioning he'd proved uncertain about nearly everything. He couldn't remember what clothes Cielo had
worn; yes, Cielo might have been older, might have
been heavier—it was hard to say. The dealer had gone
home bewildered and Rosalia, her hand on Anders'
shoulder, had exhaled with a slumping sag of disappointment.

The name *Cielo* clearly was not so much an alias as a
nom de guerre, a code name; *You can call me Cielo*; it
meant nothing to the police or the agency; quite possibly
it was a name adopted for one operation, as disposable
as a paper wrapper.

But then the Volkswagen had been identified by its
license number and the police had sent Perez to cover it.
Now Perez had seen the man who drove the car and
Perez had been trained to identify faces.

Anders said, "He didn't have a belly or a beard."

"No. No beard. Big in the shoulders and as tall as
you, yes? But no heavier than you are. One-ninety,
perhaps two hundred. No more."

"The face? Tell me again now."

"*Comó se dice*, square, yes? *Latino* but not too dark.
Not *Indio*. Short hair, not crew-cut but short and neat,
and not bald. A, how do you say, widow's peak, yes?"

"Then he didn't wear a hat."

"No, no hat." Perez scowled. "The face, yes. I have
a good picture here." He tapped his temple. "A square
face, heavy bones, is hard but not stupid, you understand? Wide face, very wide."

"And the clothes?"

"Khaki jeans, a light windbreaker jacket, faded gray.
Work boots like a car mechanic. Your clothes would fit
him."

"When you first saw him he wasn't coming out of a
house, you're sure of that?"

"He came out a driveway between two houses. From
behind, the next street I think, yes?"

If it was Rodriguez, Anders thought, he'd have been

smart enough to leave his car parked several blocks from his destination. It made for the dreary prospect of house-to-house inquiries.

Perez said, "If he is in these pictures I'll find him. It's a promise, yes?"

"All right. I'll check back with you." Anders left the second cup of coffee for him.

The federal building looked like something the Spaniards might have constructed to contain lunatics and violent offenders. The agency had borrowed a desk for him in an office attached to the Department of Agriculture; officially he was out-of-bounds on U.S. soil. At least the office had a scrambler phone. He found Rosalia there—she gripped his tie and pulled him down, licking his mouth lasciviously.

Anders poked both fists into his kidneys and reared far back. "You yank at me like that again, you'll have me in traction for a week."

Rosalia leaned leeringly forward, straining cloth with breasts. "Your place or mine?" She was in a springy droll mood.

"You've got fabulous boobs," he told her. "But it's the wrong time of day to be caressing each other's erogenous zones. Did George Wilkins call in?"

"Not yet. If we got married could we still work together?"

"I doubt it. Against regulations."

"Then we won't get married until you retire."

"Got it all worked out, I see."

From the beginning she had amused him with her cub-reporter bounce and cuddly lovability; she'd inculcated in him a kind of playfulness he thought he'd lost. It was beginning to occur to him that perhaps she was the girl to whom he wanted to be faithful: Despite her overt sexuality she possessed the soft nesty instincts of a purring kitten.

"Oh dear. I've forgotten what I was going to say." She rummaged through papers. "Here it is. Mr. O'Hillary wants you to call him."

"God." He fixed his glance on the phone as if he expected it to serve a subpoena on him.

"Also there was a call from Harry Crobey."

"How the hell did he know where to find me?"

"I gather he called the FBI and they transferred him to the Justice Department and they transferred him to—"

"No. I mean how'd he know I'd be in San Juan at all?"

"Are you asking *me*?" She ripped the page off her pad. "He'd like to meet you tonight at half past seven for dinner at the Tres Candelas in Old Town. He said he'd be bringing a guest."

"Carole Marchand?"

"He didn't mention a name."

"All right. Why don't you come along?"

"Love to. I'll put on something slinky."

He regarded her husky ripe shape. "Sure. You'd better ring O'Hillary for me and put it on the scrambler."

O'Hillary—smooth, avuncular, elegant: "Glenn, how are you? Any fix on Rodriguez?"

"Not yet."

"Can you be overheard?"

"Only by my assistant."

"Ask her to leave, will you?"

Anders cupped the mouthpiece. "He wants privacy."

With genial disgust Rosalia lifted her nose into the air and went out, pulling the door shut with a quiet reproachful click.

"All right. I'm alone."

O'Hillary said, "This project of yours has consumed a lot of time in briefings and meetings. It's becoming a tedious football."

"What am I supposed to do about that? Drop the ball?"

"It's not quite that simple, as I'm sure you appreciate. As you know, Glenn, there are varying factions of opinion on this issue. There is, not to put too fine a point on it, an ambivalence in the Administration's attitude. On the one hand an Ambassador was victimized, an American murdered, and the Administration can't be seen to condone terrorism—"

Can't be seen to. That summed up O'Hillary all right.

"At the same time," O'Hillary went on, "there's also the matter of the current efforts to ameliorate relations with Cuba."

Anders could picture him tipped back in his wingback swivel chair with his silk-clad ankles crossed, gently palming the distinguished wave in his silver hair and staring whimsically at a point about a yard above the President's official photograph.

O'Hillary said, "Conversely Castro is still, in an unofficial way, the enemy. There's the sticky affairs in Somalia and Ethiopia—and we have people among us who still haven't forgotten the history of the Angola affair. In certain eyes Fidel Castro remains the bad guy. In regard to the Rodriguez group, there's still a faction here that takes the understandable position that he who is my enemy's enemy is perforce my friend. To be blunt, this faction—numbering not an inconsequential few persons in high places—is engaged in the attempt to persuade the Administration to let Rodriguez run and see if perhaps he won't take care of Castro for them. As a result we're in dubious straits, my friend. We're in grave danger of being short-circuited by conflicting orders."

Whenever O'Hillary turned pedantic and longwinded it meant he was preparing a smoke screen. O'Hillary had an abstract fondness for intrigue as an end rather than a means. He had an infallible intuition for gothic complexities—he thrived on deceptions even when they were superfluous; he was a success in his profession because he had mastered the skill of trick marksmanship—shoot first, then draw a bull's-eye around the bullet hole.

The principal of survival in Langley was Cover Your Ass; ultimately the decision would come down on one side or the other and O'Hillary would be ready, either way, to end the match with a perfect bull's-eye—a neat trick and one that might require the sacrifice of a subordinate or two.

Anders knew he had to listen very carefully to O'Hillary now: It wasn't what O'Hillary said but what he didn't say.

"I do hope you're not recording this, Glenn. If things backfire we mustn't make the error of leaving tape-recorded evidence of our misstatements about, must we." Like a disagreeable schoolmaster, Anders thought, O'Hillary selected his tone for its prim offensiveness.

"It's not being recorded."

"Good. Your instructions—from me, not from above me, and not in writing—are to proceed with the investigation, to locate this man Rodriguez and his little Sherwood Forest band, and to report personally and directly to me and to no one else. You'll consult with me before taking action of any kind. And you will not take the police or anyone else into your confidence. In other words you must proceed henceforth without police assistance."

"Then how am I supposed to find them?"

"Wits. Ingenuity."

"And what am I supposed to tell the police?"

"Tell them the leads proved false. Pull them off the case."

"You honestly expect me to find Rodriguez without any help?"

"I do. If there's a man who can do it it's you."

"You can butter me up all you want," Anders said, "but you can't have me for breakfast. This opens up a provocative can of beans. You want me to find Rodriguez but then keep hands off him. That's pointless."

"We must be prepared for whatever decision comes down, mustn't we. We can do that only by performing thoroughly the task to which we're officially assigned— the task of intelligence-gathering. Once we fix Rodriguez's location we can then take whatever action we're ordered to take. In the meantime nothing is to be filed through normal channels. You're on your own and I'm your only contact with the company. Understood?"

"In other words if the Administration decides to let him run you don't want the record to show we knew where to lay hands on him. You want to keep it private because you don't intend to produce it until it's absolutely clear you'll be applauded for producing it. Christ—what a grisly waste.''

"Regardless of provocation you're to take no action that might jeopardize security. You understand your instructions, don't you? You're to find Rodriguez. But you're to do it in such a way that no one except me knows you've done it. Not Rodriguez, not the police, not the agency. No one.''

"We'll see." Anders smiled, anticipating the response.

"Don't give me evasive answers!" He could have heard O'Hillary without a telephone.

It made him laugh aloud. "You're so easy to string along. Mind your blood pressure. I understand the orders—we may have an argument about it when I get back but I understand them. Anything else on your mind?''

"As long as you're on the phone you may as well bring me up to date."

Chapter 12

She awoke stiff and grumpy to the buzz of a distant tractor. Sunlight stabbed in through holes in the cheap blind.

It was too rustic for words. She had to pick a barefoot path across weeds to the privy; she accomplished her morning *toilette* at the kitchen sink with the aid of the compact mirror from her handbag.

There didn't seem to be a soul in the house. She was glad of that; it gave her time to collect herself. She dressed in a plaid shirt and blue jeans and desert boots; and rummaged through the Spartan kitchen.

Last night, she thought, they seemed to have reached an understanding of sorts. Her last glimpse of him had discovered a defiant and lascivious grin. She had responded in kind.

It was inevitable, in the circumstances, that she would be tempted toward an unhealthy attachment: Crobey was the only remotely familiar object in this alien world, the only bridge between her and the sanity she'd left behind. But she had to guard against trusting him too much.

As if summoned by her mind a car crunched into the yard. She went to the kitchen door and looked out—it was Crobey but it wasn't the same little shoehorn car he'd had last night. This one was a high square Bronco, a coiled-cable winch on the front bumper, a drab green paint job and big-lugged tires that looked like cross-country equipment. Undoubtedly it was four-wheel-drive. Crobey stepped down and glanced at her, not smiling, and reached into the back of the truck, from which he lifted a heavy rucksack. He carried it toward the house.

Carole made an ineffectual and self-conscious swipe at her hair. "Good morning."

"Yeah." He squeezed past her into the house. When she followed him into the front room she found him dumping the contents of the rucksack on the parson's table—a jumble of oily blue-black machinery that she belatedly recognized as disassembled guns.

He began to sort things out on the table. There was a flat red steel box; he slid the lid off it and revealed a collection of ramrods, white cloth patches, cans of oil and solvent.

He assembled something out of the parts—it looked like the kind of stutter gun that airborne commandos carried in war movies. Stubby, ugly, wicked. Crobey worked its action with a great deal of sinister clacking.

"I see you've been to the arms dealers."

"One of 'em. If he's been approached by Rodriguez he's not admitting it. I've got a few more on the list—then we'll have to widen the net. Caracas, Rio, the Azores." He gave her a direct glance for the first time. "Glenn Anders is in San Juan."

"Oh?"

"Flew in last night."

"How do you know?"

"I haven't altogether wasted my time since I got here. You've got two other people on your payroll besides me and Santana. I slipped them a little something to keep their eyes open—I check in with them now and then."

"Who are they?"

"It doesn't matter."

"Crobey—"

"Part of the reason they're willing to deal with me is they know I won't name them. All right?"

She conceded it. "So Anders is here. Why?"

"I suggest we ask him."

"We?"

"He wants to meet you. When I was in Mexico City I told him I'd try to set it up."

"What have you told him?"

"A little bit of the truth. Not too much." He went back to work on his toys.

She said lamely, "Where's Santana? Working the farm?"

"No. He's out looking into the Rodriguez family background."

"Have we stirred them up at all yet?"

"I'll ask Anders when I see him."

"I'm asking you. You're supposed to be my expert."

"An expert's a fellow you hire because he's the one who knows what experts to call in, and when to call them. Are you going to dispute everything I do? Because if you are I don't see much point in carrying on. I can't function if I'm harassed from both sides at once. Do you want me to pack?"

"Don't throw ultimatums at me," she said. "I might call your bluff."

"Then you're ready to give it up?"

"No. I'll look for somebody a bit less prickly. You can't possibly be the only man alive who knew those people in the Bay of Pigs days."

"Ducks, I don't think I can be happy here if we have to have this conversation twice a day. It doesn't give me a sense of job security."

"Security? You?"

"I'm not talking about the long term. I'm talking about maybe getting the rug pulled out from under me at the wrong moment."

"You don't trust me."

"Ah, ducks, tell me why I should."

She touched a finger to one of his guns and twirled it on the table, picked a stray hair off her cuff, leaned back, crossed her legs, put an elbow on the table and her chin in her palm, looked him in the eye and said, "Nobody can do that. It's a trick question and you know it. The only way to find out whether you can trust someone is to trust the person and see what happens."

"You're a truly contrary creature." He stood, pulling the Levi's down from his crotch.

She watched him limp toward the back door. "Where are you going?"

"To the loo, ducks."

"Why've you started calling me by that awful epithet?"

"Ducks?" In the doorway he turned; the smile was more sardonic than amiable. "When I use it, it's a term of endearment." Then he went.

She heard the slap of the privy door and realized she was smiling. She straightened her face. She kept catching herself trying to ingratiate Crobey—it was a warning sign; she had to guard against it. It wasn't a contest of will or pride; in effect he'd imprisoned her and rendered her ineffectual; if she remained she could only sink into passivity. That wasn't what she'd come for.

When he came in from the yard he said, "I wasn't intending to switch cars right away but there was a problem in town—I left it parked while I went to see the man about the guns and when I came back I found it jammed in by two parked cars that hadn't been there before. One of them had a couple of smokers in it. So I stepped into a hotel and got lost. I phoned the rent-a-car people to go pick it up and we got the Bronco from a pal of Santana's."

"Who were the men in the car?"

"Locals. I've no idea whose."

She said, "If someone's putting pressure on the police to scare you out of Puerto Rico, it shouldn't be impossible to find out who that is. If the police are impressed by this person or frightened of him, it means they know who he is."

"I realize that. But I can't think of any coppers I'd like to talk to right now."

"Would Anders know?"

"Anders could find out," he conceded.

"Then let's arrange to see him."

Crobey said, "A while ago you were chastising me for consorting with him."

"Consistency is the hobgoblin of little minds." She smiled. "Besides, I want to give you a fighting chance."

"Good. I already made a date for tonight: seven-thirty at the Tres Candelas."

The Tres Candelas struck Anders as a Harry Crobey sort of place. The long dismal narrow room was mostly bar. A row of tiny tables, a back room with half a dozen tables-for-four. There was a Wurlitzer jukebox that might have fascinated a dealer in fifties *kitsch*.

Anders had his jacket hung over his shoulder by one fingertip and Rosalia held his hand like a teen-ager. The bartender, in soiled apron and halfheartedly trimmed beard, waved them toward the tables in back. No one was back there. Anders seated Rosalia under a cockfight poster and selected a chair from which he could watch the entrance. According to his watch it was 7:05. He was surprised by Crobey's absence.

Rosalia reached for his wrist and heaved it around to see the face of his watch. "We're awfully early."

"Once in my life I want to be somewhere ahead of Harry."

"He's got some kind of hex sign on you, hasn't he?"

"Not really. Sometimes I envy him a little." He was looking at her breasts, not smiling. "Want to know what I'm thinking?"

"I think I already do," she said in a mock-cool voice. She had extraordinarily long natural eyelashes and knew how to use them; she batted them at him. Anders made a point of tracing the lines of her body with his eyes. Rosalia began to chuckle. "How'd you ever turn into such a lout?"

Anders shook his head gloomily. "You see it was like this. When I was nine I ran away from home and got picked up by a very smooth hair-tonic salesman who hooked me on smack and used me as a courier until he got run over by a Chinese tank, and then I was all by myself on the streets mugging old ladies until this kindly fat man took me in to his establishment and I worked upstairs there on the line until I got arrested for selling atomic secrets, and after that things just started to go wrong somehow."

Mirth captivated Rosalia, making her shake. Anders

laughed at his own absurdity. Then he looked up in time
to see Harry Crobey walk in, escorting a striking
woman.

Anders watched the brisk-gaited clipclip of the
woman's good long legs as Crobey limped beside her.
She wasn't especially tall but she managed to carry herself as if she were. The skin of her face was drawn over
precisely defined bones—she was at least forty and
didn't attempt to look younger; very little make-up and
she'd been out in the humid wind but dishevelment
suited her. In a rust-hued skirt and brown satiny blouse
she managed to look cool. Her eyes were shaped for
scorn and for easy laughter; her hair was reddish but not
red and something made him certain she didn't tint it.
She wasn't pretty in any of the usual ways—the bone
ridges were prominent, the nose sharp, the impression
one of planes and angles rather than soft curved
features—but she was extraordinarily attractive and it
was clear by her carriage that she knew it and was
assured and confident in herself. Possibly it was a pose
but if so it was one she'd had plenty of time to rehearse.

Anders shook Crobey's hand and introductions went
around: Rosalia gave Carole Marchand an ingenuous
beaming smile. Crobey held the woman's chair for her,
an event that astonished Anders—he'd never seen
Crobey do that before—and she sat down with un-
studied grace; she seemed almost wholly without self-
consciousness.

Crobey hooked an overhand wave toward the bartender and sat down with a wince that betrayed the
chronic troublesomeness of his knee. "Christ, this
humidity. Like Dante said, it's a nice place to visit
but. . . ."

The bartender distributed menus enclosed in fly-
specked plastic. Rosalia was asking Carole Marchand if
it was her first visit to Puerto Rico—it was all very
desultory; Crobey seemed in no hurry to get to business
and Anders decided Crobey wanted the delay in order to
give his client an opportunity to size Anders up.

After a time Carole Marchand wrinkled her nostrils in
the direction of the kitchen. "Do I hear someone

rattling my dish? I'm famished. It had better be edible, Crobey."

"I doubt it comes with a written warranty, ducks. Last time I was in here it wasn't half bad."

Anders said, "Harry's a connoisseur of greasy-spoon dives from Macao to Dar-es-Salaam. He's got an unerring nose for the worst food in town."

"That's what I was afraid of." There seemed to be an easy tolerance in Carole Marchand's acceptance of Crobey's eccentricities and Anders wondered how much of it was sham. It was difficult to believe she didn't actually dislike the man; Crobey wasn't her sort—the juxtaposition struck him as something like thowing a groomed show-bred poodle into a cage with a timber wolf.

Crobey said obliviously, "I didn't have to be the world's greatest pilot, you know. With a little education I could have been a gourmet."

"Don't be sickening," Carole Marchand drawled; she turned mischievously to Rosalia. "Harry takes a mulish delight in pretending he's an ape. Actually beneath that rough crude exterior beats the heart of the first man in Liverpool to climb down a tree without having had to climb up it first."

Crobey's smile was a bit strained. "The lady likes to turn on the fan and wait for something to hit it."

Carole Marchand breathed in slowly and expressively through her nose; she tried to suck her mouth in with a tight look of disapproval but her lips began to quiver. "Keep it up, Crobey, keep it up." She reached sternly for her glass but then began to laugh; Anders realized to his astonishment that she actually enjoyed bantering with Crobey. Finally she drank and held the glass away from her with critical suspicion. "What the devil is this?"

Crobey said, "I suspect it ain't Dad's Old Fashioned Root Beer, ducks. Beyond that it's hard to say, in this dump. Could be horse piss."

"Philistine. Infidel."

The dinner that ensued was edible if not palatable; finally the bartender cleared the dishes away with a surly crashing of porcelain. Soiled espresso cups alighted on the table like moths; Crobey lifted his, peered dubiously into it and said, "Confusion to our enemies."

"And I believe we're here to discuss our enemies," Carole Marchand said. Her voice had hardened—no longer the cool acerbic drawl.

"Right," Crobey said, "we want to win the war and get home by Christmas, don't we?"

Carole Marchand considered Rosalia; then her glance came around to Anders. "Not to be indelicate but—"

"Rosalia knows what I know."

Crobey smiled at the girl, full of insincerity.

Carole Marchand said, "Let's take the man's word for it, shall we, Harry?" She looked down, then quickly up into Anders' face—as if trying to catch him off guard. "How do you tote it up, Mr. Anders? Are we on the same side or not?"

"That would depend."

"You sound like O'Hillary."

"I try not to do that." He smiled a bit.

"I intend to pin these terrorists to the board," she said. "Just so there's no misunderstanding of my position."

"We understand your position."

"Talking like that could get you elected to Congress," she said. "My first objective is to goad your agency into doing the job it ought to have done without goading. If that fails I have every intention of doing it myself. And I ain't whistlin' 'Dixie,' Mr. Anders."

Anders put his head down, thinking. The phone conversation with O'Hillary ran through his mind. Defiantly he made the decision. "Rodriguez—if that's who he is—seems to be running under the code-name Cielo. He tried to buy ordnance from a broker in Fajardo. The broker wasn't selling but that only means Cielo's shopping somewhere else. Incidentally a couple of policemen spent most of the day today surveilling a car that turned out to be yours, Harry."

"The two smokers? They were about as inconspicuous as two giraffes in a bathtub."

"Anyway two days ago the subject, Cielo, was here in

San Juan driving a Volkswagen. He spent a night in the
Rio Piedras area. We don't know which house but at
least we've got it narrowed down to a neighborhood. He
may have contacts there—maybe other terrorists,
maybe a safe-house, maybe a girl friend. Whatever. He
may never go back there again, of course, but it's a sort
of lead. We've checked the municipal directory but
there's no Rodriguez or Cielo listed at any address
around there. He was spotted by a cop named Perez and
we had him go through the pictures and he's identified a
photograph of Rodrigo Rodriguez taken in nineteen
sixty-two.''

Carole Marchand said, ''All *right!*''

''Take it easy, ducks. The man could've been
wrong.''

Anders said, ''Perez thinks it may be the same face.
But nineteen sixty-two? The man was young then. Perez
admits it's not a positive make. We ran the old
Rodriguez fingerprints through the computers and got
no particular results—evidently he hasn't been arrested
or identified since before the Bay of Pigs.''

Crobey kept watching him, filled with reserve. ''Why
the cooperative candor, Glenn?''

He'd expected it. Now Crobey had put it to
him—bluntly, so that Anders couldn't evade it without
exposing the evasiveness. He knew half truths wouldn't
convince Crobey. ''I have to stonewall that. I'm not at
liberty to break security. All I can tell you is I've got instructions to find Rodriguez. Beyond that I can only
suggest you don't look a gift horse too carefully in the
teeth.''

Carole Marchand said, ''It's a matter of the national
security.'' She looked at Crobey. ''If we find Rodriguez
he expects us to report it to him—but if he finds
Rodriguez before we do, why do I get the feeling he
won't tell us a damn thing?''

''Maybe I won't,'' Anders told her. ''I won't make
promises I might not keep. But look at it this way: You
know more now than you did before you came here
tonight. It hasn't hurt you to talk to me.''

"Then what do you want?"

"Co-operation. Quid pro quo."

The woman scowled at Crobey. "How would you play it?"

"Under an assumed name." Crobey smiled a little. "I know Glenn. He wasn't born devious but he's been playing these games a long time—I guess he knows how to finesse. He's got something in his wallet he hasn't put on the table. If we knew what it was we might change our minds."

"Suppose I told you you're wrong, Harry."

"I doubt I'd believe you. I have to jump to that conclusion—you've laid on this fog of facts that don't get me anywhere when I stop to think about them. A gift? Sure—but what's it worth? Give us something worth trading for."

Rosalia, flashing with anger, turned on him with low-voiced hissing savagery: "Glenn's told you everything we know. If you think he's lying I don't see any point continuing this meeting."

Carole Marchand said—ignoring Rosalia and addressing herself to Anders—"As soon as Harry began asking questions here he was given a warning by a police detective. Between the lines the policeman gave him to understand there were powerful interests in Puerto Rico who wanted him to leave. Does that suggest anything to you?"

"Such as what?"

"Clout. Local political clout. If it's true the local police have no leads on Cielo-Rodriguez, if they don't even know him, then obviously he's not the one applying pressure. Someone else is. Someone known to the police. Someone who's either fronting for Rodriguez or being fronted for *by* Rodriguez. Someone here in Puerto Rico."

Anders was unimpressed. "You do stretch a point."

"Humor me."

O'Hillary's instructions ragged him. He'd already disobeyed them tonight but if he started poking around San Juan police headquarters asking questions, it would get back to Langley in no time at all. That was no good. Then he turned to look at Rosalia. "It might be worth flirting with a cop or two."

She made a face at him.

Crobey said, "I think our best shot's still the arms merchants. If we find the dealer we might follow the shipment to Rodriguez."

Anders said, "I doubt he'll be that obliging. He doesn't leave a lot of tracks—you said that yourself. I'd like to concentrate on looking for the connection in Rio Piedras. He spent the night there with somebody."

"You go poking around down there," Crobey warned, "you could get your guts handed to you."

"On the other hand," Carole Marchand said, "you can't steal second base if you insist on keeping one foot on first."

"I don't follow the game, ducks."

Anders said, "Can I take it we've agreed to join forces?"

"For the time being," she said.

Crobey was dubious. "It's your money."

"I think it's money well squandered," she replied. "Let's not tiptoe, Mr. Anders. If we keep secrets from one another we'll have terrific problems questioning each other because the nature of our questions will have to describe the limits of our own knowledge. Miss Rojas assures us you've turned the bag upside down and shaken it—Harry's obviously not convinced of that and neither am I. It seems to me you've had minions upon minions working on this case. Haven't they come up with anything more than what you've told us? Haven't they tried to check up on sales of paperback science-fiction books, for instance, or Gauloise cigarettes? It's the kind of grinding legwork that requires a flat-footed legion of peons—I'd have thought your organization would have done it."

"Inquiries have been made." Anders regretted his stiffness as soon as he couched it that way. "They've looked, they've asked around. They haven't come up with anything. A lot of people buy paperbacks and cigarettes. You can't stake out every shop on the island.

Nobody's got that much manpower. There's a limit—you're new to this, I guess, but believe me we've tried to follow every lead. Keep in mind this case isn't right at the top of the San Juan police department's list of urgent matters."

"It's at the top of mine." The intensity with which she spoke drove him back like a physical blow to the face. "What about yours, Mr. Anders?" The challenge was harsh, and she was throwing it in his face.

Anders said lamely, "My instructions are to find Rodriguez. It's my full-time job right now. I've got no other assignments. Does that answer you?"

"To find Rodriguez—and do what?" She was as persistent as a dentist's drill.

Anders said, "Let's just find him first, shall we?" Rising, he reached for the back of Rosalia's chair. "Where can I reach you?"

Crobey said, "We'll be in touch. You're at the Sheraton, right?"

Carole Marchand was still watching his face; she hadn't cooled. Anders paused and tried to smile. "We'll find him, you know."

"Yes, I know." She wasn't giving an inch. He'd failed to put anything over on her; she was shrewd—she didn't trust him. He felt a touch of shame, as if he'd been caught with jam on his face.

She said, "Do you have children, Mr. Anders?"

"No."

"Imagine if you had," she said. "Imagine what you'd do if someone murdered your child."

It was impossible to find a parking space in Old San Juan; they hadn't even bothered—they'd come by taxi. Now and then you could find a cab in the plaza; they set out that way on foot with three or four blocks to cover. Rosalia said, "One tough lady."

"Not all that tough," he judged. "But angry."

"Didn't you ever want to be a father?"

"Not with the wife I had then."

"How about with me?"

"A whole mess of kids."

"I love you," she said.

"Is there any truth to the rumor that an unidentified male made an ass out of himself in the restaurant back there?"

"None," Rosalia said. "She was trying to get your goat—that's not your fault."

"I don't mind lying, it's part of my job. I do mind when somebody catches me at it. Makes me feel like a foolish little boy."

"What lies did you tell them? I didn't hear any."

"Lies of omission, *querida*. A lot of things. I didn't tell them they're to be shunted off into the cold as soon as we get anywhere near Rodriguez. I didn't tell them I'm using them because I've been disconnected from the machinery and I need all the manpower I can get now that we've got no staff, no connections no police privileges. I didn't tell them how badly I need their help, or how high the odds are that I'll have to betray them later. In short I didn't level with them and she knew it."

"So did your friend Harry," she said. "He just wasn't so obvious about showing it."

"Well Harry understands. He won't get sore if I push him overboard—he knows how to swim. Let's cut through here, save a block." It was a steep cobbled passage walled by crowded stone-and-stucco buildings; a drainage rut ran down the center. An old man with a collapsed mouth sat on a worn step nodding, reeking of wine, looking back past them. The old man sat under a twenty-five-watt bulb in the doorway. Beyond it the passage was dark—at the top was the glow of the plaza. Anders was saying, "I don't feel sorry for Harry but the woman's another thing. . . ." And then he let his voice peter out because it occurred to him that the old man hadn't looked at him but had looked behind him, which meant the old man had seen something back there more interesting than Rosalia or Anders. He looked over his shoulder with sudden sense of alarm.

There were two of them, big in the shoulders, soft caps over their eyes—menace in the speed of their approach: Now they began to run and Anders took the girl's arm. "Come on." And bolted for the head of the

passage, ankles twisting on the cobblestones, leather
soles slipping. At an awkward shambling pace they
scrambled for it—he couldn't hear the two men behind;
they ran on rubber soles; then he stopped and swiveled,
propelling Rosalia away: "Go on—keep running."

One of them was nearly on him; the other unaccountably was sprinting away, back toward the street,
rushing past the old man in the doorway whose head
swiveled to indicate his bewildered interest in the
dashing to and fro.

The assailant slowed to a jog and Anders saw the glint
of a knife and aimed a kick at it but the cobblestones
unsettled him and he careened against the wall, all but
going down; the assailant half circled to cut off escape
and then moved in fast and Anders hauled the jacket
around—he'd had it hooked over his shoulder—and
dragged it against the knife, snagging the blade, a
desperate parry: He'd never been good at this, and
science always went out the window when panic set in.

He heard the knife tear through the cloth but it was
deflected just a little and he went for the man's wrist
left-handed, trying for a grip. He nearly missed.

He let go the jacket and flung a fist toward the man's
face but the man knew that one and went under it,
twisting his knife wrist out of Anders' grip and
swiveling: The knife plunged forward and Anders got
his arm up, forearm against forearm, batting to one
side—the snife scratched stucco but then the man's knee
grenaded into Anders' thigh and he felt himself go over.

With his back against the wall he slid off his feet,
thrusting his arm out to break his fall. The assailant
loomed.

Anders tried a scissor kick but he had no purchase,
slithering on the stones, and the man stepped right
through it, stooping; the knife poised to slash upward
through Anders' belly, the man waiting only for a clear
target, and Anders tried to bicycle his way out of it,
lying on his side, but knew he couldn't make it.

He tried to reach out for the knife—better to lose a
hand than be gutted—but the knife jinked easily to one
side and jabbed toward him and Anders squeezed back

from it, knowing it was hopeless, eyes popping and mouth wide open in the rictus of terror. Feeling like an utter fool. And then the man howled and sprawled away, falling across Anders' legs—he heard the clatter of the knife when it fell.

Rosalia tugged at his arm. "Come on—"

"What the hell did you hit him with?"

"This." The wooden heel of her shoe. She was hopping on one foot trying to get it back on. Anders clambered to his feet and steadied her; then he made a dive for the knife and got it in his hand before the assailant rolled over. The man was groggy but not out. Anders waved the knife in his face and hissed at him: "Hold still, you bastard."

Something screeched up at the head of the passage. Rosalia said: "Glenn—"

"I see it. Come on."

Up there a car had slewed across the opening and the driver was getting out and Anders suspected the dark shiny thing in his hand was a gun. Together they ran down the passage, bouncing off walls. Anders risked a glance over his shoulder.

Blind luck: The big assailant was lurching back and forth on his feet trying to clear his head and blocking the sight lines of the man above.

Anders knew the second man had run back down to the bottom, got in the car and driven around to the head of the passage to cut off escape; the man up there with the car and the gun was the same man who'd come after them on foot, the assailant's partner. That meant there were two men and one car. It should be possible to elude them.

Steering Rosalia by the elbow he skidded around the building corner at the foot of the passage and ran her catty-corner up the street.

Dimly he heard the slam of a car door and the race of an engine: It meant the gunman hadn't waited for his partner but was coming after them with the car but he had to get around several corners and hope not to encounter traffic in the narrow one-way streets of Old Town. The chances were getting better every moment.

There was a drugstore half a block farther, lights splashing out onto the sidewalk—Anders made for that, hauling Rosalia by the arm.

Tires screeched not far away. They ran full tilt toward the doorway.

"Oh shit," she said. "It's closed." A lattice gate was padlocked across the drugstore; the lights had fooled him.

He led the way on toward the head of the street: a sharp left into another passage—blank walls, locked doors, poor light. But he could hear the car again and there wasn't time to turn back. At least this one wasn't cobbled. They ran fast and hard, the shirt pasted to him by sweat.

At the corner he pulled her around the edge and they flattened back against the wall. Fighting for breath Rosalia said, "Why don't they go crawl back under their rock? Those are the most persistent muggers I've ever—"

"I guess they're not muggers. Come on." He moved out slowly, looking for the shadow that shouldn't be there.

Rosalia said, "Who are they?"

"Rodriguez or his friends."

"But how did they know?"

"Either they followed us or they followed Crobey. Come on, keep moving." An L turn, no choice which way to go—and the passage was leading them back toward the street they'd left. The crime rate here was on a par with that of Spanish Harlem and as a result everything was locked and bolted; no way to get out of the street.

A sign under a tall hooded whip-lamp on a silvered stalk: *Calle Del Cristo*. Street of Christ. He tugged her out of the pool of lamplight.

He wished he'd paid more attention to the field courses that trained you how to get out of places; he wished he'd had more aptitude for this sort of thing.

Above them was the veranda of El Convento. A quartet of tourists was getting into a taxi. He rushed her forward, waving, shouting to the taxi—and then a garish baroque automobile, some dinosaur of the fifties, came down Sol Street like a seed squeezed from an orange, horn-honking the length of the passage, sliding maniacally around the bend and slamming with a tremendous racket into the taxi. The old Buick bounced off and kept coming like a juggernaut, leaving the hard-hit left side of the taxi destroyed, the sheet metal looking like a crumpled paper napkin. On the sidewalk the taxi driver and the four tourists flung themselves belatedly against the wall in terror.

The Buick was bearing down on Anders and Rosalia, its right-side wheels climbing the curb—above the sidewalk was an iron fence six feet high and Anders flung Rosalia toward it. They leaped off the ground, clenched the wrought iron overhead, drew their legs up—and the car cannoned past, the driver at the last minute lacking the nerve to crash the fence.

The car lost a hubcap—it went rattling away bouncing off things—and the Buick slewed toward the intersection below, the driver trying to control it, fishtailing for a U turn and another try.

Anders dropped off the fence, helped Rosalia to her feet—"You all right? Jesus!"—then they were racing for it again, heading for the battered taxi. The five people had fled into El Convento but the veranda was too long, the door too far away—the man in the Buick had a gun. Running past the taxi Rosalia said, "They don't build those things the way they used to," and giggled, on the near edge of hysteria. "I bet you haven't had this much fun since World War Two."

"I'm not *that* old—" and he never finished it because the Buick had stopped and the gun started shooting and Rosalia dropped like a stone beside the taxi's fender.

Something plucked at Anders' sleeve. He dived for the pavement, rolled, heard something whine away, got an elbow under him and flung himself toward Rosalia. *"Querida—querida?"*

"Shit, I think he's shot me. *Jesus Cristo*—I'm bleeding!"

He crouched over her, lifting her with an arm behind her shoulders.

"Get up, Rosalia, we can't stay here."

She cried out when he touched her and he felt the sticky warmth of her blood; he couldn't see where she was injured.

Over the hood of the taxi he saw the Buick start to move.

Rosalia had her feet under her after a fashion. He slid backwards into the taxi on his rump—the tourists had left both doors wide open—dragging Rosalia into the cab with him. She slumped, head lolling back, and he had to reach across her to pull her right leg into the car.

The Buick at the foot of the street was maneuvering back and forth trying to get turned around, its wide turning radius incompatible with the narrowness of the intersection. But the taxi's engine was reluctant and Anders could hear every turn of the starter inflict its drain on the weak battery and if it didn't start soon it would be dead and they were trapped in the thing now and the Buick was starting to accelerate, coming up the hill right at them.

Nearly twisting the key to breaking point Anders stared ruefully at the approaching juggernaut, yelling at the top of his lungs a strained litany of oaths—then it caught, coughed roughly, revved screaming high: Anders jammed the lever into drive and the taxi roared forward, jerking his head back, making Rosalia cry out.

He spun the wheel left to get out from the curb and almost took the skin off his knuckles—the Buick had smashed the door in too close to the steering wheel.

The only way through was to bluff the Buick out: a deadly game of chicken and Anders had the rage for it now, he wanted nothing except to kill the son of a bitch in the Buick and he aimed straight down the steep narrow street, knowing just the point where he'd thrust the wheel left and drive his front bumper right into the driver's door.

The taxi's rear wheels scrabbled for purchase, the tail sliding a bit from side to side as it gathered speed and settled in. He had the pedal on the floor and that prevented the transmission from shifting up; the engine whined painfully to its highest revs. Collison course and

he had the momentum for it now; he clenched the wheel
and only then did it penetrate his awareness that the girl
sagging beside him was injured and not strapped in and
that the impact would crush her against the dashboard:
At the last minute, with the Buick slowing and hugging
the far wall, Anders straightened the wheel and shot past.

Anders knew where the hospital was and that oc-
cupied everything in his mind except for the portion that
made him keep searching the rear-view mirror. The
Buick never appeared. By now its driver knew he'd lost
his chance; probably he'd known he'd lost it when they
got too near El Convento—that was why he'd started
shooting at them: If they'd got inside the restaurant
he'd have lost them.

It was madness. Anders' pulse throbbed; he blinked
in quaking disbelief. The hospital—he slewed into the
ambulance driveway, stopped the cab by the emergency
ramp and started to yell again. After a little while they
came out with a stretcher and took Rosalia inside.

He sat on a hard bench watching the wall clock. The
waiting room was crowded with people sick and people
bleeding. It was the kind of sultry night that provoked
violence and disease. Anders kept watching the door,
half afraid his assailants would appear again.

They wouldn't; by now they'd have disappeared into
the *demimonde*. Rodriguez's people, he was sure. It
gave him pause, sudden concern for Crobey and the
Marchand woman.

He looked at the clock again, got up in anger and
presented himself at the desk and demanded news of the
heavy-set nurse. She had nothing to tell him: Miss Rojas
was undergoing emergency surgery, he must wait.

The bullet had struck her in the back; it had hit bone
somewhere, for there hadn't been an exit wound in
front. It was all he knew for certain—that and the fact
that she'd been unconscious when they'd removed her
from the car.

God, God. He'd only just found her. . . .

Those two with the Buick had exceeded their orders;

he felt morally certain of that. They'd had instructions to follow the quarry and attack them where there were no witnesses: with knives to make no noise. Mugging victims found dead in an Old Town alley—nothing to stir up much of a fuss. The thing had gone awry because the man with the knife had been knocked down by a shoe and Anders and Rosalia had got away from them. The man in the Buick had got mad. The continuation of the attack, beyond all reason, had taken place because the man in the Buick was angry and at the same time atavistically shrewd enough to know that if he killed Anders and Rosalia he'd have no witnesses against him.

I didn't even get the license number, he thought savagely. Not that it would matter. The antique car would be easy enough to find; but it would prove to have been stolen. Not even an amateur killer set out on his nightwork in a car that could be traced to him.

Anders tried to remember the face of the man with the knife. The police would be here soon; the hospital had called them. He had to clear his mind, make a decision: Give a description to the police or keep it to himself? He wanted someone to nail the bastards but at the same time he was unable to lose sight of the fact that the two men, if he could find them without police help, might lead him to Rodriguez. And he wanted Rodriguez now, not just the hired guns. It was Rodriguez who was responsible for what had happened to Rosalia. The hired guns were only tools.

It had been dismally dark in the passage. Mainly he'd seen the knife; it had drawn his attention. The man's face? He thought he'd know it if he saw it again—big, blocky, young, a bit of a double chin, clean-shaven except for the mustache: It might have been the face of Pancho Villa from an old photograph. Yes, he'd know the man again.

And the man in the Buick? No. Anders had never really seen that one's face—only enough of him, running in the cobblestoned alley, to know he was a fairly big man.

He decided to tell the police he hadn't got a good look at either of them.

The nurse summoned him to the desk. "The doctor will see you now."

The doctor was a tired young man with dust on his glasses and fresh creases in his white smock; clearly he'd just changed into it. He was scrubbing his hands in a lavatory sink at the side of the cubicle. "Sit down."

"How is she?"

"I'm sorry," the young man said as if by rote, "she didn't make it."

Part Four

Chapter 13

Crobey drove, as always, with one eye on the mirror. She was accustomed by now to his sudden turnings and doublings back. All the same when they reached the highway she was exasperated enough to say in a caustic voice, "I trust you're sure you've lost them."

"Right."

She cast an eye at him. "You mean you *were* being followed?"

"Right."

And she believed him. Crobey had the peripheral vision of a professional basketball player.

She said, "Why are you angry with me this time?"

"Forget it."

It didn't take her long to work it out. Insects smashed into the windshield and the Bronco jounced her gently. Crobey's profile was pale in the dashboard's reflected illumination. She said, "If you didn't have me along you'd have let them catch you, wouldn't you?"

"It might have been useful to ask them a few questions."

"Suppose they'd asked first?"

Crobey only crooked his lip corner in a tidy smile. Feeling rebuffed she said, "Tell me something: Is there anything you do badly?"

"Yes. Lose."

"Your conceit is absurd."

"I told you before: We'd get along faster if you'd go home."

She began to retort, then curbed her tongue. It was occurring to her he might be right. He tolerated her because he was a mercenary and she was his employer;

he resented her because she was a woman and an amateur.

She wondered why he put up with her at all.

She said, "Who were they?"

"I've no idea."

"But they might be some of Rodriguez's people?"

"Might."

She didn't comprehend his equanimity; she said bluntly, "You want me to leave, then."

He made no answer. They were approaching the turnoff. Crobey punched the button, extinguishing the lights, and used the hand brake to slow the truck so that the brake lights wouldn't flash. They rolled slowly off the main road into that total darkness that had frightened her so much the first time. The truck eased to a halt; she heard the ratchet of the emergency brake. Crobey hooked his elbow over the back of the seat and twisted to watch the road behind. He didn't take the revolver from under his jacket but she knew it was there; she'd seen him put it there before they left the house.

He had a stalking predator's steady inexcitability. It wasn't tranquillity; it was the cool command of an otherwise tumultuous temper. His cool passivity came across as menace.

That morning he'd instructed her in the manufacture of a Molotov Cocktail. "You mix soil and gravel, and a little bit of soap powder to make it grunge together. Fill the bottle about one third with this gunk. It weights the bottom and gives you throwing ballast—and the gravel makes good shrapnel. Now we fill the rest up with petrol—gasoline from the pump, the octane doesn't matter. Right to the top. Tear off this much rag, see—wad it up with this little bit of clotheslines for a fuse. Stuff it in the mouth like this to soak up gasoline from inside and make sure the clothesline pokes out an inch or two. When you light this thing get rid of it fast—throw it hard and drop on your face. Drop behind something that'll shield you from the blast and the heat, if you've got a choice. In Hungary they took out Soviet tanks with these things."

"Why the hell are you showing me these horrible things?"

"Because the kind of people we're dealing with, ducks, you may find yourself getting chased into the woods by people with guns and machetes and maybe all you've got is your little car and your handbag. You've got gasoline in the car—suck it out through a hose you strip off the engine, if you have to—and I never met a woman who didn't carry half a dozen little bottles in her handbag."

She'd stared with revulsion at the fused bottle of gasoline. Crobey had said, "When the crossbow was introduced in the twelfth century the Pope called it an inhuman engine of destruction and banned its use."

"If I were still a college sophomore I might find that world-weary cynicism of yours dramatically mysterious. Right now I'm not too thrilled by it."

"Cynicism," he'd replied, "is idealism corrupted by experience, like Machiavelli said. Remember one thing: You haven't been there. I have. Listen to old Harry once in a while."

Now, watching him peer back into the darkness with his chin on his forearm, she remembered the quiet tolerant tone he'd used.

He faced front and let the brake out and put the vehicle forward at a crawl, hunching over the wheel to peer through the night. Carole couldn't see a thing. Branches slapped the truck, coming out of nowhere; the suspension bucked and pitched as roots and rocks went under the wheels. But Crobey seemed to know where he was going. Finally he switched on the headlights. When she looked behind she saw nothing in the red taillights' glow except forest—the road was out of sight back there.

After a while they reached the yard of Santana's farm and Crobey parked the truck behind the house; they went inside and Santana, dressed as if he planned to go somewhere—a shabby seersucker jacket, a white shirt frayed at the collar—stood up in deference to Carole's presence. He had an open can of beer in his fist: He looked, she thought, rather like a can of beer himself—stubby, squat, cylindrical.

Santana's face was animated. He began to speak in something approximating English but neither of them understood it and Santana lapsed into Spanish. Crobey snapped a few monosyllabic questions at him, got answers and translated for her:

"He thinks he's got a line on Rodriguez's family."

"Where?"

"Here. Rio Piedras."

Santana spoke again, with gestures, and Crobey said, "All right, but keep your head down. Don't show yourself."

An adventurously brash grin and Santana was gone, the screen door slapping shut behind him.

"Where's he going?"

"To stake out the house."

"He knows the house?"

"Sure. Probably the one where Rodriguez spent the night when Glenn's cop spotted him."

"Then why send Santana? Let's question them ourselves." She was already turning toward the door.

"Calm down, ducks. We'd get nowhere."

"What?"

"Elementary security—if you've gone to ground you don't tell civilians where you are. Not even your own wife. We could torture the children and force the wife to talk but she wouldn't be able to tell us what she doesn't know, would she? All we'd do is expose ourselves." Crobey tossed his jacket onto the couch. "If Rodriguez turns up Santana will spot him. I kind of doubt he'll turn up. He knows people are looking for him."

She was shocked. "Don't you even want to know—"

"Know what? What his wife and kiddies look like? I don't care all that much, ducks. Go on—go to bed. You've got to learn how to wait things out."

She lowered herself into one of Santana's ruined chairs. "How did he find them?"

"Mostly on the telephone. He hunted down some of the old-timers from the days we all worked training fields in Alabama. You know how it goes. You dig up one veteran and he gives you the number of two others.

It's like a chain letter. The first nineteen don't know a thing but number twenty happened to bump into Rodriguez's wife in a supermarket or whatever. It's harder to disappear than most people think it is. Especially if you've got reasons to stay around an island where people know you. If Rodriguez had really wanted to evaporate he'd have had to move to Africa or the Philippines. But he didn't because he's a soldier, of sorts, and this is where his army is.''

"And Santana was able to make this contact while all Glenn Anders' minions couldn't?"

"In the first place I kind of get the feeling Glenn's minions have dried up on him. I don't think he's got police co-operation any longer. If he did he wouldn't be so eager to have our help. And in the second place Glenn didn't know all those people the way Santana did. Santana was one of them. He knew who to ask."

She was still tracking Anders. "Why wouldn't he have police co-operation?"

"My guess is they've told him to soft-pedal the investigation."

She tipped her head back onto the top of the chair and closed her eyes. She'd been running on her nerve ends too long; exhaustion was overtaking her.

Crobey said, "Maybe tomorrow we'll show ourselves again and let them follow us around a while. Maybe we can pull them in and ask them questions."

She opened her eyes. He stood in the middle of the room looking down at her, lamplight reflecting frostily off the surface of his eyes. She said, "We? Us?"

"You wanted to be dealt in, didn't you?"

It made her sit up. "You've changed your tune."

"Have I?" He turned away. "Go on to bed, ducks."

He stood with his back to her; his spine seemed rigid—defensive; but against what?

Too tired to resist his suggestion, she went into her cell—she thought of it as a cell: the cot, plaster flaking off the wall. There was no shade at the window; she took one or two things out of her case and then switched off the light before undressing. A narrow rind of moon had come out, throwing a bit of light through the glass, and for a while she stood taut in tawny underwear looking up toward the mountain peak. It was quite clearly silhouetted against the stars.

The floor creaked; she turned; and knuckles rapped her door.

"Yes?"

She watched the knob turn. She could have spoken; she didn't. A bit of faint illumination bounced around corners from the kitchen and outlined Crobey when the door came open. He didn't advance, he only stood there.

"I sort of was wondering what you'd look like without your clothes." His voice had gone raspy.

Almost with relief she stirred, with a slow, carnal smile. "Ah Crobey," she murmured, "you've got twenty-four hours to get out of my bedroom."

He flipped the door shut with his heel. His hands lifted to her shoulders and dropped upon them. He stood at arm's length. His hands seemed weightless. 'You're vibrating."

"I'm terrified."

"Tell me to leave. I'll go."

With hesitant fascination she reached up, palms against his grizzled cheeks. Crobey had a face like a leather coat, she thought; the kind that looked better the more battered it got. He turned his lips into her palm, kissing her hand; everything seemed to move at sixty-four-frame slow motion. She felt the pound of a pulse in her throat and an odd vertigo—her head thrown back to look into his eyes, she felt as if he were bearing down on her like an avalanche. She cried out; but what emerged from her lips was only breath. Then he tugged her forward.

His face loomed an inch from her own. His eyes had gone wide and the preposterous idea struck her that he was as intimidated as she was—that the monumental self-confidence was all facade.

Astonishingly tender, he bore her down.

Sex, to Carole, was always followed by feelings of starvation. She came back from the kitchen with a plate of cheese and half-crumbled crackers. Crobey was crowded far over on the edge of the narrow cot, hands under the back of his head, long hard body full-length. She almost tripped over the heaped tangle of his clothes where he'd left them on the floor. Even in the faint light she could see how his eyes explored her body when she sat down on the cot and set the plate beside her and began to nibble.

Crobey hiked up on one elbow and helped himself to a snack. Holding the cracker in his hand, regarding it, he mused. "For what you're about to receive may you be truly thankful, Harry."

"Do you have any children?"

"Probably not."

He'd have been a good father, she thought; he had the strength to be gentle.

Robert. . . .

Robert, she thought, looking at Crobey's naked form, would have liked Crobey. Robert had no snobbery.

She had no fear of Crobey now.

She said, "That was terrific, you know."

"It's an old trick I learned in the South Seas," he told her gravely. "What the Trobriand Islanders call the missionary position."

"You're demented."

Crobey laughed casually. "Maybe I am. Hell, I don't know what I am any longer."

"What's the matter, Harry?"

"I don't know. Postcoital depression."

"Tell me." She'd buried her face in the hollow of his throat; her voice came up muffled.

He said, "Will you promise not to laugh if I tell you something?"

"No, but I'll promise to try not to laugh."

"Supercilious bitch."

"Ill-mannered lout."

He said, "Would you find it possible to believe a slob like me could ever long for the sanctuary of a home?"

"Why not? Everybody needs a hand to hold onto. Even me."

"Right. Somebody to be around to pick up the soap when I drop it in the shower." He stirred, hooking a leg over her; his fingertips trailed up her spine. "I'm a mean tough two-headed son of a bitch, ducks. My job is terror. I did it, you know, for a while, believing in it. Then it was just a job. You fly them in, you fly them out. They put bombs in the plane and point you at a target and you go. You can destroy them so easily. The day comes when for the first time in your life you realize you can't just keep killing them. You can't ever kill them all. I'm too old for this foolishness and too far gone to repent. Going downhill and maybe getting scared: I never was any good at coping with failure. I'm trying to learn to accept my changing limitations, I expect, but it's hardly a propitious moment for—this, you and me, us. Shit, why should I tell you all this?"

"Maybe it's time you told someone."

"Thing is, I'd tucked myself into a hole in the ground over there in Nassau to try and sort myself out—I was ready to chuck it in, find myself another line of work. Then you hit me with recollections of your brother Warren, who was a guy I liked and maybe owed. I didn't think much of this job, you know. I thought you were around the bend. But you were right up there on your supercilious high horse and I never sat at a table over drinks with a woman like you before. I got it into my head to take care of two things. I was going to take you down off the high horse and I was going to get you into bed to prove you weren't any different from any other woman."

"You succeeded."

"Wrong, ducks. Nobody's ever going to knock you down and as for the other thing, you're not the same as any other woman."

"Why not?"

"Because no other woman ever got to me the way you do."

"Go to sleep now, Harry."

"Right." And, amazingly, he did.

She drifted in a soft haze of contentment, not trying to think. Her awareness was limited to the physical present: the weight of his hard body against her, the sound and warm flutter of his breathing, the rise and fall of his ribcage under her outflung arm, the abrasive stubble on his cheek.

After a time she heard him whimper softly in his sleep.

She woke up feeling an absolute wreck; she opened her eyes slowly and Crobey took on a sort of surrealistic substance limned in red—the back of his head: Somehow he'd contrived to roll over without knocking them both off the cot.

She got up gingerly, ran her tongue over her front teeth and stumbled out side carrying rudiments of clothing. By the time she mastered the use of the eccentric outdoor shower she was in a state of shimmering rage.

Crobey laughed at her.

"Shut up," she told him.

"What's wrong?"

"Nothing."

"Oh. I see. You grind your teeth every morning at eight, that's all."

"One of the basic freedoms is the right to be irritable before breakfast, all right?"

"Come on," he said, "come over here."

"Can't you see I need to be left alone right now?"

"Be reasonable."

"No." In high dudgeon she left the room, hauling the doorknob after her, and winced when the door slammed.

In the kitchen she got out her compact and looked critically into its mirror. Then Crobey appeared, naked, a bath towel in his fist. She backed up against the sink to let him pass. Crobey made as if to walk by, then turned and pinioned her.

He was grinning: His face came down on hers but she kept her lips stiff and still under his.

Crobey lifted his face away. "Come on back to the bedroom."

"Man does not live by bed alone."

He backed away, defeated. "A record-breaking fit of pique."

"Beat it. I feel my temper going."

"I can see that. You're more than just a bit glacial today, considering. Wasn't it Catherine the Great who commanded the farm serfs into her bed at night and ordered them back to the fields next morning?"

"Harry, please, for Heaven's sake!"

He went.

By the time he returned—hair all wet down, towel strapped around his middle—she had fried four eggs and poured coffee. They sat facing each other across the Salvation Army table and she pushed the eggs around on her plate with a fork until Crobey said, "Stop looking like an injured cocker spaniel."

"Shut up. Will you please just shut up?"

"What the hell do you think I am, ducks? An extra on your movie set?"

"You're leading the witness," she warned.

"Come on. Spit it out."

She almost upset the coffee when she reached for it. Vexed, she lifted it with great care and drank from it and set it down, absurdly proud of the face that she hadn't spilled a drop.

Finally she said, "You just don't give a shit, do you?"

"About what?"

"Last night. Me. Anything."

"Come again?"

" 'The world is my whorehouse,' " she said bitterly. "Well you proved what you wanted to prove. You could get me into bed just like any other woman." She mocked him: "Ah, ducks, take it easy, what the fuck, a little roll in the hay never hurt anybody."

Crobey put his fork down and laid both palms on the table. "Now listen to me: Don't confuse someone who doesn't parade his feelings with someone who doesn't have any feelings. You think it was a game? A one-nighter?"

Subdued, she said, "I wouldn't care, if only—"

"If only what?"

She began to cry then—surreptitiously at first, hoping

he wouldn't notice, but it turned into great gasping heaves and she didn't know how but he somehow got her up and guided her into the front room and sat her down on the couch and folded her against him so that she cried it out with her face buried against his hirsute chest, baptizing him with her tears, clinging to him, clutching him in an insane desperation because sometime during the night she had awakened and realized with a sudden explosion of terror that she would not be able to bear it if he left her.

She had never felt this with anyone. Never known such an agony, never known what a tender sad thing love could be. She'd got up this morning hating him for making her long for him, for destroying all her carefully constructed defenses with his muscular embrace or his harsh laugh, for subverting her prejudices by making her love him in spite of—because of?—his ridiculous masculinity, his reckless gaiety and resolute foolishness, his violently assertive intensity. It was melodramatic, absurd—she truly was obsessed by him: In the night she'd thought of all the years she hadn't known him; and she'd been jealous of all the women he'd ever known; and she'd kept thinking that at best he'd make the kind of bully husband who never touched the dishes.

He kept patting her shoulder and there-thereing her. It was imbecilic. She pulled herself away, snuffled, dragged a sleeve across her eyes. "Don't just let me sit here with egg on my face."

She peered at him, trying to clear her eyes. "God damn you, it's not that I don't want to live without you—it's that I can't. And I don't know what the hell to do about that."

"I wouldn't worry about it, ducks." He took both her hands. "You've eaten your way right through me like termites."

"What a suave line you have there."

He wrapped himself around her, more like a wrestler than a lover but his rough kiss dissolved her, made her feel as if her colors were running and blending into his own.

They were tangled together on the couch. Past

Harry's shoulder she saw Santana in the doorway, not smiling.

"God invented the fist so that we could knock before entering." She began to sit up.

Santana's expression never changed. He had a rolled newspaper in his hand. She watched him approach: He unfolded the paper and held it out for them to see. It was in Spanish but she recognized the photograph—Rosalia Rojas very young, her hair straight down over her shoulders and her smile bright and expectant: yearbook photograph.

Harry swung his legs around and got his feet on the floor. She saw his jaw creep forward to lie in a hard straight line. He looked from the newspaper up into Santana's face. "*Donde está?*"

"*¿Pues—a la policia?*"

She said, "God*damn* it. What is it?"

"Sorry, ducks. Seems the game's been called on account of death."

"Rosalia?"

Harry, naked, left the towel when he strode across the room. "Get yourself ready to travel." He disappeared.

"Oh, the poor thing. She was so—" She followed him as far as the door. "Why her?"

He was climbing into underwear. "Gunning for both of them, I guess. The paper makes it out to be a mugging."

"Isn't there a chance—"

"No."

She pressed her cheeks with her palms as if to reassure herself of her own reality. *I must look a fright:* She ought to do something about her hair. But she didn't move from the doorway. "You want to put me on a plane."

"Ducks, I want you to stay alive."

She said, "She was such a breezy kid."

"She was all right," Harry acknowledged.

"Maybe now at least they'll reopen it in Washington."

"I doubt it. They'll just pull the covers up over their heads. They've got an out, haven't they—nobody can prove it wasn't an ordinary robbery attack.'' He buttoned up his short-sleeve khaki shirt and left the tails out over his Levi's. Then he sat down to lace up his roughout-buck boots.

"What are you going to do?''

"Find out how Glenn wants to play it. Give him a hand if I can.'' He looked up. "This gives him a stake in it, doesn't it?''

"What about you?''

"Ducks, you're my stake in it.''

"I don't want you killed, Harry.''

"People have been trying to kill me for twenty-five years. Don't worry about me.''

She went back across the front room for her boots. Santana stood in the kitchen doorway—neither drinking nor smoking nor eating nor reading; simply waiting.

She tried to comb her hair. Turmoil enveloped her—she had always tried to exercise control over the events of her life and because she was able and intelligent she usually succeeded but now they were racing by too quickly and she felt adrift.

Harry was with Santana talking Spanish when she emerged. Santana came away, heading back past her to her room. She said, "Don't bother, I didn't pack it.''

Santana hesitated and Harry scowled. She said, "Down in the Amazon basin the jaguars hunt in male-female pairs. When two of them pounce on a big tapir that outweighs both of them put together, the battle can be kind of fierce. We were down there on location once and I saw it happen. It can look right dicey, as you'd say. But the outcome's always the same.''

"That's kind of fanciful.''

She said, "Please don't sell me short.''

Santana looked on with stiff disapproval.

Harry said, "Okay, ducks. We'd better pick you out a gun.''

Chapter 14

Cielo walked fretfully to the edge of the cliff and peered down into the thin mist. Kruger was down there striding back and forth like a colonial officer, whipping a stick against his britches; Cielo measured the distance again with his eye and turned back toward the mountain.

Vargas's eyebrows lifted—he was awaiting Cielo's signal. Uneasy, Cielo shook his head and went back to the trees, crossing the flat rock where the helicopter had set down last night, passing two field guns and the crated mortars. The field pieces were small ones, three-inchers.

He had another close look at the oak to which the block-and-tackle was cabled. It was the biggest tree in the vicinity and looked as substantial and monolithic as a granite mountain and Kruger, the engineer among them, had passed on its suitability as an anchor for the cable but Cielo was troubled by doubts because water was easy in the rain forest and the rock subsurface was close beneath the soil—even the biggest trees had no need to drill roots very far down; it made for a shallow purchase.

Kruger had dismissed it. The oak, he'd pointed out, was old enough to have survived a hundred hurricanes. It would support the weight of a Sherman tank, let alone a small mountain howitzer or a crate of rockets.

Vargas came across to the oak. "Before long the sun will burn this off. We need to be under cover by then."

"All right." He still felt nagged by reluctance but he forced himself away from it. "Let's get started then."

He went to the rim and watched the cable pull taut over the guy pully. The crate—twelve hundred

pounds—began to skid and tilt; then it was lifted off the
ground and swung far out. Vargas and two of the men
prodded it with poles to slow its pendulum swing. After
a time it settled down, twisting a bit in the air, hanging
clear out over the face of the cliff.

Down below Kruger was watching with his neck
craned back, his face pale in the mist. He began to make
beckoning gestures with both hands and Cielo relayed
these signals to Julio who shifted the gears and began to
pay out cable from the donkey engine's winch drum.
The heavy crate began to descend, well out away from
the face of the cliff, and Cielo sat back on his haunches
and relaxed; it was working splendidly.

The donkey engine banged away methodically and
down at the mouth of the cave Kruger had stepped to
one side and was reaching up to guide the crate to its
seat on the flatbed cart that waited to receive it. Four
men clustered around the swaying load while it dropped
slowly amid them. There was a second donkey engine in
the cave, only seven horsepower but enough to winch
the dolly into the cave.

For the next hour Cielo squatted on the rim relaying
hand signals from Kruger at the base of the cliff to Julio
at the hoist engine. It gave him a kind of peace to per-
form this near-mindless repetitive job. There were two
small howitzers, four mortar crates (one containing
mortars and three containing ammunition), two crated
rocket-launchers and four crates of rockets. The rocket-
launchers doubled up on one load; at seven minutes per
load Kruger had calculated it would take an hour and a
quarter to finish the job but it was running a little slower
than that and Cielo realized the mist probably would
clear before they had everything put away. But that did
not particularly exercise him.

In any event near the end of the first hour the clouds
came scudding over the peaks and by half past eight it
had begun to drizzle, a very fine spray that pricked his
face and made him smile.

The donkey engine ran out of gas. There was always
something you'd neglected. They had to pause while
Cielo tossed the end of the rope down to Kruger and a

man went off to the camp to bring back a five-gallon
jerrycan from the Jeep. Julio came over to the rim and
gave him a hand hauling it up; it was heavy and the
work made him sweat. Julio said, "Almost done
now—just the two guns left. Then I can get back to my
book. I've only got a couple of chapters left—I want to
find out how it comes out."

"I can tell you how it comes out. The computers take
over the universe."

"Very funny." Julio stumped away lugging the
gasoline. He was in a good mood; the helicopter had
brought him half a dozen science fictions.

Vargas and his crew hooked up the first field gun and
Kruger down below waited with his arms folded on his
chest, head tipped back, blinking when raindrops struck
his face; brooding. To Kruger everything had come out
of kilter with time. The tragedy of Kruger's existence
was that he hadn't been born early enough to be a storm
trooper.

The engine coughed and started up again. Cielo
looked back toward the cliff and thought of checking up
on the oak tree again but he was feeling a bit lazy and
his earlier unease had been settled by a gentle calm. He
wagged a finger at Vargas and then at Julio; the field
gun dragged along the ground a bit and then swung
aloft and swayed out over the drop.

Down below him Kruger's men stood out well away
from the cliff. Kruger walked across the hardpan and
dragged the dolly aside; they wouldn't need it this time,
the gun had its own wheels. Coming back onto the drop
zone Kruger looked up and watched the gun descend; he
began to wave the others forward and they moved in
like scavengers toward a carcass. Old men now, all of
them—old for this at least; they were over forty, some
of them fifty or as near to it as made no difference;
Vargas was what, now—fifty-six? For men like these
this kind of life was nothing more than simulation.

They'd been nurtured on patriotism and old Draga's
monstrous calumnies. Time had betrayed them. When
Draga was gone Cielo would have to face up to the
dismal grief of disbanding them. Some of them would

take it with relief, he knew—Vargas for instance. Others would lose their moorings and be swept away by the guilt of their failure: He could picture one or two of them on skid row and he didn't know how he could prevent that. Julio had his own plans, Cielo thought—but they involved business, not insurrection. As for Kruger, that one wouldn't suffer; he'd find another war and go off to shoot Communists somewhere.

For himself there was simply the money Draga would leave him. There was something curious in that—not long ago he'd had ten million dollars in his hands but he'd turned it over to the old man. When Julio had questioned that he'd explained that they couldn't double-cross the old man and survive it; the old man had tentacles everywhere and how could you spend money without his getting wind of it? But that was only a half truth. In a way he loved the old man. After the old man died it wouldn't matter if Cielo turned traitor to his cause but while Draga lived Cielo would humor him because these dreams were all the old man had left.

A boat. That was his own dream. Not a Greek yacht; just a boat—fifty feet, maybe sixty, an old one would do if it didn't have dry rot. Something with plenty of canvas and a little diesel auxiliary. A boat and a warm-water landing where he could moor it; a house by the landing where he could moor Soledad and the children and bask away his days in a soft warm nesty feeling of family and love. All he really wanted was the old man's half million dollars to see him through. *Ah*, he thought, *I'm one hell of a revolutionary*.

Musing, he watched Kruger's men drag the field gun out of sight into the cave. The cable came back up and Vargas hooked it to the last gun.

The drizzle tapered off. Steam in the air now; he could hardly see the oak back there and beneath him Kruger's face was leached of color by the gray mist. There was always rain in El Yunque but it seemed to have been heavier than usual this year—every day a half dozen squalls, some of them drenching. It was a wonder the whole mountain didn't wash away. Everywhere you

saw trees with their root systems exposed to the air
where floods had carried the earth away.

He didn't like it up here. Cabin fever was another
danger; he couldn't keep the men here forever. The
schedule of rotations permitted each man a two-day
furlough in the fleshpots; the men were away two at a
time on overlapping days; their discipline was strong
and he knew none of them would get drunk enough to
let anything slip. Nevertheless they were beginning to
think of themselves as prisoners. A few had their own
resources: Julio would last as long as the supply of
science fiction held out and Vargas had the methodical
patience of a saint and Kruger, the good soldier, obeyed
orders to the end but the others were restless and soon a
listless apathy would infect them; they would begin to
quarrel among themselves and things would begin to
disintegrate. And there was Emil, if he ever returned
from the city. But he saw no solution to it unless the old
man died soon.

The idea had occurred to him that if push came to
shove he might mount an attempt to invade Cuba, then
abort it for some reason. That would push things back
toward Square One for a while. It would take time to
reorganize and re-equip. The thought remained in his
mind as a workable contingency but he preferred to
avoid it; anything like that might cause injuries and
jeopardy. What was the sense in exposing the men to
pointless risks? Besides, an aborted attack would disap-
point the old man acutely.

Something snapped—very loud. The earth seemed to
quake under him. He was watching Kruger, waiting for
signals, but the noisy tremor spun him around and he
was in time to see Vargas diving toward a man nearby,
tackling the man, driving him down and back from the
cliff—and then it registered on Cielo's consciousness
that the derrick was coming apart.

He saw in an instant what was happening: The one
thing they hadn't been able to test—the rim of the cliff
itself was buckling. A fissure must have opened; rot in
the rock. The telegraph pole that had been pinned into
the ledge by cables and rock drills was letting go and in

that split instant of time he saw the great logs scatter like toothpicks.

He whipped around to scream a warning at Kruger but Kruger had seen it, too, and was scrambling to get out from under the plummeting field gun. For a moment Cielo thought there was time, believed Kruger would make it; the angle of perspective gave him false hope. Kruger launched himself like an Olympic swimmer—a flat dive to get away from the impact area—but his soles skidded on the wet and he belly-flopped and the gun came down on him—bounced horribly and tipped over, its cable whipping like a snake, lashing its heavy loop back toward the cliff where it knocked a man—Ramirez—clear off his feet; Cielo wasn't certain but he had the terrible feeling the cable had struck Ramirez right in the face. The man pirouetted back out of sight.

Stunned by shock and the suddenness of it Cielo climbed to his feet on rubber knees and looked left: Vargas was standing up, the man he'd rescued dusting himself off, someone else lying askew with the butt end of a telegraph pole across his chest. The donkey engine died with a sputter and Julio stared at Cielo in horror. Vargas on his big legs stumbled from side to side like a man concussed; but Cielo believed he'd not been hurt.

Juices pumped through him but he forced himself to behave with leaderly calm. He went jogging across to the man pinned under the pole. It was Ordovara and he was quite dead, his rib cage crushed; Cielo turned away, then turned back and laid a finger along Ordovara's throat to feel for a pulse. There was none. A stink of excrement hung in the air.

He went to the lip and looked down. Two men were manhandling the capsized field gun away from Kruger who lay on his belly with both legs splayed out at weird angles. Even from up here Cielo could hear Kruger's moans. Well, at least he was still alive but it looked as if both legs had been crushed.

He felt weight behind him. When he turned Vargas was there. Cielo pointed toward the body of Ordovara. "Get that thing off him and bring him down to the camp. Tell the others to clear up—get the equipment out of sight. Put Julio in charge. I'm going down.''

He strode along the rim, not hurrying, heading for the trail they'd cut down the side slope. It would take him fifteen minutes to cover the circuitous course but it was the only way down, short of rappelling down the cliff on a rope.

The fault, he thought, was no one's but his own; he could lay the blame at no one else's door. *And how do I expiate this sin?*

Ramirez was dead, half his face taken off by the whipping cable. The two dead men were not a major problem—only a major grief. It was Kruger who commanded his attention.

It wasn't as bad as he'd feared it might be—the undercarriage of the field gun had landed square across the back of Kruger's thighs but it was a pneumatic tire and that had absorbed a bit of the impact; the bones of both Kruger's legs were broken but the flesh hadn't been badly severed. Nevertheless he was already swelling up and it was obvious a good many blood vessels had been crushed. With immediate sophisticated medical attention it might be possible to save his legs. Up here there wasn't much they could do but splint the fractures.

He took Julio aside. "You'd better break radio silence. Call in the helicopter. We'll have to carry him up there.''

"You want to risk everyone for Kruger?''

"Do you think I should let him lose his legs, Julio?''

"He's lost them anyway.''

"Now you're a surgeon, are you?''

"Rodrigo—listen, think what will happen if we break security. The old man, what'll he think? What'll he do?''

"I don't care right now. We owe Kruger a chance to keep his legs. Call Zapatino.''

"What if I can't raise him?''

"You'll raise somebody.''

Emil met Cielo at the door. The big youth's eyes were

filled with scorn. He conducted Cielo through the house
to the tiled deck where his grandfather sat in a cane
chair with a newspaper across his lap. Through an open
door Cielo glimpsed the cathode screen of a stock
market quotations machine. The old man sat with his
chin on his chest and appeared to be dozing but then the
newspaper rattled in his hands and he tossed it to the
table beside him and lifted his eyes. He did not look
well, Cielo thought. It was something other than old age
or irritation; a malaise. For some time the old man
seemed to have been shrinking into gauntness—Cielo
wondered if he had cancer.

The old man said, "How is Kruger?"

"The chances are pretty good, they said."

Emil said, "It shouldn't have happened."

"I knew that." He didn't want to give Emil a chance
to exploit it; he said, "It was my fault."

"Zapatino tells me it was an accident," the old man
said.

"Accidents don't just happen. Someone's careless—
then there's an accident. We should have made surer of
the rock before we bolted the derrick to it."

Emil said, "It's easy to say that now," and the old
man, misunderstanding him, nodded his head. Then
Emil said, "It's magnanimous of him to take responsibility for it, isn't it. Now that it doesn't cost him
anything."

The old man ignored him. "Kruger's the engineer. It
was his fault, then, not yours. Must you burden yourself
with feelings of guilt for every mishap that takes place
around you?"

"I'm in command. The responsibility's mine. If it
weren't for me Ramirez and Ordovara would be alive."

"If it weren't for me they'd be alive, too," the old
man pointed out, "and if it weren't for you they might
all have died long ago in a Havana dungeon, yourself included. You mustn't put on sackcloth and ashes for the
rest of your life on their account, *hijo*."

"One day I'll get over it," Cielo said philosophically.

Emil pressed his opening: "Papa, he broke security.

We can't dismiss that so easily."

"I believe we've covered the breach as well as could be done," the old man said. "We've made Kruger out to be a tourist who was changing a tire when the jack slipped in the mud and the car fell on him. It explains the imprint of the tire tread on his legs. It's not as if he had a bullet in him—there'll be no official inquiry. Cielo did the right thing. We're not savages—we don't leave men to die just because they've been injured."

"All the same. They could have brought Kruger down in the Jeep. They didn't have to violate radio silence."

Cielo watched him loom and wondered if the youth would have the audacity to challenge him for the leadership of the group. Not yet, he thought. He's not ready just yet. He's preparing the ground now, that's all.

"Breaking radio security," Emil said, "that's a serious mistake."

"I had to make the decision on the spot," Cielo replied. "I don't regret it."

"Then you're a fool!"

Cielo laughed at him. It was the only way to deal with him.

The old man said, "Emil has a point, you know."

"Not realistically. Nobody has direction finders zeroed in on us. Nobody even knows we're here. The odds were favorable and my concern was Kruger. I stand by the decision."

"You're wrong," the old man said, "at least in part. They know we're here."

Cielo looked from face to face. They were both watching him. "I wasn't told that, was I?"

"I'm telling you now," the old man said.

Emil said, "It changes things. They're getting close—we can't afford sloppy leadership any longer. We can't afford to allow accidents to happen—we can't allow security to be broken again."

The old man lifted a palm toward his grandson. "The most important thing is that Cielo didn't panic. It must have been a dreadful few moments. Cielo kept his head. That's why he's in command."

It was a vote of confidence but Cielo thought

gloomily, *I wish you trusted me less.*

The old man said, "They've traced the kidnapping of Ambassador Gordon to Puerto Rico."

"How?"

"I don't know. I'm not blaming you. You have a distressing tendency to shoulder the responsibility for everything—I'm not putting any fault on you. The fact remains, they've traced you—at least they know you're on the island and perhaps they know who you are. I believe you know two of the men involved in the investigation—Glenn Anders and Harrison Crobey. I remember the names from years ago when you trained in Alabama. Your reports mentioned Crobey several times."

Cielo stood at the parapet. A white sloop gamboled offshore. The sun gave it the look of a hovering butterfly. Crobey, he thought. He'd always been a little afraid of Crobey, but he liked him.

"I've heard of Anders but I never met him."

"He was Crobey's liaison with Langley."

"Yes, I suppose he was."

"There was a young woman with Anders. Presumably a member of his staff." The old man squirmed a bit in the cane chair and spent a moment clicking his teeth and it occurred to Cielo the old man was having trouble for some reason—searching for the right words. "There was a certain—breakdown in communications here in my headquarters. When we learned of these people's activities we attempted to shadow them and take certain steps to throw them off the scent and discourage them. You know how these things are. Orders pass down a chain. A few links in the chain turn out to be imperfect conductors of the current—information is garbled and there's an excess of zeal or a misunderstanding of instructions."

Emil's face was getting red; he was turning his back and his shoulders lifted defiantly.

The old man continued: "The young woman with Anders was killed. Not by my order, but it's happened. Like you with your accidents, I must take responsibility for mine. The killing of this unfortunate woman may

stir up the hornets in the nest. I've no doubt the search
will be intensified. Of course the girl may have been
simply Anders' lover but I doubt it, and it makes no
difference anyway. What has happened is tantamount
to what happens when a police officer is killed. The
department tends to drop everything else in the rush to
apprehend the cop-killer. We can expect a good deal of
pressure. For that reason I propose that you discontinue
further shipments and arms purchases for the time
being.''

Relief flooded him; he tried not to let it show.

The old man said, ''We must pull in our horns and
wait it out. Cover our tracks completely.''

''This killing—was it Luz?''

''No. You don't trust Luz, do you?''

''No, I never have.''

''You needn't be concerned about him. Luz obeys my
orders without question and without deviation. He will
continue to do so even if the orders come from beyond
the grave. Do you understand me?''

''Yes.'' The meaning was clear and it proved once
again the old man's shrewdness. After the old man died
Luz would deliver the safe-deposit key to Cielo and
Julio. The half million dollars: the house, the landing,
the fifty-foot boat. That was the leash to which Cielo
was tethered. That and his loyalty to this absurd old
man.

Then he understood something else. The anguish with
which the old man had skirted the issue of the CIA
woman's death, and the way Emil had flushed and
averted his face—it could only mean the woman had
been killed by young Emil, or by others at Emil's command.

Cielo said, ''It means postponing the attack on
Havana then.''

''It can't be helped. We must go to ground. Keep all
your men in the camp, don't let anyone out on furlough. Keep your radio receiver switched on at all times
and have a man monitor it twenty-four hours a day. If
we learn of any danger approaching you we'll give you
warning by radio, but you're to use it only for receiving

and you'll make no transmissions. Questions?''

"Harry Crobey—is he in charge of the investigation?''

"We don't know. My sources in the government are not master spies, you know. I acquire dribbles of information here and there. I know that Anders is a sort of troubleshooter for a department of the CIA headed by a gentleman named O'Hillary who seems to have all the earmarks of a clever and ambitious civil servant. Up to now the handling of the investigation of the Mexican kidnapping has been guided more by political considerations than by legalistic ones, but the murder of this girl may change that. We don't know yet. I don't have a private pipeline into the White House or the CIA's top echelons. I have only friends, here and there, with their ears to the ground. Of course I have friends on the police here in San Juan. They know about Anders well enough. They haven't been able to tell me very much about Crobey, however. He's here and he met with Anders—just before the girl died—but the nature of his official function is obscure. We're not even certain who he's working for. He told a police detective he'd come to Puerto Rico to scout film locations for a Hollywood director. That's patently ridiculous, of course, but it shows how little we've learned. There's a woman with Crobey, too—either an associate or a courtesan.''

"What's her name?''

"Marchant, I think. Or Marchand. Something like that.''

"Carole Marchand? She's the mother of the boy Emil killed.''

"Then perhaps that's who she is." The old man didn't seem interested. "I keep my lines open to the police, of course, and any information they have tends to filter back to me. But if Crobey is free-lancing we'll have no way to anticipate his movements.''

Cielo said, "Crobey's like a mamba. I know him—he's dangerous.''

"We'll see that he doesn't find you. Your job now is to go to ground and keep the others in the burrow with you. Don't communicate with Soledad.''

''I know that well enough,'' he said irritably.

''I'm sorry. Love of a woman often makes a man foolish. I'm fortunate to be so old. Pretty girls no longer turn my head.''

That wasn't true at all; the old man was only having his little joke as a way of easing the admonishment. There were always delectable girls around the old man. Cielo didn't like to think how they probably must service him.

''I wonder how they traced us here,'' Cielo said.

''I've no idea. But Puerto Rico's a big country. Let's just make sure they don't trace us any farther than they already have.''

''Will you have Anders and Crobey killed, then?''

''I haven't decided yet. The decision will depend on how close to us they come.''

Emil, throughout this, had wandered about the deck with his hands in his pockets. Cielo said, ''What about Emil? Do I take him with me?''

''No. Emil will remain here and go about his business as if nothing were amiss. His absence from this house might create suspicion.''

Cielo was relieved not to be harassed by Emil's presence; things in the camp would be tense enough without him.

Emil said, ''While you're waiting up there you might draw up the plans for the coup in detail. I'll have a look at them afterwards. This investigation will die away like they always do. When it does we'll make our final decisions. There's not going to be any more foot-dragging.''

The old man smiled. ''To the young everything must happen quickly.''

It was more than that, Cielo thought. Emil wanted to get the job done while the old man was still alive because only in that way could Emil be sure of securing the power he wanted for himself. The old man would see to it that Emil was looked after: Perhaps Emil even had designs on Castro's position. Without the old man there wouldn't be a prayer of that happening—Emil had no constituency. So he had to move fast.

All I have to do, Cielo thought, is delay things until the old man dies.

After that it would be possible to deal with Emil, because he could be isolated.

Emil watched him angrily: For an instant Cielo was afraid the youth had read his mind. Emil was clever in his brutal way.

The old man reached for the newspaper beside him. "Luz will drive you back. I know you'd prefer another chauffeur but Luz is the one I trust to make sure you're not followed."

On his way out of the house Cielo felt a measure of dulled contentment. The predicament now was in the old man's lap. The old man would die soon and everything would dwindle away—all Cielo had to do was go to ground and stay there.

Chapter 15

The message at the hotel desk advised Glenn Anders to call a phone number between four and six. He took it to be the number of a public telephone. He made the call from a booth in the lobby of the Sheraton; Harry Crobey answered on the fourth ring.

"We heard about Rosalia." It was, in its tone, sufficient expression of shared sorrow. Crobey's voice went on: "We should meet."

"I agree. Where and when?"

Crobey gave him instructions and Anders broke the connection. He made another call immediately, to the Department of Agriculture office where they'd given him a desk. The GS-8 on the front desk, a pale man whose name he kept having trouble remembering, exchanged identifying greetings with him and said, "We're all awful sorry about that young lady, Mr. Anders."

"Did Langley call back after I left?"

"No sir."

"No messages of any kind from O'Hillary?"

"There's a Telex, sir. Plain English. It's only a confirmation."

"Read it to me anyway."

"Yes sir. Message reads, 'Prior instructions remain in effect until further notice. No change in orders.' That's it, sir—just the signature."

"All right. Thanks."

He went outside with his hand on the flat automatic pistol in his pocket. There were taxis at the curb; he boarded the first one and rode it to the north gate of the university and paid it off there and walked through the campus, stopping twice to check behind him. Students milled about the lawns and a couple was necking under a palm tree; a fat youth sat on the grass reading a comic book. Anders drifted aimlessly among the buildings, going in and out, upstairs and down, from one building to another, staying within crowds when he could; he kept an eye on his watch and at exactly half past five he emerged from the south gate of the campus and walked a block to Calle de Diego where a taxi was just pulling up: Anders stepped in and the car pulled away and Crobey, on the other side of the seat, twisted around to look back through the window.

"Nobody came with me," Anders said.

"All right."

Crobey dismissed the taxi and they walked together through a dusty passage, bordered with scrubby bougainvillea and oleander; Crobey led him erratically through the turnings and kept looking back. No one was following them; Anders was beginning to be annoyed by the excessiveness of the precautions when Crobey led him out onto a paved street where a Ford Bronco waited at the curb with Carole Marchand behind the wheel. Anders tipped the passenger seat forward and climbed into the back; Crobey got in and Anders said, "Good evening."

"My condolences," she said, "and I mean that."

"Were you two followed last night?"

"Yes," Crobey said. "We shook them."

His hands wrenched at each other; he turned his stare out the window because he didn't want to cry again, not in front of them. "You know she was a little wacky, all right, she was far too young for the likes of me, none of it made any sense anyway—just a kid from the office they assigned to run errands for me. She was Cuban herself, you know. For a while I even suspected she might be a plant. Then after a while I didn't give a damn."

"Now you know she wasn't a plant," Carole Marchand said mildly.

No, he thought, actually he didn't know that at all. Maybe Rosalia had been the target after all—how could he be sure they weren't afraid she'd expose them?

Maybe they'd known she was falling in love with Anders. Maybe they'd killed her to keep her silent.

What he said was, "They're going to pay for it. I don't much care why they did it."

Then he thought, Pull youself together, you've got to be cold now. He needed dispassion. He said, "This bastard Cielo—presumably Rodriguez—bought some fairly heavy weapons from a dealer in Mayaguez. Mainly mortars and a couple of small artillery pieces. They were delivered to a farm. That's all the dealer knew about it—he took the money and delivered the merchandise. I ran a check on the serial numbers of the banknotes. They match the numbers on some of the ransom bills—if we need more confirmation of that kind. I had a look at the farm where he delivered the guns. Nothing there now, they've cleared out. Most likely they used it just once and they'll never use it again."

"Do you mind coming to the point?"

Anders said, "I reported to O'Hillary. A few hours later he got back to me. This is off the record now. Officially we're still engaged in the hunt for these terrorists. But unofficially my orders, as of noon today, are to lose the file down behind the file cabinet somewhere. You see the connection?"

"Right," Crobey said. "The arms buy makes our boy respectable."

"Spell it out for me," Carole Marchand commanded.

"They're picking up heavy ordnance," Anders said. "This buy will be one of dozens, I imagine. They'll spread the purchases around to avoid drawing too much attention. It begins to look like a major paramilitary operation. You can buy a lot of weapons for ten million dollars. O'Hillary's analysts likely have it sized up that Rodriguez shows every sign of intending to mount a well-equipped mobile striking force for an attack on Castro's headquarters."

"With a handful of men?"

"We don't know for sure how many men there are, do we? Anyhow look what the Israelis accomplished at Entebbe with a handful of troops. It's not numbers that count in a palace coup—it's tactics and planning. They could wipe out the Cuban leadership if they handle it with enough sophistication.''

She said, ''That's a farfetched extrapolation from a few flimsy clues, isn't it?''

''The agency works that kind of scenario all the time.''

''In other words O'Hillary thinks Rodriguez may have a chance of overthrowing Castro so he's ordering you to keep hands off?''

''It's one possibility.''

''It's what I thought all along,'' she said, ''more or less.''

''There's another possibility,'' Anders said. He felt so weary he could hardly get the words out. ''Your idea that there had to be someone here in San Juan with enough political clout to sic the local police on Harry—somebody with that much clout might also have enough influence in Washington to put pressure on the agency to soft-pedal the investigation.''

She said, ''And the murder of Rosalia—one of your own agents—doesn't even put a dent in those policies. You folks sure are expendable.''

Anders managed a lopsided hint of a smile; and Crobey said, ''Are you filing for a divorce from O'Hillary?''

''Not yet. Officially I'm still under orders to locate the terrorists. Locate 'em but keep hands off. Those are the orders I'm obliged to obey, aren't they? After we locate them—we'll see.''

Crobey said to Carole Marchand, ''The first rule is cover your ass. Glenn doesn't think of himself as a bureaucrat but it rubs off on everybody.''

''As opposed to Harry here, who's of pure and noble character,'' Anders said without heat. ''You're both missing the point. If I can show legitimate orders then I can maintain my freedom of action. There's no point going out of my way to shut off communications. I may as well keep making use of the apparatus as long as it's available to me. And to hell with O'Hillary's private instructions.''

"Watch closely, ducks, and you'll notice that amazingly enough, at no time do his hands leave his arms."

"As of now," Anders went on, feeling the anger rise within him, "I'm in this right up to my hairline. No more reservations. I want to nail these bastards and to hell with Fidel Castrol. Put a gun in my hand and Rodriguez in the sights—that should settle the question quick enough."

Something made a sudden noise—a slam of sound: The truck jiggled and Anders went into his pocket for his gun, whipping his eyes around—it was two kids: Their baseball had bounced off the truck fender.

"Jesus."

Crobey climbed out and the kids scuttled back. Crobey went along the curb and picked up the baseball. He talked in Spanish to the kids and tossed the baseball to one of them; the kids swallowed and nodded their heads and put their backs to him and ran like hell. Crobey got back into the truck. He glanced at Anders. "Shooting them wouldn't have done a whole lot for your image, Glenn."

Anders was rattled; it was clear to all of them; excuses or apologies wouldn't change it. He didn't really care. His future had been shot down last night with a bullet on the steps of El Convento. That had been his second chance; now he'd missed it. It was time to quit: Take early retirement and put O'Hillary out of his life and mark time in an Arizona suburb ranchette writing letters to the editor and taking up hobbies.

There was only one possible escape from that: The sense of justification he might derive from destroying the destroyers who'd taken Rosalia from him.

Crobey said mildly, "That house in the next block with the pink Pinto in the carport—that's Rodriguez's house."

"What?"

"He hasn't been back since that night he ditched your plainclothes cop," Crobey said. "Will you relax a little?" He tipped his head toward the house he'd indicated. "The wife's name is Soledad. They've got three girls, various ages, the oldest about fourteen I think. Or maybe twelve—kids grow up faster these days, don't they. The family name on the mailbox is Mendez. Ernesto Mendez, that's the name he goes by when he'd not being Cielo and/or Rodrigo Rodriguez.''

A battered camper-bodied pickup truck came crunching down the street, turned in at a driveway and let off a woman with her hair in yellow plastic curlers who began to unload brown grocery bags from the seat. Crobey's voice went on, droning in his ear with that faint Liverpudlian overlay: ''The neighbors believe him to be an adjuster for a casualty insurance company, which is a fair dodge because it explains his absences—he's away investigating claims. He belongs to a local National Guard regiment, the kind where they train every Thursday night and one weekend a month. A couple of old pals of mine have been asking questions around. They've come up with some interesting bits and pieces. This National Guard outfit has a little rat-pack of noncommissioned officers all of whom seem to have served with Mendez-Rodriguez at some unspecified time in the past, for which I tend to read Bay of Pigs. It turns out, on inquiry, that every last one of the members of this little rat-pack happens to be away on important business at the moment—extended business trips.''

''You've been busy. What else have you found?''

''We're still about thirty bricks short of a full load but we're getting there,'' Crobey told him. ''These two buddies who've been working for us on Carole's payroll have talked to several of the National Guardsmen in that outfit. Not rat-pack types but other chaps in the same unit. It seems the first lieutenant in command of that particular platoon is one Emil Draga, age twenty-four, graduate of the University of Florida at Coral Gables.''

''The name sounds familiar.''

''The family name ought to. Try this on—Jorge Vandemeer Draga-Ruiz.''

''Ah. The boy's father?''

''Grandfather. The old boy's pushing ninety.''

Anders looked at Carole Marchand. She hadn't

spoken for a long time. Between the bucket seats her hand lay across Crobey's; Anders marked that and drew its meaning. He said to her, "That could be the source of the police clout you were looking for."

"I know."

Carole Marchand said, "What if we asked him a few hard questions at the end of a gun?"

Anders smiled a little at her naïveté. "I'm sure that man's guarded by a security system as heavy as a medieval baron's moat. You'd never get within half a mile of him."

"We could get him to come to us," Crobey said.

"How?"

"Leave that aside a minute. The question is, if we get the old goat under a gun, do you go along with it or do you blow the whistle on us? He's a powerful old bastard. He's probably got four senators and a dozen congressmen in his pocket."

"And that's supposed to scare me off?"

"It's the kind of thing that'll cost you your job and your pension."

"I doubt that. These old Cuban families aren't that influential anymore. They've turned into White Russian emigrés—nobody pays that much attention to them."

"Draga's just a little bit different from most of them," Crobey said. "To the tune of maybe three hundred million dollars."

Anders kept glancing fitfully up the street toward the Mendez-Rodriguez house, reassuring himself that no one was going in or out. He said, "I'd be happier if we had better evidence the old man's involved. Suppose we get him under a gun, as you say—suppose he turns out to be the wrong man? Suppose he doesn't know anything about this business? We'll have made ourselves an enemy strong enought to blast us out of Puerto Rico permanently. Then what happens to the hunt for Rodriguez?"

Carole Marchand said, "Harry and I are willing to take the chance. We believe Jorge Draga has got to be the power behind Rodriguez."

"A minute ago you were accusing the CIA of jumping to conclusions on the basis of flimsy fragments.''

"All right, the shoe's changed feet—we bought your reasoning. Why shouldn't you buy ours?''

Anders picked at a ragged fingernail. Carole Marchand said, "You can get out of the car right now if you like. We'll do this by ourselves if we have to. But we're a little short of manpower and we could use your help. I thought, in view of what happened to Rosalia, you might be inclined to throw in with us. . . .''

The last of the day's sunlight was creepihg up toward the low roofs across the street. The two young baseball players had disappeared—gone inside for dinner, probably.

Crobey said, "The two blokes I've been using here are Cubans. They owe me favors and I've been collecting. But they hate Castro. I don't think we ought to depend on them to help us do anything except collect information. I'm sure they won't go up against Rodriguez in a firefight—there's a limit to their obligations to me. They wouldn't have strung along this far except that Carole's paying them good money. What I'm doing is giving you the full picture. Odds against. There's only the three of us, unless you can recruit people from the agency.''

"Not much chance of that. I couldn't do it without O'Hillary getting wind of it.''

Carole Marchand said, "Then it's just three of us. If you're in.''

"And just two of you if I'm not. What happens then? How can you fight him by yourselves?''

Her reply was a defiant stare.

"I think you're nuts." He looked at Crobey. "She's nuts. I never thought you were. What's in this for you? I hope it's enough to pay your funeral expenses.''

"Don't worry about it. I've arranged to sell my body to science.''

"Come on, Harry. If I buy in, how do I know you won't disappear when we need you?''

"I trust him," Carole Marchand said.

"Sure—but you're infatuated with him.''

It only made her smile, a reckless bawdy sort of grin. She was, he thought, a remarkably likable woman. Clearly she had captivated Crobey; and he found that to be an amazing thing.

Anders sighed out a long exasperated breath. His chin dropped toward his chest and he contemplated the veins in the backs of his hands. He made a few faces and glimpsed the tail ends of various rationalizations and in the end he said, "All right. How do we get our hands on Draga?"

Chapter 16

She felt cramped in the truck seat—too many hours of sitting. The night was muggy and the shirt was pasted to her; she felt unclean. She said, "What if someone has to pee?"

"You go in the bushes, ducks."

The armory was a low pink stucco shoebox. A high chainlink fence enclosed a paved yard on which squatted two dark green tanks, their cleated treads glistening under the lights, and several trucks and Jeeps. Beyond the armory the road rolled away through open fields.

Anders, in the back seat, yawned audibly. It was the only sound any of them made until Carole shifted in her seat to ease her rump. They had run out of conversation more than an hour ago.

Harry seemed imperturbable but she'd detected signs of unease in Glenn Anders. The death of the girl had unraveled his nerves.

Along both shoulders of the dusty road cars were parked—she'd counted forty-odd. Crobey had told her to ignore the rest; they were only interested in one of them. Nobody intended to start a fight with the entire platoon.

She felt conflicting pulls toward Anders. There was an urge to comfort him; but something else held her back—a lingering distrust. He was one of *them*, the *apparatchiks*. She dealt with his kind all the time: the people who ran the studios. A movie executive was a sorry creature whose guiding principle was fear: "Let's take another meeting. We want to keep our options open." Things were stalled forever by their dithering. And in the end the decision usually was negative; very few heads of production had ever been fired for turning down a project. It was always safer to say no. Soon Anders might begin to remember he was an organization man. He had never altogether forgotten it: *I'd be happier if we had better evidence.* . . .

Harry's hand dropped casually upon her shoulder and she tipped her cheek against his knuckles, wondering what would become of them.

There was a plan of sorts—she wasn't sure she had faith in it. The first step was to isolate the old tycoon and force information out of him. That was dicey, as Harry put it. But if they could pry the location of Rodriguez's hiding place out of the old man then they would keep the old man on ice while they made their way to what Harry with a straight face had designated as the Bad Guy's Hideout.

The weapon of Harry's choice was gas and they'd spent nearly twenty-four hours and the major part of Carole's cash to obtain cartons of Mace canisters, tear-gas grenades and the military handcuffs that now crowded the rear compartment of the Bronco beside Anders' seat. Ballistic arms were there as well—the light automatic guns Harry had been disassembling in Santana's house—but if they had to resort to those they would fail. The guns were only for defense: to cover a running retreat.

She stirred, lifted Harry's hand off her shoulder and tried to read the luminous dial of his diver's watch. "How much longer, for God's sake?"

"Settle down. This is *mañana* country. A couple hours of lectures and then the boys probably shoot a few racks of pool—most of them haven't got all that much to go home to."

It was frightfully hot, a night for long cool drinks; she squirmed in her sweat and poked her head half out the open window in the search for air. Below the truck a crowd of red ants were dragging a huge dung beetle stubbornly across the earth. She had done her hair up with a few pins in an attempt to leave her neck bare and cool but it hadn't helped. She desperately wanted a shower.

Harry had withdrawn his hand and she sat far over on her side of the seat, not so much watching the armory as thinking about Harry. It was always her tendency to expose the ludicrous side of things: Can you honestly picture yourself facing this man across the breakfast table every day for the rest of your life? If what she felt toward him was infatuation, what would happen when it wore out? God knew she was not at ease in Harry's world. She could not bear the thought of losing him—but what was the alternative? *Think about the derivation of that word "wedlock."*

Then she thought, *I am putting the cart ahead of an unborn horse.* But she had no pride left. She would demand that he marry her. Or at least live with her. It came to the same thing; in her tradition—inescapable— marriage was not an experiment but a contract. And now she felt like a Victorian belle—setting her cap for him.

And then what?

Abruptly she turned to face his profile. "Harry?"

"What, ducks?"

"You could be a stunt director."

"A what?"

"In the movies. Stunts. Airplanes, special effects. You know."

"I did that a couple of times. In Yugoslavia a few years ago. A guy I knew was making war pictures."

"Didn't you like it?"

"The truth. I love it. But I felt like a damn silly ass, play-acting at war."

"You were young then."

From the back seat Anders said with a nervous laugh, "Harry'll never be old."

But Harry kept his eyes on Carole, grave and gentle—she felt an outpouring of love: She touched his cheek fondly. She was thinking that in nature, no matter what the species, only one male in a hundred was any good. *I'm not about to let him go.* And to hell with the impossibility of it.

Harry said, "If that's a job offer I think I'll take it.
This was going to be my last caper anyhow, wasn't it?"

She breathed, "Oh, Harry!"—like an ingenue; and
threw herself into his arms.

"Heads up," Glenn Anders said, very mild. "Here
they come."

Entangled with Harry she twisted her head to bring
the armory into her field of vision. Men emerged in
clusters, all of them in fatigues. A good deal of talk;
some calling back and forth, good nights and *hasta
luegos*. She straightened in the seat in abrupt alarm.
"How do we know which one he is?"

"He'll be wearing a silver bar," Harry said.
"Scrunch down a little."

She slid down in the seat until she could barely see
over the rim of the windowsill. Anders hissed, "I don't
see him!"

"Give him time."

The soldiers were separating, going to their cars.
Right in front of the Bronco the battered ruin of a
pickup truck started up, flicked on its headlights and
gnashed away down the two-lane. By ones and twos the
Guardsmen climbed into vehicles and the parking
shoulders gradually emptied, streams of red tail-lights
retreating in both directions. No one paid any attention
to the Bronco. After five minutes nothing was left on
the road shoulder except a glossy Trans Am with
discreet racing stripes, parked directly opposite the entrance to the armory.

Anders said, "I guess he didn't come to the meeting
then." Was it relief in his voice?

"Wait it out," Harry said.

"That's the only car left. It must belong to the night
guard."

"No. Leave a car alone on this road overnight and
you'd come out in the morning and find you didn't have
any tires or battery. The night guard's car must be
parked inside the compound."

"That's a point."

The scheme had been to follow the car and, given the
opportunity, run it off the road and trap the driver. Ap-

parently that no longer was going to be necessary—if in fact the Trans Am didn't belong to a watchman.

The armory door opened. Harry tensed beside her and she heard a quiet click behind her—Anders getting out a pair of handcuffs.

For a moment the man stood silhouetted in the open doorway—she had an impression of size: big shoulders, a squarish head, legs too short for the powerful torso. Then the door closed and the man came down the steps under the exterior light; she saw then that he was quite young. The lights glinted off the insignia on the collar of his fatigues.

"My God in Heaven," Glenn Anders whispered. *"Him!"*

"What?"

"That's the guy. That's the guy who killed her."

Harry paused with his hand on the door handle. "Nothing stupid now, Glenn."

"What? Come on—let's go, what's holding you up?"

"We don't want him dead," Harry said in a firm but quiet way.

The big youth was crossing the street toward the Trans Am, tossing a casual glance at the Bronco. He took car keys out of his pocket and stooped to find the lock in the door.

Harry was out of the Bronco by then; Anders clambered over the tilted driver's seat and squeezed out after him, hurrying. Carole felt everything tighten—muscles, gut, throat. She saw the big young man recognize the gun in Harry's fist and straighten up beside the car, going bolt still, his face rising into the light—fear, but defiant stoic acceptance with it.

Anders was moving in fast from one side and Harry spoke quickly, harshly: "Glenn." Anders slowed down and looked back briefly—a head-shaking frown like a puzzled baffled bull.

"Easy."

The big youth's eyes flicked back and forth from one to the other. He looked once toward the armory and she thought he might yell but Harry spoke again, his words too soft to reach her ears this time, and the youth slowly deflated. Anders was right beside him then and she found she was holding her breath expecting a shot from Anders' pistol but he only showed the handcuffs to the young man and the youth slowly turned around and crossed his wrists behind his back, staring into the muzzle of Harry's revolver.

Anders fitted the handcuffs onto him and propelled the prisoner into the back seat of the Trans Am and then Harry crowded Anders aside and climbed in alongside the prisoner. Anders spoke—some sort of objection— and Harry must have answered him from within the car, for Anders threw his head back and she saw his chest rise and fall with a full slow breath. Then Anders looked back at her, at the Bronco, and made a vague signal with his hand: He managed to convey both instructions and bitterness with that gesture; then he got into the driver's seat of the Trans Am and pulled the door shut. The exhaust puffed smoke and the lights come on.

Trembling, Carole turned the key. The Trans Am rolled away and she put the Bronco in gear and followed it.

She still didn't know the way; she had to follow closely through the forest. Ahead of her the Trans Am, low-slung and sporty, bottomed several times in the ruts—she heard the clanking. The Bronco pitched her around on its hard springs but she had no trouble handling it and her only moments of fear came when, for brief intervals, she lost sight of the car's red lights in the deep woods ahead. Each time, however, Anders waited for her. Then finally they were running down the bumpy track into Santana's yard.

By the time she'd parked Harry and Anders had the prisoner out of the car. She saw that Harry had tied a black cloth blindfold over his eyes. The big youth stumbled as they guided him across the weedy ground and hustled him inside. She followed them in through the back door and the kitchen.

In the front room Santana switched off the television and looked at them all with a commendable lack of visible surprise. Santana must have been out in the fields; he smelled of it. He stood picking sunburnt skin shreds from his nose.

Harry said, "You probably won't want to know about this." And Santana with a shrug and a nod picked up his can of beer and left the house.

Anders went around turning off all the lights except one in the kitchen, which threw enough light into the front room to see by. When Anders came back into the front room he was trembling visibly, anger coursing through him and flooding his face with color.

The prisoner, head high, hands shackled, waited with tight-mouthed endurance. The black velvet over his eyes gave him a slightly comical look—like a blindfold trick-shooting act in a county-fair carnival.

Harry said, "In here," and turned the prisoner toward the door of the cell Carole had been using as a bedroom.

She waited at the door while Anders went in past her; she stood in the doorway to watch, too ambivalent about this to enter the room. Harry looked up at her—he had sat the prisoner down on the cot and was locking another pair of handcuffs, fastening the youth's ankle to the crossleg of the cot. It wouldn't prevent him from hobbling around but it would be an unpleasant anchor to drag—no chance he'd get far with that hanging from his foot.

Harry took a wallet out of the pocket of the young lieutenant's fatigues. He looked through it and held it up so Anders could see it. Anders' face never changed; it was as if he feared any shift in expression might break the tenuous skein of his spurious dispassion.

The young man was making surreptitious attempts to explore his boundaries: a tug and shift of the shackled ankle, sly shiftings of hip and elbow. He said, "Do you people know who I am?"

"Emil Draga." Harry tossed the wallet into the young man's face. It was a gentle toss but Emil Draga, blindfolded, jerked away from it violently, almost upsetting the cot.

"How much ransom do you plan to get for me?" It was mostly a snarl.

Harry got to his feet. Anders watched him: "You going to make the phone call?"

"Maybe we won't need to."

"Now there's a thought." Anders thrust his automatic pistol toward Emil Draga. "Maybe you're right."

"Why don't you stop waving that thing at him? He can't see it and you're not going to use it until we've found out what we want to know."

Anders didn't lower the pistol. "Ask him fast, then."

Carole said, "You'd better take it away from him," to Harry, and afterward she was surprised because she had no doubt he could.

Anders looked at her—a wry sour face—and then at Harry, who only stood there monolithically; Anders put the pistol in his pocket with a rueful show of reluctance. "Ask him now," he said again, and stalked out of the room.

Under the black blindfold Emil Draga had a waxen and slightly concave face—ugly but shrewd and arrogant, a rich youth who must have learned early that everything had a price and could be purchased— probably the only sexual love he'd ever had was the kind you bought.

"I suppose you people know what the penalty for kidnapping is."

Carole said, "Maybe you should have thought of that before you kidnapped—"

"Let us handle this part, ducks."

"All right." She propped her shoulder against the wall, folded her arms and smiled at Harry to show her trust. "I'd just as soon be watching this part from an airplane anyway."

Emil Draga blurted, *"Who the fuck are you people?"*

Carole only watched Harry; and Harry shook his head, mute. The whole scheme was Harry's: *We'll keep him blindfolded throughout. For one thing we don't want to put Santana in jeopardy, do we. For another thing if the kid knows anything we'll want to get it out of him. Deprive a man of one of his senses and he'll begin to go up the walls pretty fast. The blindfold stays on.*

The plan had been to telephone the old millionaire and force him to come out of his lair. But that was before Anders had identified Emil Draga as one of Rosalia's killers. If he was that deeply involved then he probably knew everything and that suggested there might be no need to drag the old millionaire into this.

Abruptly Harry said, *"Draga!"*

The youth almost leaped off the cot. He tried to control his trembling.

Harry let the silence run on. Anders came back into the room and stood just inside the door with his hands in his pockets and his face closed up tight. He'd gone outside to collect himself; but he'd been unable to stay away. His eyes ran around, alighting fitfully on Harry, on herself, on the blindfolded prisoner.

"What do you want from me?"

When Emil Draga got no answer to that he began to shout. Tendons corded his neck and he screamed obscenities until Harry stepped forward calmly and slapped him hard across the ear.

Emil Draga fell across the cot, struggled back to a sitting position and snapped his mouth shut, breathing hard and fast through his nose. He was, she saw, a youth who probably had the battlefield sort of courage—he could run screaming right into the guns—but he'd never had to learn endurance. And there was the torture of anticipation. . . .

She turned away, not wanting to watch this, but Harry said, "You'd better stay," and she understood: This was on her account and he meant her to accept the responsibility.

Anders said in a chilly voice, "I guess it's time we had a word with this citizen." With a deliberation that shocked her Anders stepped forward, leaned down and slammed the barrel of his pistol against Emil Draga's shin.

The youth screamed.

Anders stepped back, pocketing the gun. Harry gave

him an unpleasant look but didn't speak.

Anders lifted shaking fingers and ran them through his hair.

Emil Draga began to flay about him wildly with his free leg. He flung his torso off the cot and crashed painfully onto the floor and scrabbled about like a half-crushed beetle until Harry's toe slammed him in the ribs and Harry bellowed something at him and the youth curled up fetally, cringing, trying to hide his head between his knees, the cot overturned across his legs.

Harry let him whimper for a while and then got down and unlocked the ankle cuff from the cot. He set the cot back in place and beckoned to Anders. Between them they lifted Emil Draga to his feet.

Harry motioned with his head toward the door and they man-handled Emil Draga outside, the loose handcuff clattering behind his right foot.

Feeling nauseous, Carole followed them across the front room into the kitchen, where Anders held Emil Draga upright while Harry plugged the stopper into the sink and began to pump water into it.

Immediately she understood, without having to be told, what they had in mind; she turned her face away and stared at the gray television screen.

Somehow she comprehended without the need of explanation that it was in their minds to break him first—then ask questions. Unprepared, he would have no opportunity to rehearse lies.

They were torturing Emil Draga by depriving him of basic sensory information. Harry was right, it was astonishingly effective: It was working on her—and she wasn't even blindfolded.

Harry's mouth was screwed up in an expression of sour distaste. Two things amazed her: that he was capable of this, and that having learned the capacity he nonetheless took no pleasure from it. It was something essential she'd learned about him: Harry was hard but there wasn't a shred of sadism in him.

But Glenn Anders. . . . Anders looked on with his lips peeled back from his teeth, a burning intensity in his eyes: She'd never seen the hunger for revenge written so clearly on a human face. The eager glow sickened her. *A week ago did I look like that?*

Harry abandoned the pump handle. A final gush flowed into the sink—it was about two thirds filled.

Emil Draga said in a dull voice from which all feelings had been sucked, "Please—what do you want?"

Anders snapped, "Before long you're going to be geting your emissions from dreaming that this is over. Well it's never going to be over, I promise you—it's never going to finish. You're in Hell, Lieutenant."

"Why—*why?*"

But Anders only grinned unseen.

Harry made a harsh gesture: *Calm down, get a grip on yourself*.

Harry took Emil Draga from behind by both shoulders and pushed him gently forward until he stood facing the sink with his belly two feet from its rim. He moved to one side to position himself; Anders stepped in behind Emil Draga and hooked both hands strongly in Draga's web belt. Draga stiffened, utterly rigid.

"Spread your feet out," Harry said mildly.

When Draga didn't move Anders kicked his Achilles' tendon, not hard but it was enough to provoke reluctant co-operation: Draga slid his foot out to one side, then the other foot until he stood splayed, hands flicking open and shut in the manacles, head whipping back and forth and breath sawing through him. Then Harry's fist slammed into his gut.

It doubled him over. A gasp, a little cry—not so much pain as dread—the breath punched out of him and his head poised over the sink and that was when Harry shoved him down into the sink face-first.

Draga struggled every way he could but there was no chance—he was pinioned by four strong arms and had no way to get loose. Carole gripped the doorjamb with both hands and pushed her face into it and clenched her eyes shut, hearing Anders' tremulous voice: "Amazing how a man can drown in just a few inches of water, ain't it."

In the end she was unable not to look. The silent struggle had abated; Draga's body was lurching with the heaves of choked nausea and he'd slumped so that the only thing holding him up was Anders' powerful two-handed grip on his web belt.

Harry lifted him by the epaulets, pulling his face out of the water. Draga blurted water from his mouth and nose. A choking cough; wheezing to suck air back into him—eyes popping, mouth working, panic.

The sounds he made were so agonized that she had to leave. She stumbled into the front room, fell across the couch and covered her ears with both hands.

But the not knowing got to her and she turned her face to listen.

Draga was coughing now—a painful wheeze, a sucking gasp.

Then Harry: even-voiced, firm, giving away nothing. "I'll ask a question once. You've got one second to answer and then you go back in the water and you stay there twice as long next time. Are you listening? *Where's Cielo?*"

A mutter, then a cough; then, "El Yunque."

Anders was pacing back and forth, shoulders jerking with each turn. Harry sat at the table leaning over the topographical map. Sitting on the couch with her elbows on her knees she held the glass of rum in both hands and sucked at it. The door to the bedroom cell stood open and she could see one of Emil Draga's feet at the end of the cot: They'd manacled him there, flat on his belly with his hands cuffed together under the cot. The chloral hydrate capsule would keep him unconscious for at least a few hours.

Anders said irritably, "It's no good using a helicopter. They'd spot it."

"And nothing with wheels. It's got to be on foot," Harry said.

Carole shuddered. She spilled a few drops of rum and wiped ineffectually at her shirt.

Harry picked up on it. "Sorry ducks but you're in that part of the world now."

"I'll be all right."

"Sure. I know you will." Harry watched her a

moment longer and went back to his map and put his finger on it again. "The farm's here. The track goes back into the hills from there. There'll be false trails and it'll take us a while but we'll have to get all the way back in there and scout them out. We can't decide how to handle them before we know the position and the defenses. He said there are fourteen men—but suppose they've recruited more?" Harry glanced toward Emil Draga's door. "Someone's got to keep him on ice. That'll be you, ducks. Take out whatever guards they've got on the place, seal up their exit route and Glenn and I will go in on foot while you sit on our friend there."

She said, "You've been looking for an excuse to leave me behind, haven't you?"

"Use your head, ducks. You're hardly a veteran guerrilla. And we've got to keep little Emil and those guards locked up and fed until this is done."

"I don't see why we have to wait hand and foot on them," Anders said. "Remember what they did to Rosalia."

"When we get the job done," Harry said, "you can take your choice of turning Emil Draga over to Castro along with the rest of the bunch or delivering him to the police and testifying against him for the murder. If you don't mind going up against the Draga interests in court. That'll be up to you—but you try putting this lady's neck on the block and I'll find things to do to you."

Anders put his head down. "I'm sorry. Wasn't thinking."

"You're doing a lot of that right now, Glenn. Not thinking."

"Don't worry about it. I'll cool down." Anders trudged into the kitchen; she heard him filling a glass from a bottle. Harry began to roll up the map.

She sat behind the wheel of the Bronco with the revolver in her lap and tried to ignore the sensation that Emil Draga, handcuffed to a chain in the back seat, was burning holes in her back with his eyes.

Farmland rolled away in all directions and the mountains lifted soft and green under the bellies of the clouds. Harry and Anders had been gone a long time. She kept looking at her watch. *Get hold of yourself.*

She twisted the rear-view mirror to get a better view of Emil Draga. Blindfolded still, he sat groggily with his head slack against the window, mouth open. The drug was half worn off and in another thirty minutes he'd be alert.

She was going to have to get used to being his jailer. She tried to steel herself.

On the horizon a smoke-chuffing tractor moved very slowly, pulling some sort of harvesting machine. She could see the driver's tiny silhouette and wondered if he would become curious about the vehicle parked by the fence. He was a good quarter-mile away and she hoped his curiosity wouldn't be sufficient to goad him into crossing the distance.

After a time the tractor went out of sight. A few fine drops of rain touched the windshield. She thought about switching on the radio for company but decided against it; it might awaken Draga. She didn't want to have to converse with him.

She covered her eyes with tinted glasses and tipped her head over against the frame of the door. The few droplets were all; a false alarm—the cloud moved on, the windshield dried. Ten minutes more and the sun poked through.

She heard him stirring behind her and looked up in quick alarm but he was only shifting position. His head lolled to the left and he uttered a somnolent murmur, something in Spanish and too slurred for her to guess at it.

Tensions and anxieties had drained her of the will to think. She tried to see ahead but preoccupation with the present kept crowding everything else aside. A kind of hyperacuity had infected her, sensitizing her to every signal: the flight of a bird from a tree, the shuddering tempo of Draga's breathing, the smells of farming, the very motionlessness of the truck seat.

A figure approached on foot—Harry, there was no mistaking his limp even at a distance. He emerged from

the trees and waved her forward and she started it up
and drove bumping across the field, Draga awakening
and grumbling in the back seat with petulant loqua-
ciousness. He was still talking in Spanish when she
stopped the truck and Harry opened her door.

"Everything's fine. There was one man—he decided
not to fight the drop. Glenn's got him under cover."

"Get in, then."

"No hurry." He offered his hand and helped her
down. Looking in at Draga he said, "He'll keep," and
walked her away—a copse of trees, a hummock of grass
in the shade. It was hot but she was getting used to the
sticky closeness of the climate.

She understood right away that he wanted to be alone
with her here because they'd have no chance once they
joined Anders. She turned toward him. Her hands
touched his shirt, shyly, and slid up to the back of his
neck.

There was no heat in it; it was only a touching of lips,
very light, but she needed his touch, needed to draw
strength from him. They sat down on the earth with
their backs against the same tree and leaned against each
other, shoulder to shoulder. Harry crooked his good leg
and looked at the bottom of his shoe. "These are the
times that try men's bootsoles." There was muck
smeared on it.

She took off her sunglasses and swung them back and
forth by one earpiece. "What's the program?"

"We'll backpack a few gas grenades. If it looks
promising we'll try to knock them out. Otherwise we'll
pull back to the farm and think about raising rein-
forcements."

"From whom?"

"I can maybe call in a few friends and acquaintances
from various ports. It'd cost you some money."

"Wouldn't it be safer to do that first?"

"Ducks, we don't know how long Rodriguez is going
to sit up there on the mountain. He could bug out any
time."

"Don't be too heroic, Harry. I can only take nobility
in small doses. You were the one who used to keep in-

sisting the wages didn't include walking into the jaws of death.''

"There won't be any trouble."

"You're lying and I love you for it but I don't believe it."

"Then I'll lay it out for you. There's a good chance they've got some central gathering place up there. A tent, a cave, a hut, whatever. There'll be one or two men on guard and we'll have to take them out. Then we find the camp and we wait for all of them to congregate. If it's an enclosed space we're all right. We hit 'em with tear-gas grenades and exploding canisters of chemical Mace. In less than ten seconds that stuff disables a man completely. It takes him quite a while to function again and by that time we'll have handcuffs on them. It'll work if we can take out the guards without alerting the camp, and it'll work if Draga's told us the truth and there's only a dozen or fourteen men up there."

"Have you counted the ifs in that?"

"If it doesn't work out that way we'll pull back."

"Promise me."

"I'm not a fool, ducks. Sure."

"How far is it? To the camp."

"Not too far as the buzzard flies but we may waste a while chasing false leads. I've tracked VC through country thicker than this—if they're up there I'll find them but I don't want you to come apart at the seams if I'm not back right away. Give it a couple of days before you start to panic. On the morning of the third day you're on your own. How do you feel about this?"

"Scared."

Harry nodded. "That's the right answer."

"Maybe it's like what Mark Twain said about Wagner: It isn't as bad as it sounds."

"You just need to worry about two things, ducks. Keep on eye on the mountain because if anyone besides Glenn and me comes down that hill it means you're in trouble. Get in the Bronco and run for it—forget everything, just run. Head for the federal building in San Juan and don't stop till you get there."

The unspoken addendum was that if the terrorists

came down the mountain it would mean Harry and Anders were dead because that was the only way Rodriguez was going to get through them.

He said, "And the other thing's your charges there. You've got two prisoners to look after and they'll try every trick they can think of to get loose, especially when they realize they're being held by a woman alone. Keep them ankle-shackled to water pipes in separate rooms. Spoon-feed them but never undo the handcuffs behind their backs. You listening to me? Keep the revolver cocked and if you're even a little bit uncertain of their intentions start shooting. You've got five loads and you may as well burn them all up because one of them's bound to knock the man down if you keep plugging in his direction. Are you going to get gun-shy and not pull the trigger?"

"No."

"Remember this: If you get humane and one of them gets away, all three of us are dead. There's not a chance in a thousand that Rodriguez hasn't got a radio receiver up there on the mountain. If Emil Draga or the watchman gets away from you they'll head for the nearest phone and we'll be finished."

"I understand."

In a different voice he said, "Do you regret it, ducks?"

"Doing this? No, I don't think so. I regret that it has to be done."

"You're not wrought up anymore. Not the way Glenn is."

"I haven't forgotten my son if that's what you mean."

He said bluntly, "Your son's dead whether or not we go through with this."

"But Rodriguez is free. Until we do it."

"Which is it then—revenge or justice?"

She shook her head. "God knows. It's not an obsession—but it's a compulsion. Does that make any sense?"

"Bet your bottom," he agreed.

"Harry, tell me something."

"All right."

"After this—after it's done—are we going to be able to make it together?"

"Why, ducks," he said, "do you know, I expect we will."

Harry swung the Bronco into the caved-in barn and they got Emil Draga out and took him across to the house and at the door Harry could not resist his moment of wistful comedy: He took a step backward and bowed over his extended leg with a minuet flourish. Then he kicked Emil Draga in the rump and sent him inside asprawl.

Anders, holding the door open, made a face. Glancing at him as she came past into the house, Carole suppressed a shiver. Anders' eyes had gone peculiar and she was disturbed by it: She said, "Harry, you'd better show me around," using it as an excuse to get him away from Anders.

Harry took her through the house. It was ramshackle—a bigger and more substantial place than Santana's but it had the same smell, the same taste. In the kitchen—she was relieved to see running water—she said under her breath, "Glenn's got a wire down in him, Harry. Don't trust him."

"I'm keeping an eye on him. But I want him with me, not with you."

She clutched him then, squeezed until her arms gave out. "Promise me you'll come back."

"I promise, ducks."

Part Five

Chapter 17

There was rain. In the cave Cielo sat on a crate chewing on a pencil and watching it flood down like a beaded string-curtain. The radio stuttered at him—a lightning bolt not too far away interrupted the message entirely with a burst of static and then the thunder deafened him to another few words but he had the gist of the message and Julio, switching it off at the end of the transmission, sat back against the wheel of the howitzer and said, "I wonder what drew them off?" According to the wireless message "Butch and Sundance and Etta" had vanished. But Butch hadn't checked out of his hotel. Did that mean Glenn Anders intended to return shortly?

It was unnerving. He felt entrapped, not only by isolation but also by unknowing.

Julio sat absorbed in something on the jacket of which was painted a lurid creature that looked a bit like a feathered octopus with the head of a vulture, its hues running from silver to electric orange.

Cielo was getting hungry but he wasn't quite ready to brave the downpour across the distance to the chow tent. It would require a change of boots afterward and he wasn't sure the others had dried out from the morning's storm. Fifteen years ago he'd have taken such discomforts as a matter of course but the passage of years had taught him that there were all kinds of ways to prove one's manhood and that in the end nobody cared much anyway. By now dry feet were more important than demonstrating he was unafraid of the squall.

He awakened stiff from having lain with his bones on the rock cave floor. The rain had quit. Still daylight; he checked the time: 4:10. So he hadn't slept that long, really. He glanced at Julio. "Want to get something to eat?"

Julio spoke without looking up from his book. "You have an uncanny talent for interrupting me right at the crucial point." He held up the book so that Cielo could see he was within a very few pages of the end.

Cielo picked up his rifle and went to the mouth of the cave. He had brought down two rabbits with the rifle yesterday, for the pot; he was a hell of a marksman and it was one of the things he still took pride in. The rifle wasn't a military weapon. It was his indulgence: a Mossberg #800 chambered for 6.5mm Magnums—a walnut Monte Carlo stock and a 6X riflescope sight. Sometimes he used its telescope to look at parrots in the treetops. He never shot one.

He stood a while in the shadows at the side of the cave mouth searching the trees. Right after a rain was a good time to spot birds: They came out to clean themselves and scout for food that might have been exposed by the storm.

Broken clouds sailed by overhead but high above them hung a fat roll of cumulonimbus and he knew there would be more rain. He'd had enough rain up here in the past few days to last him the rest of his life. He knew the rest of the men felt the same way. If the radio didn't terminate their restrictions soon there would be trouble in the camp. The men were already picking at each other.

Something stirred at the corner of his eyeline. He looked that way, casually curious—saw a man lift himself from the ground and move crabwise, jinking from cover to cover.

¡Chingado!

But he didn't move— didn't want to alert the man. Over his shoulder and very softly he said, "Julio."

In a moment, alerted by his tone, Julio was behind his left shoulder. Cielo said, his voice dropping almost out of hearing, "Look half left. See the acacia? Just beneath it. Wait for him to move again—"

"I see him." Something clicked in Julio's hands—the

Uzzi, probably; it had been near at hand.

"No shooting yet." Cielo lifted the Mossberg and fitted his eye to the scope socket. The rain forest came right up close and he had to play it around before he found the target. Behind him Julio was sidling away toward the far side of the cave—standard defense posture: Never give the enemy a bunched target.

How did he get in here past the road guard? Who was on the road this shift? Santos, yes. If Santos fell asleep on his post. . . .

The face of the enemy came into focus and Cielo recognized it and was not surprised. Harry Crobey— submachine gun, grenade belt, backpack.

Crobey was working his way down toward the tents. Cielo took a moment to think it out. It was no good shouting at him to surrender; Crobey would fade into the forest in half a second if he had a chance. On the other hand it was no good killing him cold; there were things Cielo needed to learn from him.

Let him know he's zeroed in. Harry won't fight the drop. Deciding, Cielo turned and made a down-pushing motion for Julio's benefit and Julio nodded, lowering the muzzle of the Uzzi, relaxing. Cielo took aim through the 'scope and flicked off the thumb safety and fired with casual ease. The racket of the gunshot was earsplitting because of the echoing walls of the cave.

The bullet banged off the treetrunk against which Harry Crobey had paused. Cielo stepped out into the open, jacking another cartridge into the chamber, shouldering the rifle again and training it so that Crobey could see the telescope and measure his chances. Over to one side Julio walked out showing the Uzzi.

Cielo saw Crobey's eyes move from one to the other. A heavy bleakness hooded Crobey's lids; he stood up with slow resignation, dropping the submachine gun out to one side.

"Come on up, Harry."

With Crobey limping between them they went down into camp and ushered him into the radio tent. Since they'd moved the radio up to the cave to protect it from the cloudbursts the tent had fallen into disuse. It was a good place to have a private talk with Crobey.

Some of the others had heard the shot and come outside to have a look. It was starting to rain again—big slow drops; in a few moments it would pour. The men clustered around. Crobey had trained most of them and there were a few hesitant smiles until Cielo said, "Scatter yourselves. Martin, go down the road and see what's become of Santos. Villasenor—a couple of you scout up through there, find out if he was alone. Look for tracks."

Vargas loomed. "Harry?"

"Hello, Vargas. Time you went on a diet, innit?" Crobey grinned—or grimaced.

Cielo pushed him into the radio tent. Julio came in after him and held the Uzzi on him while Cielo stripped him of backpack and grenade belt. Looking through the backpack Cielo discovered a dozen pairs of handcuffs. He used two of them on Crobey and when the prisoner was snugged down Cielo said, "I didn't think you'd turn against us, Harry."

"I didn't think you'd take up murdering innocent hostages," Crobey replied.

Cielo made a face; he'd had a feeling that might come back to haunt them. "An accident," he said, feeling a need to set the record straight. "It wasn't our doing. An outsider—a mishap."

"Emil Draga?"

A shrewd guess, Cielo thought, but only a guess. It didn't surprise him that Crobey knew the name. Crobey had been born a few minutes ahead of the rest of the world. Cielo fixed a dismal stare on him. "You seem calm about this."

"Well I might throw a fit and tear my hair if I thought it would help any. Is this all you've got? Eleven chaps? Hardly seems enough for an invasion of Havana."

"How many of you out there?"

Crobey said, "That's for you to find out." He was smug.

Cielo poked around in the backpack. Chemical Mace.

The grenades on the web belt weren't fragmentation, they were tear gas. The only thing Crobey had been carrying by way of a deadly weapon had been the submachine gun; there were only two thirty-round spare magazines for it in Crobey's belt.

So he wasn't prepared for a firefight.

Cielo brooded at his prisoner. Crobey smiled cheerfully back but Cielo wasn't ready to be fooled by it. Crobey was clever that way and the smile could mean anything.

"May as well give it up," Crobey said. "You've been found, haven't you?"

"Who told you to look for us here?"

"I found it in a horoscope."

Julio was nervous. "What shall we do?"

"Man the radio. If there's a force after us we'll be told of it. Post a few men in the forest—give them rain slickers. Spread everyone else out. And stay by the radio. Go on—leave me the Uzzi."

"Shouldn't we get out of here?"

Cielo watched Crobey's face. "I don't think there's any need, Julio. I think he came alone—I think he's on his own. Working for the mother of that dead boy."

Crobey grinned at him and Cielo had to smile back; Crobey had that sort of infectious way.

"How can you know this?"

"Look how he came armed. He wanted to wait till we all sat down to supper—then pop a few gas canisters into the tent and put handcuffs on us all. Harry always liked to be a one-man air force, remember? Now he's a one-man army." Cielo shook his head in mock disappointment. "We're all much too old for this, Harry. Five or ten years ago you wouldn't have exposed yourself that way."

"You're probably right about that," Crobey agreed.

"Go on, Julio. I'll be all right."

"But—"

"Am I the leader here?" he demanded.

"But what if you're wrong?"

"I'm not wrong, am I, Harry?"

Crobey only smiled; finally Julio departed.

Cielo said, "You'd like us to panic and clear out, wouldn't you. Then you could confiscate our little arms dump and put a stop to our intentions quietly, no fuss, no headlines—the proper way to support the détente between Washington and Havana. Where's Glenn Anders, Harry?"

If the question surprised Crobey he gave no sign of it. "I don't know," he said.

"When did you see him last?"

"I don't rightly recall."

"I suppose I wouldn't answer questions either if I were sitting where you're sitting. It won't help you to talk, will it—you have to assume we'll kill you either way."

"You won't kill me right away," Crobey said. "I might come in handy as a hostage."

Chapter 18

She soaked small wads of cotton in the last of the witch hazel and placed them on her eyes and tried to relax. She'd only slept in fits and starts for the past two nights and it looked as if this one would be no different. At midnight she'd gone around the house checking the restraints on the two prisoners—Emil Draga in the front room and Stefano, who was small and ruddy and middle-aged and not frightening at all, in the bedroom. He had a fuzzy mustache and comical buck teeth and a wart on his lip and he told amusing stories about his family in south Florida. It was Stefano who had told her the sequence of incidents that had climaxed in Robert's death.

And these, she thought, were the terrorists who had so exercised her.

She had spent a great deal of the past twenty-four hours resisting what Stefano had told her. She did not want to believe any of it and it was quite possible Stefano was lying: He had every reason to coat the truth with opaque paint. He claimed he didn't know which man had actually shot Robert.

Robert. . . .

Before dark she had made sure all the lights were extinguished. Now, making her hourly rounds, she carried the revolver into the front room and had a look at Emil Draga. The smell of his sweat clouded the room. He seemed asleep. She went back to the kitchen. The waiting had gone far past dragging on her nerves; it had numbed her. She drank coffee and sat with her hands flat on the table, drooping in the humid heat, listening to the rain drum against the roof. It must be two or three in the morning. She had the jitters but attributed that to the coffee; fatigue prevented her from stirring. This afternoon she'd gone into the bathroom and studied herself in the mirror and judged she must have added a minimum of five years to her visible age in the past week's time. *I look older than Harry does.*

It didn't matter. She'd taken three showers today but nothing helped. She felt sticky—the heat perhaps, but a Freudian would have found interesting speculations in that persistent feeling of uncleanness. *You see, Doctor, I feel like Lady Macbeth.*

Was it possible that one day—if she lived to be old enough—she would be able to forget this nightmare aberration? The absurdities of it piled up one upon the next and she could not cope with them any longer. She cast a dulled eye at the coffee cup between her hands. *Harry, come back here and take me away from all this. I'll show you Las Vegas and Palm Springs and we'll never be without Dewar's and cologne and clean sheets again.*

It had gone beyond the unreality of a dream. It had become the unreality of a failed movie: The kind where the director, the producer, the writer and each player in the cast had a completely different notion of what the movie was about. The sort of movie—*A Touch of Class* came to mind—that started out as a farce and ended up a dreary melodrama.

Something alerted her. She snatched up the gun and went to the window, stumbling against the sink in the dark. Nothing out there but blackness; the rain pummeling the house. She felt her way to the corridor and looked both ways. She'd left the twenty-five-watt light burning in the hall closet, the door open two inches, and it threw a bit of light both ways, enough to see the hall was empty. She looked in the bedroom: Stefano smiled, his buck teeth glistening in the soft light. She went on to the front room and Emil Draga was tugging petulantly at the handcuffs and he wasn't going to strip them off over those big knobby hands and she left him to it, prowling back through the house, wondering if perhaps it hadn't been merely the faint metallic struggle of Emil's manacles.

The back door began to open.

She lifted the revolver in both hands and pulled the hammer back.

"Don't shoot me." Glenn Anders stumbled inside, nearly capsized, shoved the door shut behind him and stood swaying, dripping, an apparition. A puddle formed at his feet and began to spread, soaking into the floorboards. "Don't shoot me."

She kept looking past him, looking for Harry. She lowered the gun slowly, easing the hammer down, waiting.

"He's not coming." Anders, visibly in the last stages of exhaustion, lifted both hands a few inches from his sides in a gesture of helplessness. "I'm alone." Then he staggered past her, pushing himself along the wall with both hands, lurching into the kitchen. She heard the muted crash when he dropped into one of the chairs; its legs scraping the floor. She went in and Anders' arms slid out across the table, knocking the coffee cup off—it shattered on the floor and Anders dropped his head onto the table.

For the longest time she only stared at him. Then with somnambulistic deliberation she opened the refrigerator door and propped a chair there to keep it open. The light exposed Anders' profile and she saw his eye was swollen almost shut and scabbed with blood.

He muttered, slurring the words so badly she could barely make them out, "They didn't spot me. I don't think they spotted me. They were banging around up there, looking for tracks I guess, but it started raining again, harder than hell and I'm sure that must have washed my tracks out. They didn't follow me. I guess they think he was alone."

In a fury she snatched a handful of his hair and jerked his head up off the table. Anders whimpered. She threw him back so that he sat more or less upright in the chair. Now she could see his face clearly for the first time: His eye was a mess and something had clawed great red welts down his cheek.

"Where's Harry?"

"They took him. . . ." She watched him gather himself with a terrible effort of will. "He was alive the last I saw of him. I heard a shot—by the time I got to where I could see through the jungle they were marching him down into the camp. He was limping but then he always limps. I don't think he was hurt. They've captured him, see. I guess they'll work on him till he talks. We found the guard they'd posted on the trail, you see, we hit him with Mace and handcuffed him to a tree with a gag in his mouth and then we went in to scout the place but one way or another Harry got unlucky and they spotted him. I don't know how it happened, I didn't see it. I was still back in the woods and there wasn't a damn thing I could do for him, there were eight or ten of them scattered around the camp and mostly they had guns. I thought about shooting the camp up, driving them to cover and giving him a chance to run for it but Harry can't run with that leg of his and it just wasn't any use. Honest to God I'd have tried if there'd been any chance. But what was the sense of getting myself killed if it couldn't do him any good? I got the hell out of there, didn't make any noise at all. . . ."

"He's alive?"

"He was the last I saw of him."

"Were they hurting him?"

"Not that I saw. Nobody was beating up on him or anything. They had him at gunpoint—they took him prisoner."

"What happened to your face?"

"I got lost in the dark. Slipped in the mud and fell into a goddamned cactus. I can still see—it didn't blind me, maybe it looks worse than it is. But Jesus, I feel sick as a dog."

"Why don't you see a vet," she said with a violent contempt. She wheeled away from him and kicked the chair aside and slammed the fridge shut and tried to think.

She tried to cleanse the wounds on his face. She found a small bottle of iodine in the bathroom and boiled up a pot on the stove and dropped a torn section of bedsheet into the boiling water, retrieved the cloth with a fork and let it cool a bit and then went at his face with it, not as gently as she might have; she was disgusted with him.

A chip of light came in from the hall closet. It was all the light she wanted; she was afraid of attracting attention to the house. When she finished her ministrations she painted his face with iodine. Here and there he was still oozing droplets of blood but that would stop soon. She let him keep the wet cloth to dab at himself.

He said, "We'll have to go to the police. We'd better get moving—the longer it takes, the less chance Harry has."

When she didn't answer he took it as a sign that she hadn't heard him. "We've got to call the police. There must be a phone in that village we came through. Listen, they'll keep Harry alive a while but in the end they'll find out what they want to know from him, or they won't find out but either way they'll kill him, won't they."

There was a plea in his tone. She perceived that he had gone up against something, up there in the jungle, and it had cracked him open; he wasn't much good for anything now.

Anders touched his face with the cloth. When he took it away he looked at the dark stains and winced like a galley slave. Then his face collapsed into defeat. "I'll stay here if you want to go call the cops."

His voice set her teeth on edge. She turned half away from him, trying to think, frowning, snapping her thumbnail against her front teeth.

"Maybe it doesn't matter," Anders muttered. "Who's going to care. Harry hasn't got a family. Just another funeral nobody'll go to."

He's got me. "Shut up, let me think."

"What for? Call the cops."

She was trying sluggishly to reason it through. Finally she said, "That's not the way."

"What are you talking about? We know where they are now. I mean I can lead the police right to them. And they're not going anywhere—they think Harry was alone, they think nobody else knows where they are.''

She was ready to retort but when she looked at him she knew it would be pointless. He was far gone past the edge; she had no idea how long he might have gone without sleep but in any case he was in shock, shivering as he slumped stuporously in the chair; berating him would serve no end.

She said, ''Listen to me, Glenn. Can you follow me?''

''Yeah—barely.''

''If we take an army of police up there Rodriguez will make a bloodbath of it and Harry will be the first casualty.''

''Harry's dead already, breathing or not. There's no way to get him out of there now. At least we can end this.''

''Maybe you're ready to kiss him off just like that. I'm not.''

Anders tried to get to his feet. ''Then if you won't do it I will. It's my job—''

''This is a marvelous time for you to suddenly remember your responsibilities.'' She snatched up the revolver.

''You're out of your mind.''

''And you're out on a limb. I may even be able to save your ass, Glenn.''

''What the hell do you think you're going to do?''

''I'm going to get Harry out of there.''

His bitter laughter followed her away down the hall.

Chapter 19

At daybreak it was still raining when she brought Anders and Emil Draga out of the farmhouse. Draga's feet prodded the earth tentatively; he was still blindfolded and manacled. Anders rubbed his jaw and came to a stop when he reached the Bronco. "What now?"

"Get in. You drive. You know the way."

"Up *there?*"

She pushed the Cuban into the back seat and wasn't particularly gentle about it: Rage swirled in her and Emil Draga was the nearest available target.

Anders stumbled. He reached for the door handle for support. The bruise around his eye was big, dark and ugly. He looked half dead. It was more than just the physical injuries; probably he was suffering from some sort of shock not to mention exhaustion and fear and dejection. She didn't know anything she could do about it except snap at him to keep him awake and functioning.

"Go on—get in. You can drive."

"I can try," he muttered, and hauled himself up onto the seat.

She went around and climbed in and sat sideways with her gun and half her attention on Draga. He sat twisted awkwardly because his hands were cuffed behind him. But he was a big brute and his feet were free now and she didn't trust him to stay still.

The Bronco lurched uphill and she sat in a chilled fury with the revolver in her fist, thinking it out. They had Harry up there—hostage or dead. Very well. Now she had a hostage, too. They'd have to tread easy where Emil Draga was concerned: The power of his grand-

father's wealth would force them to take no chances
with Emil's life and as long as she had her gun to his
throat she could go among them and stay alive long
enough to get Harry out if Harry was alive. If Harry
wasn't alive she'd use Draga as her shield to get out of
there and then, she thought, *God help me I'll kill him.*

But it wasn't going to come to that because she
couldn't really believe Harry wasn't alive.

Because if he was dead it was her fault.

Emil Draga sat rigidly upright, his shoulders wedged
in the corner between seat and window, and Anders
wrestled drunkenly with the wheel, driving poorly,
failing to anticipate rocks and potholes in the trail;
Carole clung one-handed to the armrest.

They rolled onto a flat shelf of rock and Anders
pointed vaguely to the right. "That trail's a phony. We
wasted two hours on it yesterday." He swung left into
the bed of a stream and the four-wheel-drive whined
high. He was hunched forward, using the wheel for support; he was past the end of his endurance and she
steeled herself against pity.

"How much farther?"

"Maybe an hour, hour and a half."

"Describe the camp again for me."

"What can you possibly accomplish except to get our
stupid heads blown off?"

"Tell me about the camp. Do it now."

The trail grew steeper and narrower. They had to use
the winch. Somewhere in the run of the next hour the
rain stopped but she didn't notice, partly because her
mind was elsewhere and partly because the trees kept
dripping long after it quit raining. When the sun shot a
ray through a hole overhead she said, "Where are we
now?"

"Not too—" Then the truck ran into something and
came to a dead stop, pitching her against the dash. The
revolver clattered to the floor and she felt around for it
while Anders stared at her stupidly. The engine had
gone dead and he was twisting the key but nothing hap-

pened: The starter didn't grind, nothing happened at all.

She found the revolver. "What is it?"

"How do I know? It's gone dead."

"Well get out and look under the hood!"

"I'm no mechanic, lady." But he got out anyway and lifted the hood. He looked in from one side and then went around to the other side and looked there.

She got out of the car. "What is it?"

"Maybe a wire got knocked loose somewhere."

"Find it. Fix it."

"I'm looking, damn it." He reached in tentatively, touched something and jerked back with a little cry.

"Did you find it?"

"No. It's hot, that's all."

"Oh for God's sake." She peered in under the hood, as if that would do any good, and after a moment closed her eyes and forced herself to fend off this added frustration and get a grip on her composure. All right, the son of a bitch truck had broken down, it wasn't that important, they weren't far from their destination anyway—she went back to the door and reached in and wrenched the blindfold off Emil Draga's head.

Draga winced and squinted in the unfamiliar light, cowering as if he expected a bullet.

Anders said, "What the hell are you doing now?"

Ignoring him she stood back and waggled the revolver at Draga. "Come on. Out."

Draga backed out slowly, reaching for the earth with one tentative foot, presenting his big rump to the gun.

Anders said, "Put the blindfold back on him. He's a dangerous son of a bitch."

"He'll break his neck up there if he can't see where he's going."

"I figure to break his neck anyway," Anders said with emotionless gravity. He seemed too drained to hold onto the trappings of hate; only the core remained.

"Maybe you'll get a crack at him later. Right now I need him."

"For what?"

"To get Harry out."

"You're out of your mind. They won't go for that."

"You know who this *is?* You know who his grand-father is? They need this big shit alive." She had no energy for argument; she looked up into the dank jungle. "How do I get there? Follow these ruts?"

"There aren't any more phony trails that I remember. Yeah, we just follow the ruts. A couple-three miles, I guess."

"It's not 'we'—I want you to stay with the truck and get it fixed and wait for us."

A residue of pride straightened Anders and he began to protest but she cut him off. "You're in no condition to go anywhere, Glenn. You'd be of no help to me and you'd probably give us away too early."

"You can't go up there by yourself for Christ's sake."

"Well I've got El Creepo for company, haven't I?"

"What is it, lady—some romantic urge to die with your lover? Is that what you want?"

Frogs chirruped and there was a racket of birds; water gurgled somewhere. She watched Anders lean forward, propped against both stiff arms, his palms on the fender of the Bronco, legs splayed, too weak to stand without support, tremors in his knees, head sagging, squeezing his eyes shut, shaking his head to clear it of dizziness. She wondered if the swollen eye was infected. She turned away from him and peered into the dense tow-ering tangle. "If we're not back by morning you may as well call in the police."

He gave no sign he'd heard her. She said, "Glenn?"

"What?"

"Don't pass out. We'll need this thing running—we can't get away without it."

"I told you, I'm no mechanic. I'll try. I can't promise anything."

She checked her pockets: penknife, half a box of cartridges for the revolver, handkerchief, the disposable butane cigarette lighter Harry had told her to carry. The coarse denim of the jeans scraped her thighs when she turned toward Emil Draga. His lofty eyes were narrowed to slits against the light and there was no fathoming his expression.

Anders said, "What's the point of getting yourself killed? It won't help Harry. He's dead anyway. He's seen their faces—there's no way they can afford to turn him loose."

"Is that how you'd have felt if it was Rosalia up there?"

"Rosalia." His lips formed themselves clumsily around the word. He pushed himself upright and turned his head balefully toward Emil Draga.

"Glenn, I'm counting on you to have this running when we get back." She wigwagged Emil Draga toward the trail and he began to trudge uphill. She didn't miss the glint of cunning in his eyes as he went past her. She turned back once more. "Get this truck fixed—that's all you need to think about."

Anders' bleak eye blinked at her; the other eye was swollen shut now. Too wilted to resist the force of her will, he only said, "Look out for tripwires and things. And they'll have guards posted when you get up toward those high ridges. Stay out of the road when you get up there."

She was already walking away.

The humid forest dragged at her feet, slowing her pace. It was all uphill and her legs wobbled from the strain. Emil Draga walked ahead of her in stony silence.

After half an hour she called a halt and sat down with her knees drawn up and the revolver propped on him. Emil slid down on his haunches, ever watchful.

"I expect your grandfather has some kind of affection for you," Carole said. "I loved my son a great deal, you know, even though most of the time I had a strange way of showing it."

"If it pleases you to talk," Draga said, "talk."

"Listen to me now. I want to save the life that still matters to me. You're the only weapon I have."

Draga watched her; he didn't speak.

"Maybe I'm just tired," she said, "but it's come to me that it's no good sacrificing the living to avenge the dead."

He did not stir.

"I want you to know," she said, "that I'm not going to shoot you with this unless you force me to do it. Do you understand what I'm telling you?"

"You're a fool." He showed his contempt by tipping his head back against the tree and shutting his eyes.

"I got Harry Crobey into this," she said doggedly, "and now I want to get him out of it. That's what I want—it's *all* I want. I don't give a shit about you and your misbegotten counterrevolution. Do you understand me?"

No reply. Carole lifted herself on watery knees. "Get up."

There was a tripwire and she told him to walk around through the forest to avoid it. She walked directly behind him with the gun near Draga's spine because she didn't want anyone taking her by surprise from the shadows. The sodden ground sucked at her boots. A gust of wind came along like a breath from an oven. She felt the overpowering burden of her guilt and forced herself to disregard it; she imposed calm upon herself and narrowed her thinking down to a slit through which only the most immediate practical concerns could pass.

She felt a tendon go, in her heel, and kept moving; she fastened her lips against the twinges.

Allegro and pianissimo now. Forget the pain in the goddamned foot. It can't be far now.

The trees were heavy, vines thickly entwined. Orchids and lush verdure; insects about her face. A dank smell of primeval rot.

She remembered bits of Harry's dicta. *Never talk to the enemy until you've licked him.* Well there was a time to break every rule. She worked out what had to happen and rehearsed her lines until the repetition assumed the tiresome ritual predictability of a flamenco or kabuki episode:

Send Harry out here. Send him out or I kill your precious Draga. Don't follow us. We'll turn Draga loose when we know we're safe.

It was all she'd need to say to them. All the decisions that were hers to make had been made now. The final decision would be up to Rodriguez. She had nothing more to do but play it out to the end.

It probably would go against her; most likely she'd end up killed, dead in the festering jungle and no one to mourn. But she would go through with this because it was Harry. And because she had got the poor son of a bitch into this mess. *And because I have got, you should pardon the expression, integrity.*

She moved with extreme caution now, the revolver cocked and leveled upon Draga's spine from inches away.

It was, she thought, suicidally and hysterically pointless. But she had to do it for Harry. And for herself.

Another tripwire; they went around its anchor; she said, "Stay in the trees now. Don't go in the road."

This was high ground. The primitive track skirted a jutting rock and bent out of sight, tipping down to disappear. From within the edge of the trees she surveyed it and saw no way to cross that point without stepping into the roadway. She chewed her lip. "We'll go over that rock—over the back side of it."

"I can't climb that rock with my hands behind my back."

It was true. But she wasn't going to take the handcuffs off him. Gun or no gun. He could throw a rock at her, run for it, anyway. She couldn't afford to lose him now.

"All right. Then we'll use the road. My gun in your back all the way—if anything happens you're the first to die. This thing is cocked. Keep it in mind."

She had no idea at all what might be in his head; he gave nothing away. His facade of indifference troubled her because it might mean that with Latin soldierlike *machismo* he was prepared to die for the sake of his comrades. She rather doubted it because he was too much the child of privilege for that sort of down-in-flames gesture, but it was a possibility and if it came true then she'd have lost.

She said, "Move."

"Be careful with that thing, woman. You could trip and set it off."

"That would be a crying shame," she snapped. "Move."

He stepped out into the road and she followed. Draga moved forward a pace at a time, head lifted, apparently scanning the treetops and rocks above them. She crowded close behind him with the revolver all but touching his back. She found herself waiting for the bullet that would kill her: She wondered what it would sound like.

Without warning Draga wheeled. His elbow whacked the revolver aside. Instinctively she clenched her hand—the revolver slammed her palm in recoil; the noise was earsplitting; the bullet went harmlessly off the road somewhere; and Draga was swinging his heavy boot against her—a clumsy kick, off-balance, but it pummeled her off her feet and she sprawled. She didn't lose her grip on the gun but she was still trying to roll over and face him when something—it must have been his boot—thundered against her kidney and propelled her over the edge of the road's shelf and then she was tumbling, rolling, falling down the slick mud of a nearly perpendicular mountainside—brush whipped at her, clawed her face; rocks rattled under her; she was falling in space, then sliding in muck—the world spinning.

Things went nearly black but she heard the bellowing of Emil Draga's voice somewhere far above her and she peered through the haze of her vision—brush and trees loomed at crazy angles. She heard the rush of water.

She'd lost the revolver, of course. A kind of equilibrium returned to her, she got her bearings and distinguished up from down. Above her was the track of her own sliding fall—she was incredulous at the length of the scar her body had sluiced in the mud: She must have fallen nearly a hundred feet and she wondered how many of her bones were shattered. It was a clinical thought, detached. She lay motionless, blinking. Pain gradually flooded through her system; everything ached.

At the top she didn't see anything move at the rim of the road. It occurred to her that Emil's voice was fading. He was still yelling but it was farther away. He must be running toward the camp, yelling for help.

In a little while, she thought, they'd come back and finish her.

She wondered if she could move.

She lifted her head away from whatever had cushioned it. Well at least the head and neck worked. She looked down the length of her body.

The jeans were ripped, a long slice along the left calf. There was no open cut but the skin was abraded and dappled with angry red dots.

She lifted her left hand experimentally and winced at the sudden pain in it, but she closed it into a fist and opened it and continued to stare whimsically at it. There was a nasty raw blot across the back of it where she must have flailed against something. But the fingers functioned.

Now the right hand. It was pinned half under her and she had to roll her torso back to free it. Every movement inflicted a new throbbing ache.

But nothing refused to articulate.

She had fallen into a scrub of some kind: more bush than tree. She'd crushed half of it but the rest of it supported her, a sort of latticed mattress of twig and leaves. The pitch of the slope began to level off here. It tilted down more gently—another twenty or thirty yards perhaps; trees at the bottom and she couldn't see beyond them.

If she'd come off the rim twenty feet to either side she'd have dropped into boulders. If it hadn't been raining incessantly the slope wouldn't have eased her fall. If. . . . By blind luck she was alive.

Silence now, only the rattle of flowing water below in the trees. She didn't hear Emil Draga any longer. Raindrops began to drip on her.

With a rough uncaring need to know, she curled her feet under her and attempted to stand up.

The bush collapsed under her. Clinging to it she fell another ten feet and slid to a painful halt, both hands splayed to ward off obstacles. Her palms, now, began to bleed.

She trembled with a pounding violence that she found almost comical: She grunted with effort and stubbornly climbed to her feet and lurched downhill until she blundered up against the slimy trunk of a big tree; she stood against it numbly, waggling her toes inside her boots, moving her arms about, sucking a great breath into her chest.

Everything hurt, everything throbbed, but unaccountably the organism appeared to be in rudimentary working order.

She rubbed both abraded palms against the cloth of her blouse, smearing blood and mud together. Christ. Somehow she was alive.

Then she heard them—a faint clanking; voices. Coming along the high shelf of the road above her. She recognized Emil Draga's bellowing anger.

It wasn't thought; it was primitive impulse that drove her back into the protective darkness of the jungle.

Her breasts felt as if they'd been squashed under a tractor and her hands stung so badly she could hardly stir them, and one knee had gone wonky—a ligament or something; it hurt every time she put her weight on it at a certain angle. There was a frightful bruise along her right hip, her left calf was sharp agony where it had been scraped raw and both shoulder blades felt as if they'd had chips axed out of them. She had welts on cheek and forehead; her scalp hurt frightfully where a lock of hair had caught in something and been ripped away; she had a thin bleeding line in her lower lip, like a paper cut—she kept licking it—and her teeth felt as if they'd been jarred loose. Both elbows gave her trouble and she found a new pain in her shoulder when she tried to lift her right arm to ward off a branch she ducked under.

She went slowly downhill through the stinking growth; steam eddied about her. The tattered rags of her outfit clung to her like shreds of flesh on a rotting corpse. She found the water almost immediately—the source of the sound she'd heard: a stream, birling off rocks and swirling through a big pond and disappearing through a narrow gap beyond. The noise she'd heard was a small waterfall beyond that gap.

The rush of the waterfall made it impossible for her to hear anything from above. She didn't know if they were following her track down the cliff. Most likely they'd have to use ropes to get down there—or go around, if they knew another path. Were they coming after her?

I would, she reasoned. They couldn't take anything for granted. They'd need to see for themselves that she was dead. They'd come down here and look for the body.

They'd follow her tracks.

The sudden realization shot hopelessness through her. She couldn't get away. It was only a matter of time—a few minutes at best.

No way to outrun them. The shape she was in, she could barely hobble.

She sat down gingerly.

"I'm sorry, Harry. I gave it my best shot."

She whispered the words and her eyes rolled shut.

Harry. . . .

The thought stunned her awake.

"God *damn* it—I am not dead yet!"

Cunning, now. She needed every whit of cleverness. She knelt by the pond and scooped water in her hands, rubbed her palms together gently in the water to wash off the clots of mud and blood, cupped handfuls of water and splashed it in her face. It was shockingly cold.

They can't follow tracks in water.

The pond was mostly bordered by the exposed roots of trees where the soil had been washed away. She gripped the roots and lowered herself slowly into the water, at first stunned by the icy chill, then welcoming it because it began to anesthetize her throbbing aches.

Take your time now. It wouldn't do to get swept out into the current and carried over the waterfall. She moved along with slow deliberation, clinging to outjutting roots, moving from one handhold to the next.

They'd expect her to go downstream—downhill—toward the bottom of the mountains and escape.

She went uphill instead. Pulling herself against the current. Up to the head of the pond where the water foamed over rocks in the shallow streambed. Then she trudged carefully upstream, cautiously placing one foot at a time and testing for solidity.

The stream came burbling down out of a narrow chasm. She climbed doggedly into it, moving from stone to stone, bracing herself with one hand against the wall of the chasm. The water was only a foot deep most places; sometimes she was able to walk on the tops of stepping-stones.

One of them rocked and gave way, overturning. She windmilled her arms crazily and went in up to the knees, thinking in panic that she'd twisted her ankle.

That would be the last sonofabitching straw. She put her weight on it angrily and it was all right and she realized then that there weren't any last straws—she had come too far for that; nothing was going to stop her short of death.

It started to rain again. Pelting down. Drops so big they hurt when they struck her exposed bruises. You can't get any wetter than wet, she told herself dismally, and continued stubbornly up the chasm, the water rising to her thighs once and almost pitching her over.

Exhaustion dragged her to a stop and she stood with both palms against the rock face, panting. She looked back down toward the pond but there wasn't anything to see in the sheeting rain.

Soon, she knew, they would begin searching up this way. She had to get out of the chasm. *They are the ones who killed Robert and they'll damn sure kill me, too, if I let them.*

She wasn't going to let them. Because she still had Harry to think about and she didn't intend to let him down. Cool dispassion now: This was the time to move fast, get out into the jungle and lose herself in it, because the battering rain would cover her tracks and this squall wasn't likely to last much longer.

The walls of the chasm fell away above her. She saw a narrow waterfall at the top but it looked as if there might be a way to climb out to one side of it, if the rain hadn't made the rock too slick. Trees loomed up there; vines and roots dangled thick. There was a rainbow at the top. She grinned at it: It was too Hollywood to be true. She climbed toward it but the sun moved, or the clouds did, and the rainbow disappeared.

As she approached the top she moved through tendrils of mist and realized she was actually inside the cloud. She groped for handholds, tested her weight on corkscrew roots, drew herself up six inches at a time, tearing her sodden clothes on things, planting new bruises on top of the old ones, ignoring all of it.

When she looked over her shoulder she couldn't see the pond anymore; it was screened by the trees and the curve of the chasm and the rain. She faced upward again. Not far now. *They'll expect me to run for it. They won't expect me to come for Harry.*

Chapter 20

The distributor cap had popped its clips and one of the main battery leads had slipped off its lug; that was the extent of the damage that Anders could see but he didn't know much about automobile engines and he had little confidence in his repairs until he turned the key and it actually started up.

Then he sat at the wheel engaged in sluggish debate with himself. He could do one of three things. He could follow Carole up the road—they'd been gone only an hour or so and he still might catch up before they reached the camp. Or he could do as she'd asked—remain here and wait for them. If they showed up. Or he could turn the damn thing around and do the sensible sane thing: Head for the nearest telephone and call the cops.

There wasn't much point in this first option. By the time he got up there with the Bronco they'd be in the thick of it and there wasn't much assistance he could render; he was unarmed and woozy with infection and his eyesight was going every which way. And as for the second option, it would be a few more hours at least before anything could happen here—even if by some miracle she got Crobey out alive it would take them that long to make their way back to this point. By then Anders could make it to a phone, summon help, and return to meet them. Get the cops in there: Try to rescue Crobey and Carole, and wipe out the nest of Cuban bastards who'd murdered Rosalia. There was more than enough of a case now. The murder of Rosalia and the cache of heavy weapons up there—not even old man

Draga's influence could persuade the Puerto Rican cops to ignore that.

There were some bad dangers in this last possibility though—suppose Carole showed up in fifteen minutes' time, having changed her mind or having been chased by one of Rodriguez's scouts? Suppose she ran this far seeking sanctuary and found Anders and the Bronco gone?

In the end he decided that he might as well play it for keeps. By the time help came the outcome would be decided anyway, and he couldn't risk abandoning Crobey and Carole. He wasn't that far gone.

They'd been scouring the jungle foot by foot but now some unspoken logic brought everybody together at once, by the bank of the pond. Council of war.

Julio said, "Maybe she fell in the water and got swept over the waterfall."

Cielo said, "Anything is possible."

Julio was looking at Cielo, pinning him with his gaze. "We can't let her get away, you know."

"Then find her," Cielo snapped. "What do you expect me to do about it, Julio?"

"If she gets away she'll tell everything." Julio wheeled toward two men coming in from the jungle. "Santos—Badillo—take one of the Jeeps, take a run down the trail, see if you can find this Anders with the stalled car. Where Emil says they left him."

Cielo said, "Bring him alive. We must find out how much he knows. He shouldn't give you trouble—Emil says he's sick and he hasn't got any weapons. Santos, I know you. If you kill him I'll be very angry with you."

The two men slung their Uzzis and batted away obediently through the trees.

Julio was waving his arms. "The rest of you search the stream, both banks. If she came out she left tracks. If she didn't you'll find her body in the water."

Cielo was bouncing the revolver in his fist. It was the woman's revolver. He'd found it back up the slope. Suddenly he laughed. "She's alone, she hasn't got a weapon, she must be hurt pretty bad—look what we've come to, Julio.''

The others were fanning out along the bank. Julio glared at him. ''You want her to get down to the valley and tell everybody where we are, Cielo? Is that what you want?''

Men moved through the trees, as insubstantial as fog. Cielo felt the tension inside him. His chest was lifting and falling. He cleared his throat and dragged a sleeve across his forehead. ''I'm going back to the camp.''

''You ought to help us find her.''

''They'll find her or they won't. I'm too tired to play these stupid Boy Scout games. *Cristo*—this whole stupidity is Emil's fault. Killing the Lundquist boy, killing the CIA woman. These calamitous delusions. All he wants is killing. Now we must pay for Emil's sins.''

''It's not finished.'' Julio stayed him with a hand on his sleeve. ''Listen to me. We'll find the woman and we'll bring Anders up here and find out if he's told anybody else. Listen, the killing's hardly started, you'd better recognize that. Anders, the woman—and Crobey's seen all our faces. We can't turn him loose, can we?''

''Ah, man, who cares about that anymore? Nobody wants to kill Harry. Nobody except Emil. We'll pull out, Julio, we'll leave this place, that's all. We've been here too long anyway.''

''They can identify us!''

''So? What of it? We can steal a boat. They won't find us in Venezuela or Brazil.''

''And the weapons? Just leave them here? After everything?''

''Julio, the guns will never reach Havana anyway. Forget it. It was a bad dream. The old man's hallucination, that's all.''

''You never wanted anything out of this except the money, did you?''

''I'm a realist. It's all I've ever expected to come of this.'' Cielo looked around. All the men had disappeared but now he saw two of them making their way back upstream along the far bank: They must have clambered down past the waterfall and crossed the stream on the rocks below. They went along with their noses to the ground, seeking tracks.

Julio said, "I'm a realist, too, you know. I recognize we could never bring it off by ourselves, not this handful of us. But we've got the weapons now, the money. With those we have power. There will always be people to fight the Communists—from San Juan to Santo Domingo. We can be a nucleus—barter our services throughout the Caribbean."

"You're dreaming, Julio, my ears are deaf to it. You remind me of Emil. Well let me tell you—I don't want to be a general in your crusade. I want to go out in my new boat and catch fish, that's all. You and Emil can fight it out between you."

The man across the pond stood on the bank and lifted both arms wide with an expressive shrug of his shoulders, signifying that he'd found nothing. Julio acknowledged it by pointing up toward the head of the pond. "Keep looking," he shouted.

Cielo turned away from the pond. "Better get back to camp. Maybe she's out there dying in the jungle somewhere but we can't take the chance. Let's get things packed up. We'll have to evacuate."

Julio came along after him, puffing with the circuitous climb. Off to the right Cielo could see the toboggan slide trough of the woman's fall. He marveled that she could have walked away from that. It was the mud, he thought, this damnable muck.

He felt sorrow for the woman. Crobey's woman. Well, he felt sorrow for them both. The woman would get lost out there and the jungle would kill her. If she hadn't drowned already.

"Let's hurry. I don't trust Emil up there with Crobey."

"Vargas will keep them separated," Julio said.

"Emil would slit Vargas' throat if it seemed useful." Cielo scrambled over the lip onto the road and hurried toward the camp.

Through the trees he had a glimpse of the mouth of the cave above the camp. How ludicrous, he thought.

All that ordnance—the heavy weapons, the vehicles, the tens of thousands of rounds of ammunition. All that and they couldn't even wage effective war against Crobey's unarmed woman. *Oh, we're the terrors of the Caribbean, all right.*

She crawled wincing to the edge of the high trees and looked out, panting in the thick steamy air. The rain was letting up. Pains stabbed through her and she had to wait for her vision to clear.

The flat was open to her left. Farther along the cliff she saw a fresh scar, white jagged bits of rock like exposed bone and a couple of poles that looked as if they'd fallen down. A length of cable lay curled sinuously, its end frayed like Medusan hair, and not far from her squatted a little gasoline engine with a winch drum. Someone had spent some time beside it because there were half a dozen empty beer bottles and soda pop cans.

She lay with her chin on the back of her hand, soaked through, hair matted, tattered as a barrio urchin. She was studying the camp below the cliff. Four or five rudimentary huts—thatched conical roofs, African-style. Two Jeeps were parked haphazardly between the two largest huts. While she watched, she saw two men come up into the camp from the path beyond. She didn't recognize them, though she could see neither of them was Emil Draga. They both wore green combat fatigues and military caps and she wondered if they were aware of the irony of that: Castro and his men wore the same uniforms.

The two men went past the Jeeps calling out ahead of them. In response a man appeared in the door of the largest hut: a huge man, too bulky to be Emil Draga. There was a brief exchange of words down there; then the two men went inside the hut and the huge man crossed the campground to another hut, went inside briefly and then emerged, backing out, his submachine gun leveled. Another man followed him out and, obeying the gestures of the huge man, walked around ahead of him toward the big hut. The prisoner limped a bit. She saw nothing but the back of him but it was Harry all right, and her heart soared.

Emil was pacing back and forth, rubbing the cloth bandages they'd wrapped around his wrists after Vargas had sawed off the manacles. Julio was rummaging in his duffel bag under one of the cots, looking for dry clothes to change into. Cielo stood near the door and watched while Harry Crobey stooped to enter the hut, followed by Vargas who went straight across to the radio and sat down with the Kalashnikov across his knees to fiddle with the tuner knob. The radio sputtered and hissed but there was nothing on that band. Harry Crobey looked from face to face with sardonic amusement. When no one spoke to him he sat down at the camp table and began to play solitaire.

Vargas looked up. "Emil wanted to kill him so I kept them separated."

Crobey glanced at Emil. "I invited him to try with his bare hands, since Vargas wouldn't give him a weapon, but he's a chicken-shit bastard." He leered. Emil was a head taller and forty pounds heavier than Crobey, and could spot him nearly thirty years, but Emil wasn't a fool. Not in that way. Crobey knew a hundred ways to kill a man bare-handed.

Emil declined to rise to Crobey's bait. He only said to Cielo, in an offhand way, "He knows our faces and of course he must be killed."

Cielo said, "That might be futile. There are others. We can't kill every last one of them. To you, Emil, the answer to every question is a bullet, isn't it. The fact is it probably won't matter to our security whether Harry goes free or not."

He saw Crobey's eyes flash but Crobey was too wise to ask questions.

"Then again," Julio said, "she may be dead in the jungle. That was a hell of a fall she took when you kicked her over the cliff."

Cielo addressed Crobey: "Who else have you and Anders told about this?"

"I can't speak for Anders. He's probably telling the

whole world about it by now. Me, I only told three or four friends." Crobey grinned at him. "You're right. Maybe I'm worth something to you alive, as a hostage, but it won't do you any good to waste me."

Julio said, "Of course he'd say that anyway, whether it's true or not."

"It's more likely true than not true," Cielo said. "When the others return we'll pack our personal belongings and take enough small arms to defend ourselves—in case. We'll go down the back side of El Yunque and fade into the country to the south."

Emil was looking at Vargas' Kalashnikov, possibly gauging his chances. Cielo said, "Emil, we're not taking you with us. You'll have to make your own way."

"I always knew you were a traitor." Emil said it without hate and without looking at him; he was still facing Vargas, who returned his gaze evenly, with bovine indifference. Vargas had a thick skin and a gentle soul but Emil knew better than to attack him head-on.

Emil said, "You people have bungled everything, right from the start. You've been humoring my grandfather, isn't that it? You've never had any intention of carrying through with his wishes."

"Neither have you," Cielo replied. "Your grandfather's dream is a free Cuba. Your dream is a dictatorship—your own."

Julio said, "We're going to have to kill Emil, too, aren't we?"

It made Cielo look at him. Julio's eyes were sad. "You were right, you know. Once the killing starts it never stops. Emil's the one who started it. It can only stop when he's dead."

Emil swiveled—now he was facing not only Vargas' but Julio's as well.

Crobey slapped one card down on top of another. He said, "If all you blokes kill each other I can just walk out of here. Right? It's a splendid idea, chaps. Go to it."

Emil looked about him with disdain. "Kill me and my grandfather will avenge it. Your women, Cielo, your children. My grandfather will have them killed, and you and your brother and all your men—no matter how far you go, no matter where you try to hide.''

Julio said, ''Not if you die in an accident witnessed only by me and my brother. And Vargas here.''

''And Crobey,'' said Crobey. ''Don't forget old Harry.''

''Christ, Harry,'' Cielo said, ''your presence gives me a ripe pain in the ass right now. What are we going to do with you?''

''I don't know, old sport. But I don't see as you've got anything to gain by killing me.''

''For the love of God,'' Cielo murmured haplessly, ''I don't want to kill *any*body.''

The man who'd gone to search upstream came running urgently back to the pond and stood above the waterfall summoning the others with shrill whistles. When two men came in sight downstream in the drizzle he waved his arms violently and the two men shouted back into the jungle.

By ones and twos the others appeared below the waterfall and the first two men waited impatiently while they climbed up to him. Then he led them upstream, excited, to show them what he'd found—freshly overturned stones in the stream. Someone had gone up through the chasm to the rimrock above.

''It must be the woman. Come on—we will look on top for her tracks.''

Confused as to his bearings, Anders fought to stay awake. Fever drenched him in sweat and something was going wonky with the one good eye he had left. He slammed down into a lower gear and fought the wheel. The primitive roadway had all but petered out by now. He'd have to get out and walk soon.

He clenched his stomach muscles to fight back dizziness and shoved the Bronco forward in an effort to pick up speed while he could still drive at all. Rosalia was gone but he had the illusory vague sense he could redeem himself by accomplishing this mission; at least

he had to give it his best shot. But then his eye clouded
over and he dragged his sleeve across it. He was having
trouble co-ordinating his body and hit the accelerator by
mistake. He was going about fifteen miles an hour up
the gravel when he went off into a culvert. The Bronco
slowly tipped over and fell on its side. Glenn Anders was
knocked out, and he would remain that way when the
guerrillas came to drag him back to the camp.

Listless stupidity was wearing off; she was thinking
more clearly now and her nerves started to jangle—the
terror that had muted itself expanded inside her now
and she trembled uncontrollably. All the aches and
stings of her injuries grew acute; she noticed new
agonies she hadn't felt before.

This was madness. There was nothing she could
do—nothing but make a fool of herself and get killed.
Christ, the best combat soldier in the world would know
enough to get the hell out of here. She was beginning to
remember a lot of Harry's *dicta*—among them that a
soldier's first job was to keep alive: He'd quoted
Patton's line about not dying for your country but
making the other bastard die for *his* country.

All the same she was working, moving, preparing for
the attack. The soda pop bottles, mud and gravel from
the ground, gasoline from the tank of the donkey
engine, her shirttails for fuses. She had three of them in
one hand, the bottlenecks clutched in her fingers like a
busboy carrying Cokes, and she was making her way
down the switchbacking footpath—terrified because if
anybody stepped outside the hut they'd see her on the
face of the cliff above them. There was no place to hide.
They could pin her to this wall like an insect on a display
board.

Chilly dispassion had deserted her; it must have been
the effects of the shock. She felt debilitated with terror
now and she kept thinking of all the things that could go
wrong. She made her way down the steep path one step
at a time, testing the footing with a shaking foot, sliding
one shoulder along the wall, terrified of toppling over
the narrow shelf—it was a sheer drop. The arms cave

that Anders had described must be over to her left somewhere but there were outcroppings of rock and she couldn't see it. Still, she needed to keep that in mind. If the arms were unguarded. . . . But they wouldn't be that silly, would they? No. It meant there'd be someone in the cave, and she had to remember that because it meant she'd have someone behind her when she approached the camp.

Come on now. One step at a time and don't think about anything else until you get to the bottom.

The man in the cave sat with a bottle of beer and his memories of a Norwegian girl in a fly-specked room in Guatemala. He was half asleep and didn't want anybody to catch him dozing so he got up and walked around the cave. The rain had let up but a kind of mist hung in the air, cloud tendrils prying into the cave and he felt clammy.

He stopped beside a bipod-mounted mortar and rested his hand on its uptilted muzzle. Such a primitive device, the mortar, yet devastatingly effective: An open steel pipe with a firing pin at the bottom of it, that was all it amounted to. He liked that sort of simplicity. Complicated mechanisms disturbed him; he distrusted them.

He walked across the mouth of the cave and stopped suddenly. Was that a movement over to the right at the base of the cliff—someone slipping into the trees?

He looked away, looked again: But the movement didn't recur. After a moment he lifted his rifle and sat down to watch that quadrant, alert now, ready to kill.

Coming over the rimrock the half-dozen men deployed through the trees seeking tracks; there was a shout from up ahead and it drew them all onto the rim by the donkey engine. Here they studied and discussed the evidence they saw in the earth. There were fresh tracks, made since the downpour. The tracks were hard to make out, since everything was imprecise in the squishy clay, but it was evident someone had spent a bit of time here, rummaging about.

The area beyond the donkey engine was slab rock; it didn't hold tracks. The men fanned out, a few into the jungle, two more going forward along the rim. One man began to descend the narrow switch-backing footpath that led to the camp at the bottom of the cliff.

She could see him coming down the cliff and she could see the angular one who squatted just inside the mouth of the big cave with a rifle in both hands; she saw them from her hiding place back in the sodden trees and she wondered if she had left tracks that the one on the path would find when he got to the bottom.

She saw two more men up top, fitful glimpses of them as they made their way along the rim above the cave. And there'd been voices—even more of them above her somewhere.

Madness, she thought. *Sheer utter madness: I belong in a rubber room. Stupid lunacy. But then if you figure to get killed anyway what's the point of beating around the bush?*

She felt momentarily proud of herself for that thought because it sounded like something of Harry's.

She went dizzy for a moment but she didn't faint; she only stumbled a bit and reached for a tree trunk for support. Its surface was slimy and repulsive to her touch. She took the disposable plastic cigarette lighter out of her pocket. Harry: *I don't care if you don't smoke. It's a survival weapon: Always carry fire with you.*

The rags she'd torn from her blouse and stuffed into the necks of the bottles were soaked with rain and she didn't know whether that would destroy their capillary ability to soak up gasoline from the bottles. She'd wrung them out as dry as she could but what if they refused to catch fire? In this weather it was possible to imagine that *nothing* would burn.

She put the lighter back in her pocket. It wasn't time for it yet. Then she gingerly shifted two of the bottles to her left hand, winced when she scraped a raw wound, and crept to the next tree. Her boots sank ankle-deep into the mud. She was in the jungle now and she couldn't see out past the dark thickness of trees and bamboo and lush creeping things; that man on the cliff must be halfway to the bottom by now and she didn't have much time at all.

Madness, she thought again.

And moved toward the huts.

See, ducks, the thing is, guerrilla warfare's got nothing to do with the kind of thing they teach at Sandhurst and West Point. That's what the American Army never learned in Nam. You want to stay alive, you learn to think like a magician—the kind you see doing tricks with scarves and coins and cards in cheap dives in Brighton and Sausalito. You wave the right hand around to get everybody's attention and in the meantime behind your back your left hand's pulling the pin on the grenade and they don't even see it when you roll it under their table. Simple misdirection—diversion's the whole thing, you get their attention by making a big noise to the right and then you sneak up on 'em from the left.

All she could do, really, was provide Harry with his diversion.

She'd made it as far as the first Jeep and she was crouched beside it peering up through the mud-stained windshield: Four or five men were coalescing at the top of the cliff and starting down the narrow shelving path; the man who'd started earlier was down out of sight now but when she turned her head she could still see the man in the cave, standing up now, watching the jungle, rifle held ready across his chest.

She dropped a bit lower and looked across the seats toward the big hut. She'd seen Harry go inside that one; she had to assume he was still in there, even though she'd been out of sight of it.

She set the three bottles on the muddy clay by her feet and dug the plastic lighter out of her pocket.

Crobey was playing the ten of clubs on the jack of hearts when concussion from the blast knocked him off his chair and drove the woven-bamboo door into the room like a projectile. It caromed against the table, knocking it down across him and spilling cards all over him.

The deafening racket echoed inside the hut and he had quickly-glimpsed impressions of everybody in action—Vargas peeling himself off the radio and groping for his Kalashnikov; Emil ducking, arms over his head, then straightening and searching wildly for a weapon; Julio Rodriguez wheeling toward the door lifting his Uzzi; Cielo scowling in that baffled I-knew-it way of his, lifting the revolver in his hand as if he considered it a futile gesture demanded by protocol.

Crobey's ears were still ringing when his mind focused on one object and he rolled toward it—the knapsack they'd taken off him when they'd captured him. It lay open beyond the radio, its contents exposed. Vargas was tramping toward the doorway through which the explosion had burst; flames were climbing both sides of the doorframe now, erupting very fast, and the Cubans began to shoot—spraying ammunition blindly through the fire and smoke. Emil was yelling at the top of his voice and for a moment none of them was looking at Crobey and he pounced on the knapsack. He did all the rest of it in continuous fluid motion: Plucked a gas grenade from the open bag, jerked the pin out, slid it across the floor toward the Cubans, got his good leg under him, and launched himself back into the shadows behind the bulk of the radio. There was a back door in that dark wall—you never built a military hut without a back way out—but it was bolted on the inside and he wasted precious time trying to find the bolt in the bad light. Gas exploded through the room and he began to choke on it, tears streaming, but then he had the damned thing open and he plunged outside, fell three feet into the mud and rolled fast.

He heard them coughing in there and then the second explosion knocked him about and something stung his cheek, laying it open—he felt the sudden warmth of spouting blood before the pain hit. A great blaze of fire erupted at the far corner of the hut and Crobey scrambled to his feet and wheeled to run for it. Then he heard Carole:

"Harry. Over here!"

He heard himself mutter: "Good grief." Then he was running toward the Jeep, bent over, weaving from side to side. Bullets were still flying through the flames from inside the hut but that dwindled fast—the gas would be disabling all of them now but then the shooting picked up again and he realized it was coming from elsewhere. A string of bullets from an automatic weapon sewed a swift stitch along the mud in front of him, little geysers spouting, and he threw himself flat, skidding in the muck, sliding behind the Jeep and aware that there were men on the cliff shooting down through the flames.

She stared at him, not moving, and he took the blazing Molotov cocktail from her hand and heaved it mightily. It exploded in the air and rained shards of blazing petrol over the camp. Bits of gravel and shattered glass banged against the Jeep and he realized that was what had cut his cheek—a sliver of glass from the previous bomb. He gripped her hard, by the wrist, yanking her away. "Run for it!" And hurled her into the trees ahead of him.

She tumbled into a rotting moist pool that stank of compost; she flailed weakly in protest when Harry hauled her out of it.

His face was ghastly—a long ragged slit below the cheekbone, blood matted everywhere. But a smile came into his eyes. Feeling nearly burst her throat.

"Hello ducks."

"Harry—"

"Come on, keep moving, keep moving."

He propelled her through the morass. She nearly left a boot behind in it. He was half carrying her—bullying her along: "Get your goddamned *ass* in gear, woman."

Smashing through twigs, stumbling against trees. He reached for a hanging vine and hauled them both up over a tangle of roots. Then the way was blocked by a stand of bamboo, its trunks as thick as drain pipes—a solid wall of it, looming into the sky. Harry pushed her to the left and she resisted. "Not that way. The cliff—we'll be trapped."

"Only place to go now, ducks."

"But—"

"Shut up. Come *on*. He gave her a violent heave and she lurched wildly, spinning her arms; he caught her by the elbow and then they were running, Harry gasping in her ear: "Have you got a gun or anything?"

"No. . . ."

"It's all right, never mind."

She couldn't see a thing but tree trunks and creepers; she'd lost her bearings and went helplessly whichever way Harry's arm guided her. She ran awkwardly, her body in agony, legs protesting but Harry's hand was like a tow rope. Vaguely she was aware of it when the shooting dwindled back there—a single ragged aftervolley, then no more guns, just voices hollering in confusion.

Then abruptly he jerked her to a stop. He tipped her against a tree. "Stay put a minute."

"What?"

But he was leaning away from her and she stood half blind, heaving with the effort of getting air into her lungs. Her head spun and her knees had gone loose and she choked on her own saliva and began to retch. She tried to stifle it but she was drowning and she put her head down and sucked air with panic-stricken greed. Then something pummeled her between the shoulder blades—Harry, and her throat popped clear and she whooshed in a grateful breath.

"He's gone to find out what's happening. Come on."

"Who?"

"Bloke from the cave." Harry hauled her forward and in a moment they were out of the trees and the edge of the big cave was right there; Harry was saying something—"This is right where the bastards caught me. Clumsy fool, getting too old for this shit." He pulled her into the cave and she felt him push her away toward the interior: "Get back in there out of sight. Pick something to hide behind—something that doesn't look too much like a tombstone."

"Harry, we're trapped in here!"

"Go on, disappear. I'll be right with you."

But she stayed and when he started to wrench at the

boards of a crate she helped him pry it open. He didn't object again. He tugged with frantic haste at the Cosmoline-soaked wrappings and finally tore the oilpaper away from a stubby black weapon of some kind and thrust a magazine into it and then went around the cave peering at stenciled heiroglyphs on crates until he exclaimed, "Ha!" and kicked at the edge of a lid until it splintered; he got his fingers under it and peeled boards back on their nails and she saw the ugly serrated pineapple shapes of hand grenades. Harry began to force them into his pockets.

Then he ran to the front of the cave and peered out. She stumbled along behind him, afraid to be separated from him by more than an arm's length.

The camp was in flames and the smoke had turned black; there wasn't much to be seen through it. "God knows what they're up to," Harry grumbled. He turned then; his big hands slid around her. "You looked like the bloody cavalry, ducks. Christ, I'd given it up. Mostly they didn't particularly want to kill me but we were getting to the point where it was the only thing they could do with me. Old Harry was dead—and then you dropped in. The last bloomin' thing I ever—"

"Did you think," she said softly, "I wouldn't come for you?"

Around the perimeter of the camp the angry rifles stirred. Cielo kept wiping at his eyes and coughing in spasms; the rolling smoke didn't help.

Emil loomed in the smoke, outlined against the burning hut; somewhere he'd found a weapon—one of the Uzzi automatic rifles. "It was the woman. A couple of Molotovs and Crobey threw tear gas—that's all it was. I just spotted them going into the cave."

Cielo gasped stupidly at him. He kept doubling over, coughing, and couldn't focus on what Emil was saying.

"You're all through," Emil said with grating scorn. "You're used up. I'm taking command here—you want to dispute it?" The Uzzi stirred toward Cielo.

He only coughed and rubbed at his eyes. Emil was walking away bellowing orders and he saw some of the men go trotting along after him.

They went away through the smoke and Cielo didn't move. *To hell with it all*.

After a little while he heard them start shooting.

Far back in the cave they lay behind crates of rifles. Bullets crashed around, caroming, whining, smashing things up. Crobey pulled the pin from a grenade and hurled it out of the cave and she felt him drop on top of her, shielding her; the racket drove her half crazy and shrapnel pelted off the walls and ceiling. Something cracked the heel of her boot, hard. Crobey said, "Probably didn't hit anything but at least it'll keep them back." Then he resumed prying at the stubborn lid of the crate beside him. By the stenciled label it contained mortar rockets.

She said, "Sooner or later the ricochets will get us or their bullets will set off something explosive in here. We haven't got a chance, have we, Harry?"

"Might cool them off if I can get to that mortar and lob a couple into them. There aren't but eight or ten blokes out there."

He tossed another grenade and they ducked again and the noise seemed to explode inside her. Sudden tears rushed from her eyes and she clutched at him. "Harry, oh Harry. . . ."

"Come on, ducks, we ain't licked yet." He kissed the top of her head and then he dived away, cradling two of the mortar rockets in his arms, skittering across the stone floor toward the uptilted mortar out front. Bullets began to spang around the place again but she followed him forward, yanking the pin from a grenade and throwing it with all her strength and watching it soar out of the cave before she threw herself flat and heard its devastating bellow.

Harry, she thought. Reckless indomitable Harry. She crawled behind boxes to reach him. He'd dragged the mortar back to cover and somehow hadn't been hit but the Cubans were invisible out there in the trees and their bullets were crashing all over the cave, bouncing around like stones in a tin can, and it was only a matter of time.

"I'm scared, Harry, but I'm not sorry."

"Right, ducks. Never apologize. Here, hold this a minute."

Weak in all his fibers, Cielo leaned against the Jeep listening to the noise of battle. Julio came in sight, then Vargas; the two of them trudged forward batting smoke away from their faces.

Cielo said drily, "He'll shoot both of you for desertion."

It made Julio grunt. "Let him try."

Something blew up—louder than a grenade this time and Cielo's head rocked back as he tried to identify the sound. Vargas murmured, "Harry's got one of the mortars working."

"Christ he'll kill all of us," Julio complained, and glowered petulantly toward the cliff.

Cielo drew himself upright. "Let me have that." He reached for Julio's submachine gun.

Julio relinquished it without objection. "What are you going to do?"

"What I should have done at the very beginning. If I'd been young enough I wouldn't have taken so long to make the decision." He started to walk uphill, then looked back: "Wait for me here. If I don't come back, I depend on you to look after Soledad and the girls."

Vargas and Julio began to follow him but he waved them back. He took a deep breath and held it in his lungs while he walked between the burning huts. When he came out of the smoke he started to breathe again.

The mortar whumped again and the explosion chewed up some timber. He headed that way, assuming Crobey wasn't shooting entirely blind.

He made his way with care the last hundred feet or so. He could tell where the men were easily enough—their guns made a steady racket for him to guide by—but he didn't want to get nailed by one of Crobey's mortar bursts. He heard one of them coming in, dropped flat behind a tree and felt the earth shudder when it impacted. Leaves and twigs rained on him. Then he got up and went forward again. Presently he found Emil, squatting behind a tree fitting a fresh-loaded magazine into his Uzzi.

Emil looked up and found Cielo there, and Cielo watched him for a moment, trying to think of the right words. They didn't come to mind, and after a brief moment he simply pulled the trigger and killed Emil without fuss.

Crobey had a wicked-looking bullet burn across the back of his hand. Carole had a new bruise on top of an old one on her thigh. Pretty soon, she thought, they'd both be picked apart to splinters this way. But she handed another mortar round to him and put her hands over her ears waiting for him to drop it down the spout.

Crobey began to lift it toward the muzzle but then he paused.

The shooting had stopped. She heard somebody yelling in Spanish. Crobey slowly lowered the shell to the ground and reached for the submachine gun on the stone beside him. He was scowling, listening to the voice.

"What's he saying?"

"I can't make it out."

"Harry Crobey! Hold your goddamn fire a minute. Want to talk!"

She reached for a grenade and put her finger through the pin ring. "Don't trust the bastard, Harry."

"Nothing to lose," he replied. Then he let his call sing out: *"Come ahead and talk!"*

She saw the man emerge from the smoke dragging something heavy along the ground. The man had a weapon in his free hand but it was down at his side and not aimed anywhere in particular. He had a wild hard face, very primitive, huge cheekbones, a look of savagery.

"Is that him?" she whispered. "Rodriguez?"

"Yeah." Crobey didn't lift his weapon. He only watched Rodriguez struggle upslope, dragging whatever it was.

"Maybe they want to make a deal," Crobey said *sotto voce.*

"Don't listen to him, Harry."

Rodriguez was halfway between the trees and the cave—perhaps forty feet away from them. He stopped there, out in the open. With powerful effort he lifted the object he'd been dragging. She saw it was a man—then she recognized Emil Draga. Rodriguez propped Emil Draga more or less upright, holding him in both arms, the submachine gun loose on its sling over his elbow.

Rodriguez shouted, "We've got Glenn Anders. They just brought him in."

Crobey gave her a long look. She had nothing to say; she felt helpless. Crobey looked at the heaped ordnance and then lifted his voice: "No trades, Rodrigo."

"The hell with trades. This is the one who killed the Lundquist boy." Rodriguez dropped Emil and Emil fell like a stone, quite obviously dead by the way he collapsed. "I guess we've had enough of this, Harry," Rodriguez shouted. He flung his submachine gun away into the mud and shoved both hands in his pockets. His stance was defiant. He glanced over his shoulder in the direction of the smoke that poured up from the camp. "That's my goddamn fishing boat you just burned up, you know that, Harry?"

She said, "What's he raving about?"

"Shush a minute, ducks."

"Listen, Harry—you hear me?"

"I hear you fine, Rodrigo."

"You can have Anders, you'll find him back in the trees there. And you can keep that stuff in the cave, Harry, it's a gift from me to you. We're taking both Jeeps. You'll have a long walk down and you'll have to backpack Anders but I need a half day's jump on you. Time to get my wife and my girls out. All right?"

She murmured suspiciously. "It's too easy."

Crobey shook his head. He yelled, "Fair enough. Go on, Rodrigo, beat it."

Rodriguez turned around and walked away, head down, hands in his pockets, kicking at stones in the mud. He disappeared into the trees. There were voices—a bit of argument, possibly—and then she heard movement in the woods down there. Silence after that, and she sat tense with her hands on the grenade ready to arm it; Crobey watched the trees unblinkingly. Then after a time they heard the Jeep engines roar, and growl away.

After that they heard nothing and Crobey slowly sagged back on his haunches.

She shook her head in disbelief. "It's a trick, Harry."

"No." Then he leered at her. "You look like hell, ducks."

"So do you." His cheek had stopped bleeding but he was a mess.

"Can you walk?"

"I guess. But what if he's left somebody out there with a rifle?"

"He hasn't." He took her arm. She had no resources left—only the fear that somebody out there was waiting to snipe at them when they exposed themselves. Harry cocked the Uzzi and held it one-handed, ready to shoot, and helped her walk out into the hazy dripping twilight.

Below the cave the fires were dying. She brooded for a while at Emil Draga's corpse.

They went down slowly, Harry half carrying her, limping. "He's not a bad bloke," Harry said. At first she didn't know who he was talking about. Then he said, "Mostly I guess it's a mistake to get to know your enemy. You might turn out to like the bastard. I think you'd like Rodrigo."

"Maybe."

"Ducks—"

"What, Harry?"

"Thanks."

She began to smile a little. She looked down at the wreckage of her clothing and the bruised patches of exposed skin. "I am a lovely sight for you, aren't I," she murmured. "I'd like to get cleaned up and then I'd like to get into a nice cool bar. With you."

"Right, ducks. Let's find Glenn, now."

"Ah, Harry, I hate to admit such a ghastly cornball thing but I do love you. Without reservation. And I guess that will do," she mused in surprise, "for openers."